Praise for *Rearview Sunset:*

"Beautifully written, you will find your ~~...~~ ~~...~~ ~~...~~ to overcome his bad decisions and find his true path. A first novel by Brett Champan, I expect we will see more from this Wisconsin author. I thoroughly enjoyed this book and predict it will be a winner."

Joyce Laabs, *"Ageless", The Lakeland Times, Minocqua, WI*

"I'm not a reader but I couldn't put it down..."

Marlene, *60's, Volunteer, Waukesha, WI*

"I enjoyed this book. Kept me interested the whole way through."

Brian, *20's, Construction Manager, Chicago, IL*

"I really enjoyed this story. I felt like I could connect with past experiences in my own life to the tales in these pages... There's a raw character that draws you into Beau's life and the stories that anyone can relate to and appreciate."

Erin, *20's, Mother, Chicago, IL*

"I thought it was a great book that gives one hope when they feel too far gone from their ideals...I would think many people would be able to connect with this literature."

Diana, *40's, English Teacher, Chicago, IL*

"Flowing in a fashion similar to *'Tom Sawyer,'* this is an inspiring story of hope that challenges all of us to let go of our preconceived notions of self in order to attain a life of true fulfillment. Earl is the wise but always winking grandfather I never had but always wanted."

Paul, *30's, Pharmaceutical Quality Assurance Professional, Madison, WI*

"I couldn't put it down, even when I was with my fiancé!"

Toni, *20's, Retreat Camp Assistant, Hendersonville, South Carolina*

Rearview Sunset

A Novel

BRETT CHAMPAN

NorthWaters Press

Published by NorthWaters Press, Wisconsin

Copy Edited by Wendy Huska

Formatted by Publisher's ExpressPress, Ladysmith, WI

ISBN: 978-0-9823873-1-3

Printed in the United States of America

To the Maker of sunsets and dreams,
thank you for all things—for life, hope, strength, and quiet streams.
To family and friends; sojourners near and far,
you bring light to the journey, shining bright like stars.
To those yet to join me in the race home,
I look forward to riding beside you through the land
where angels roam.

There was a child went forth every day,
And the first object he look'd upon, that object he became.
And that object became part of him for the day or a certain
        part of the Day,
or for many years or stretching cycle of years.

                                                Walt Whitman

The blue skies that lingered overhead became part of this
        child.
And the bright white snow and the sparkle of the sword-
        shaped icicle,
And the thin yet sturdy birch and tamarack pines, and the
        needle-covered trails woven in between them on the forest
        floor,
And the glare of the sun as it bounced off the lake's ripples
        and the illusion of weeds as he looked in the deep, dark
        waters,
And the glow of the ever-abundant stars and the radiance of
        the moonlight that brings life to the darkness of the
        midnight hour,
And the modified colors of the mid-evening sky, and the soft
        summer breeze and its soothing presence upon the skin,
And the serenity of the falling rain, and the friendly suspense
        of the faint thunder, all became part of him.

A Splash in the Water

August 25, 2006, early Saturday morning
Dreams are mysterious things. This I have always believed and know to be true. Some are nothing more than the residue of the day's thoughts or worries that have been taunting the soul. Others are something far greater, sometimes discernable, other times revealing deep things that are often too wonderful for the recipient to fully grasp in the present time.

And then there are some that appear to be a combination of the two, like the one I had just moments ago on this cool August night. It was so lucid and detailed, so much so that it has taken what seems to be minutes after waking for me to regain my senses and realize that I am in bed in our northern Wisconsin cabin, right where I had gone to sleep hours earlier.

Coming out of the dream, I shot up from my pillow into sitting position, beads of sweet dripping from my forehead, a deep breath escaping from my body as if it had been locked up for years. Other than the moonlight gently pouring in through the skylight, all is dark, still, and silent. Within me, though, there is little silence. Rather, a subtle angst roars from the deep, one that has been brewing for a time. I have little doubt that this angst influenced the dream, and I replay it over and over in these fleeting moments while sitting here, pondering its significance.

In the dream we were sailing over the Atlantic, cutting steadily forward through the large, gentle swells. I can still taste the sweet air as we moved up and down and can hear the hoarse sound of our fiery British captain's voice, *"Men, do not forget these times ... "*

Then came the mounting tension that steadily grew as a mighty storm rushed in. For hours we fought it, our captain maintaining a proper air of reverence and confidence that fueled his crew's hope for safe passage through the writhing ocean. I can still feel the salt water splashing my face, and more than anything, I recall the burning desire to survive in order to reach the shores of North America, where the heart of a beautiful young woman hung in the balance, awaiting my return. Despite the danger and lack of control over the situation, a sturdy peace existed within me that said I would see her again. "Not yet," I said while looking into the sky through the pouring rain. *"Not yet ... "*

The dream didn't end there. Like a mist, I was taken from the small vessel into a forest where I ran with all my heart, dodging trees and jumping through puddles and over fallen logs, a sense of something ominous and dark lurking. I had to swerve to avoid hissing snakes and low-hanging branches, which appeared more like bony hands and fingers reaching out to harm me. I lashed out at them, pushing them away, but there were so many. I remember sunlight bursting through the trees, which took my eyes off them and filled me with hope and strength to keep running.

I eventually reached a trail, where a powerful, good-natured horse was awaiting my arrival. In a way that can only happen in a dream, I was whisked up onto the saddle and began galloping faster than the wind down a well-trodden trail of soft earth, thunderous sounds rising from below as the hooves mercilessly beat the ground. Looking back once, I could see a trail of dust left in our wake. We rode for what seemed to be hours, the wind whipping me in the face as the horse cut swiftly through the trail.

The ride eventually took us into the night, where a touch of moonlight lit the trail and brought the shadows of the trees to life. The steed pressed on, his eyes able to penetrate the darkness, of which he had no fear. I just held on, feeling alive in every part of my being.

With the emergence of dawn, we finally came to the shoreline of a small lake. I dismounted and peered across the water. There, standing alone on the opposite shoreline, was a beautiful young woman with long, dark, flowing hair looking sullenly down at the ground to her side, as if a fire in her heart had been extinguished. Her face was not foreign to me.

I plunged into the lake at the sight of her. I swam towards the beauty with long, hard strokes, and after emerging from the water and rushing to where she stood, I reached out to take her hand and was met with a radiant, blinding white light.

And then I woke…

Beau closed his journal, blinked hard, and turned off the small bedside lamp on his right before lying back down. He then turned his head to the right and reached over again to take hold of the alarm clock. He pressed the light button—3:45 a.m. After giving his mind a few more seconds to grasp what time it really was, he let out another deep breath and shook his head to clear his mind.

Drawn by the moonlight and a pull on his heart to go outside in hopes of finding rest for the soul, he quietly slipped out of bed and put his robe and slippers on. He walked like a feather out of the room and down the hall toward the spiral stairs, just past the room where his two children slept. Along the way, he stopped outside their barely-cracked door and put his ear up close. Sounds of quiet breathing could be heard from within. Comforted by this, and still only half awake, he continued onward to the stairs and descended to the first floor. He crept to the front door, traded slippers for outdoor shoes, and slowly turned the door handle so as to not wake anyone.

Yet not everyone would remain asleep, despite his stealthy movements. Highway, their trusty yellow Labrador, lifted his head and began to wag his tale. He whined just loud enough for Beau to hear and released a big yawn that stretched his jaw to near-breaking point.

"You stay here, okay buddy? I need to go out alone for a little while…" It seemed the dog understood, for down went his head, resting his chin onto his paws in a sad-like fashion that tugged at Beau's heart. His tail continued to wag, though, just enough to make it known that his master could still change his mind and ask him to come with.

"Not this time, Highway. We'll be together out there on the water soon enough."

He exited the front door and walked down toward the dock with a brisk pace. It was a cool night, typical of the season. Upon reaching the dock, he stepped onto the solid wood boards and looked into the moonlit sky, which caused the water to glisten wildly. Inside, he was struggling with all the thoughts and energy running through his mind, body, and soul.

"In order to move forward, one must first look back." These words, as they often had in recent times, entered his mind. They were quoted by a pastor at the funeral of an old friend that had passed away a few weeks earlier. He was a noble man of great character who lived a simple but fulfilling life marked by an equally simple but powerful faith, and as a result, had accumulated great honor and many stories that had left a legacy for his children, grandchildren, and beyond. It was for his family and others that he lived, and he had impacted a great number of people along the way. He was much like a man that Beau had known years ago, a man whose life left an indelible mark on him.

The words at his funeral moved Beau to act on a desire that had previously been planted in him. Though still very young by most standards, he felt it was time to take a closer look into his own journey, well aware that each day could be his last and believing that, in some way, it would benefit those close to him. And perhaps he had more reason to feel this way than the common man. Just a year earlier, he sat in a hospital room, where his doctor gently informed him of a liver condition, fraught with uncertainties as to origin and nature, which would likely take his life in one year's time. He swallowed hard upon hearing those words, unsure of what emotions to display or even what he was feeling at that moment. Thoughts of every conceivable aspect of life flashed through his mind.

One year had now passed, however, and in a way that his doctor and his staff could not and cannot explain, the condition had subsided. For now, he lived, more so than ever. He hoped, God willing, that many more adventures and experiences might find him, though he was ever aware that the number of his days was out of his hands. He might have influence over the relevance of them but not the duration.

Now he stood out on the dock, the dream that led him down there still moving through his mind: the voyage over the sea, running and galloping on the horse through the woods, reaching out to the beautiful girl—just a few glimpses into the story that led him to this day. A story comprised of many stories that all seemed to piece together and stretch far beyond happenstance. A story that was just one small but significant piece of an even greater tale, one that travels beyond past, present, and future.

Part of this small story included an old, wise man who lived not long ago, who Beau called a great friend. There was also a host of others, including a beautiful young woman and what may have been angels, who helped him find his way home after he had wandered far from it—farther than he knew. Some of those faces he knew he would never see again, except perhaps in heaven. Others he hoped he might see one day, though something told him that they were sent across his path only for a time, not to be seen again for a long time, if ever. Of this he could not be certain, and therefore, he believed it warranted no further pondering, though of course he did sometimes anyway.

What he did know was that they helped him find life, saved him from certain death. They were instruments that led him through dreadful darkness, where all vision and hope was obscured, if not completely absent, to an unexpected destiny and true love that rocked his soul. And even when he later encountered death and pain via the departure of one who meant so much to him, even there he found life and joy in its purest form. He would learn that pain is sometimes one of the surest signs of life.

He would never forget those people and times that carried him across the highways of the Midwest and beyond. For that he was forever grateful, forever shaped, forever changed. And the best part was that so much lay ahead, whether in this life or the next.

So now he was left with the task of illuminating his piece of the great tale, the people and places that decorated it and made it what it is. Though he wouldn't right out say that God told him to do this, he did feel divine approval was on his side, just like when King David's servant told him to go and do whatever he had in mind, for God would be with him.

Yet of this task he was now in angst, not really sure where to begin or understanding some of the emotions running through him. It wasn't the first time he looked back, though he was going deeper this time, and there was so much. And he knew it would not come without challenge. Though he loved depth in life and was no stranger to solitude, which would be plentiful, part of him moaned at the thought of it. Men can achieve great feats and risk much in life, but to step out into the silence to unearth the deep places of the heart for oneself and others to see is perhaps one of the greatest challenges. Who knows what one may find down there.

To dig up old memories is to invite both the joy and pain in life, and that was exactly where Beau was heading. Some memories produce laughter and warmth; others result in sorrow and tears. But in the end, it can lead to greater freedom, both for the individual and those in his life. It was for this freedom he pressed onward.

Opposition and its ally, darkness, would accompany the process as well. All good things face evil resistance. Darkness hates light; it's always running away from it, always trying to keep people from it.

"There is just so much!" he growled under his breath with a reverent ferocity into the sky, breaking the silence. He couldn't help but pace back and forth on the dock, unfettered by the howls and other sounds of the night that surrounded him, somewhat surprised by these emotions. His eyes, which burned in the crisp air, traveled to the ground and then back up to the heavens. As he often did when on his feet, he prayed aloud, with an ever-increasing and confident tone with a few pauses in between, hands and arms swinging and flailing about at times to add exclamation to his words.

"I know I need to look back and share this story…all the stories. But where do I begin; how do I pull it all together?" His breathing became heavier, intensity rising. "And I cannot do this alone…I will not do this alone." He continued to pace around, various combinations of thoughts coming out of his mouth that could not find their way into complete sentences. Frustration mounted.

"And Highway doesn't count!"

Just then, right as he was about to implode into the early morning and become a memory to all who knew him, a swift, explosive splash took place just feet from the edge of the dock from where he stood. *"Whoosh!"* With a slight gasp, his body jolted, and he was shaken loose from his previous train of thought. He looked down toward the commotion and saw the end of a muskrat's tail go swirling into the depths in the direction of the dock. After a few moments of silence passed, he could hear the animal settle right below the wood boards under his feet. Sounds of rustling came from underneath, as if the little critter was snuggling up to bed, uneasy that this large, uninvited guest stood above his resting place.

Soothed in a way he couldn't understand right then and there, he stopped pacing. His arms fell down to his sides, and he just looked forward into the moonlit lake and the dark shadow of tree tops that lined the horizon, then up into the starry sky. Peace settled over him, one like a river that breaks through an old dam and sweeps through a small village, removing debris and old branches as it flows.

"Okay..." The words left his mouth. He felt lighter. His eyes and mouth closed in concession to the powerful silence that was all around him. His head lowered, and he slowly turned to return to the cabin, exhausted but relieved.

Beau slipped into bed as quietly as possible. Just before his eyes surrendered and were about to close, his wife turned over and nestled up to him, putting her left arm on his chest and resting her open palm just below his neck.

"Honey," she said softly in a dreamy tone that made him wonder if she was talking in her sleep. He could feel her warmth on his skin.

"Yeah?" he whispered, opening his eyes to the sound of her voice, somewhat surprised that she had awoken.

"It's going to be okay. You'll be given the strength and help you need to travel back there." A small sigh came out of him upon hearing this, and he was about to speak. Sensing this, she placed the tip of her finger over his lips to stop any unnecessary words. *"Sleep, honey, sleep..."* Her voice trailed off. As quickly as she awoke, she returned to slumber. Beau often marveled at her ability to do this, as he was now.

Her words settled on him like a feather, gentle yet poignant. As if drugged, his eyes closed, and he drifted away into a deep, fitful sleep.

The Canoe

It wasn't long before Beau awoke for the second time. The moonlight had now passed and was replaced by the splendor of the morning light, which crept slowly through the window on the eastern wall of the bedroom to rest upon the foot of the bed. All was silent.

Lying on his back, he heard the soft breathing of his wife and turned his head to look at her. She lay sound asleep with her hand on his arm, peaceful as could be.

He then turned to his right to check the clock: 5:55 a.m. Looking back toward the ceiling, he realized that the angst that had come and gone earlier in the morning was replaced by a great peace and eagerness to face the day, much to his satisfaction.

As the sun made its way over the distance of the bed and shone on them like a warm ray from heaven, it invited him to come outside and join in the celebration of a new day. He loved the early morning hour, and though his mind and body were eager to venture out for a quick taste of air before breakfast, he wanted to be there when his wife awoke to see her soft hazel eyes open and her morning smile that made him forget what time of day it was. With or without makeup and brushed hair, she captivated him and became more beautiful to him with each passing season.

As he lay on his back with the covers up to his neck, he resolved to get up and head outside, knowing that he could easily return to bed before she woke. Just at that moment, however, he could feel her body begin to squirm ever so slightly, and with one fluid motion, she rolled over into him, snuggling her body close and nestling her head below his chin. Her soft whimpers and calm breaths were now so close and overpowering to his senses that he knew he was not going anywhere right then and there.

After settling, her eyes opened briefly and met his. She smiled coyly before giving him a soft kiss that was followed by her return to dreaming. He again marveled at the way she was able to fall asleep, as if there was a switch to turn on and off. This even made him a bit envious, since sleep often came with greater effort for himself.

Sensing it was a fitting time to sneak out, he gently brushed her hair aside, kissed her on the forehead, and made his way out from under the covers. He set his feet upon the cool hardwood floor, which sent a shiver up his spine. After putting on a worn pair of jeans, a white cotton t-shirt, and his worn blue and grey checkered flannel that hung on a small brass hook on the closet door, he grabbed his journal from the nightstand and quietly walked to the door and opened it, taking one final glance back at her before closing it behind him.

On his way down the hallway to the stairs, he again stopped to check on the kids but this time slowly opened the door to look in. Like a brilliant sunset, the sight of them often made him lose track of whatever was previously on his mind and stand in reverence, as if it was the first time he had looked upon them. They were sound asleep with rustled hair and mouths agape, with no sign of life other than the rise and fall of the sheets that covered their bodies, evidence that life in the form of air was passing through them. A small dabble of drool dripped slowly down the side of young Wade's mouth, providing reassuring evidence as well.

As he stood there, motionless, fresh memories and thoughts of their futures passed through his mind. Looking upon these little ones, upon his family as a whole, was one of the greatest reminders of why he woke each day. "All men die, but few men really live." The time-tested quote from one of his favorite movies came to mind, as it often did, reminding him that a man is dead unless living for something greater than himself: for others. He slowly closed the door once again and made his way to the stairs and to the front door that allowed him access to all the wonders of the morning.

"Ah, Highway, my faithful comrade of the early hour...Now we can go out together." Few times, if ever, had his trusty yellow Labrador not been awake to greet his master, yearning inside and wagging his tail with sweet anticipation for their morning venture, especially when up at the cabin. Beau walked over to his hairy friend, rustled him up, and then allowed the beast to show some affection in the form of lapping his tongue over his face in a way that most people find offensive, including his wife.

"Honey, he licks himself in certain areas, you know..." she would say with a slight grimace on her face while sipping her coffee.

"My lady, this dog offers unconditional love. The least I can do is allow him to bond with me in one of the few ways he knows how."

The discussion usually ended with his wife emerging victoriously, unfairly using threats of withholding her own forms of affection if he kept it up. "Marriage and dogs...never an easy balance," he thought.

After the bonding had ended, the two proceeded to walk the sloped path to the lake below. Down a steep incline on the other side of the cabin they could hear the lush sounds of the river. Often the challenging decision of which body of water to go to presented itself, though this morning the lake won out, for on its shores sat the canoe that they would soon set out on. He wanted to give it a quick inspection before packing it and departing.

Upon coming to the shoreline, Beau looked out over the expanse and took a deep breath, inhaling the cool, invigorating air. A thick fog hovered over the water, so much so that he could not see more than twenty feet across it. The two then walked over to the canoe, and Beau looked it over, tipping it on its side to let the water from the previous day's rain drain out.

On many mornings while at the cabin, they would start the day paddling along the glassy water. There were few better ways to embrace the dawn. One of those ways was when his wife and kids rose early enough to join them, all piling into the craft. The odds of tipping improved, though Beau believed some risk was good for their souls and therefore welcomed the opportunity.

Though Beau knew God gave neither spirit nor soul to anything

made of aluminum or wood or any other kind of material, he felt there
was something special about this one.   Perhaps it was the wooden oars
that had been through so much or the memories he had of sharing time
fishing in it with an old friend of the family, who once owned it.

Most likely, though, it was the memory of a very special time in
it under the setting sun not too many years ago, one that would never be
forgotten.

Beau sat down on the craft and opened his small, black leather-
bound journal to a fresh page and took a pen from the chest pocket of his
flannel.   After a few moments, he began to pen some words while continuing to admire his surroundings that never failed to inspire.

> *Later Saturday morn, lakeside*
> There are few things in life that renew the soul and
> perspective as much as unhurried time away with loved ones.
> Those things, which on some lesser days present themselves
> as burdens and responsibilities, oft taken for granted, now ap-
> pear as rich blessings and gifts that deserve everything I have
> to give.
> I can hear the trees, water, and wind up here, and
> they all speak of the past, present, and future.   It is time to
> look back.   As a wise old friend once told me, stories are
> meant to be shared, especially ones that reach into the hearts
> of others.
> The dream still lingers in my mind.   Unlike most
> other dreams, its contents still remain clear to me—pieces of
> the past that I had forgotten, lost sight of somewhere along
> the way, until recent times, which have been bringing them
> back to light.
> I trust more will come as I venture out to
> listen.

He closed the journal, called out to Highway, who was now patrolling the shoreline, and together they walked back to the cabin.   Before ascending the steps, Beau stopped at the woodshed that sat just
behind the cabin and took hold of the time-tested maul to split firewood
for the coming winter.   He positioned several logs and unleashed on
them, swinging the instrument with precision and power.   Living in the
city, he rarely had the opportunity to use it and cherished the moment.

Often, he wished he could be a farmer, if for nothing else than to enjoy the manual labor in the morning hour that quickened the spirit.

After splitting the final log, he set the maul aside, stacked the cut pieces in the shed and gathered some dry firewood to carry inside. He was hoping his wife would still be in bed so that he could have a fire ready for her. It was still summertime, though the morning was brisk and fitting for the sight and sounds of living, crackling fire. She was already up, though, and the excellent smell of freshly brewed coffee was lingering heavily in the air, stirring the senses.

While knelt before the fireplace, Beau crinkled a few pieces of old newspaper, set them under the grate, then placed small pieces of kindling and a couple larger logs on top of them. He pulled a strike-anywhere match from a small box and ignited it by flicking it off of his top front teeth. It was a trick he learned as a kid and never let go of, and the taste of sulfur in his mouth afterward would never let go of him.

After lighting the paper, he repositioned himself, sitting back far enough to stretch out his legs while keeping an eye on the fire to make sure it grew to maturity. Other than occasionally poking and prodding the wood, he sat there, motionless, gazing into the flame.

"Is it all good and safe out there, hun?" asked his wife with a playful yet ladylike tone as she came up behind him, bending over slightly to wrap her arms around him and kiss him softly on both cheeks. "Sure is, my lady," he replied, shaking any dust off his hands before gently reaching behind him to grab a hold of her and pull her over his shoulders. She wasn't sure what he was trying to do but was relieved to find herself safe in his lap when the process was over, where she received a return kiss or two.

Soon their coffee cups were in hand, the delicate wisps of steam rising above the rim. They talked of this and that and the coming week that they would be spending apart; while Beau and Highway would be away, she and the kids would be volunteering at Whispering Pines camp just three miles up the road, a place that for years had been a part of their lives. Pleasantness surrounded their talk, which revealed a depth and transparency in their relationship that came from weathering the many challenges inherent in marriage, even one as young as theirs. Soon they were joined by the kids, who came strolling down the stairs, rubbing their sleepy eyes, drawn by the anticipation of hugs and breakfast.

With the clock ticking, breakfast was prepared, and they sat down to eat, taking hands in prayer. Though Beau usually led the family this way, Alyssa volunteered and brought smiles to her parents when hearing her sweet five-year-old voice saying thank you for Mommy and Daddy and Wade and Highway and Mommy's cooking and the water and trees and especially for the bright morning star.

"Amen."

After breakfast, Beau, with little three-year-old Wade's assistance, helped clear off the table and afterward went for a short walk outside while Mom and Alyssa did the dishes. Most of the time, Wade held his father's hand as they walked around the yard, his eyes shooting to and fro with wild excitement and curiosity into the forest and everywhere else. At one point he released his grip to bend down and pick up a small fallen branch that he proceeded to wield like a sword, hitting his father right on the kneecap with one of the strokes.

"That's my boy," said Beau with a proud, slight grimace, pleased to see the young warrior revealed in the child. He knew this was only a taste, though, and that it would be years before his son would have to pick up and carry a real sword.

By most standards their marriage was still young, their role as parents younger still. New experiences presented themselves each day, challenges that required new strategies amidst days that moved so fast that they often hesitated to blink for concern they might miss something in the kids and in each other. More often than not, it seemed like they were just hanging on for dear life, with many prayers and occasional phone calls for direction to those further along in parenting. Somewhere along the journey, a greater appreciation for their imperfect parents emerged too.

Beau loaded the minivan with his family's luggage and helped them settle in. "Bye, daddy!" shouted both Alyssa and Wade from the backseat. Wade looked especially sad that his pa wasn't coming with.

"Son, you listen to your mother while I'm away, and protect your sister, okay?" He looked up at his dad, a proud smile coming over his face.

"Okay…"

"Be careful, Beau. I want to see you in one piece when you return. I'll be waiting for you." She looked at him longingly, and they exchanged a kiss and a hug before she climbed in the van.

"Beau," she said through the window before driving off, "I thought you might want these." She handed him some note cards with writing on them. "I thought they might provide you with some light on cloudy days." With that, she ran her fingers through his hair and drove off down the gravel driveway and onto the road.

Beau looked at the cards, then put them in his flannel pocket and buttoned it, as if safeguarding a valuable jewel. As soon as the van was out of sight, he wished it was returning. Yet the time had come to go, and he took a deep breath and went to load the canoe with supplies for the week and lock up the cabin before setting out.

While walking along with Highway, he felt a strange deterrent as he approached the cabin. It was as if a whisper was telling him not to go. He was not unfamiliar with this kind of whisper, the kind that produces an uneasy feeling inside. Lifting his head to look at the sky, he kept walking and in doing so recalled the words that came down through Solomon, a king of old—words that whispered a different message.

"Let your eyes look straight ahead, fix your gaze directly before you."

That whisper he trusted, and he clung to it while his pace increased.

Beau and Highway climbed into the canoe and pushed off into the still lake. By now the sun had risen above the treetops in the eastern horizon and was shining brightly over all the land, slightly filtered by some scattered clouds. The wind was soft and mild, and he could feel it move across his face and through his hair, sending him into frequent daydreams that grew more and more vivid. Highway sat calmly in the front of the canoe, exempted from paddling and given lookout duty, staring intently into the distance, into the water and sky, mesmerized in the same way as his master by the majesty of the glassy water and thin, dispersing fog that hovered slightly above it.

"I wonder what that dog is thinking of," Beau would often wonder.

They paddled on into the distance, sending soft ripples into the lake on both sides of their small, fully loaded vessel. The shoreline of the cabin soon became a distant memory. Daydreams began to run more rampant as the beauty of creation surrounded them—thoughts of the joys and challenges of being a husband and father, friendships, parents and siblings and other acquaintances, the wonderful journey and all its twists and turns that led him to this point in his life, the unknown adventure that lay before him in the days and years to come.

"All gifts," he reminded himself as often as necessary. *"All gifts."*

With broad, heavy strokes, the canoe lunged forward. Once in a while, the two males would exchange looks, sharing conversation in their respective ways. Beau usually did most of the talking, though sometimes Highway would respond with a few low-volume sounds that fell between a bark and a howl.

After a half hour, Beau began to paddle more leisurely, realizing that he had better conserve some energy. It would take several hours, including a portage or two, in order to reach the small island that would be their fortress for the week. With one slow, smooth stroke, he looked down into the waters and up into the sky to see all the different shapes and pictures of clouds, all of which pointed to something bigger. In the haste of life, he often lost sight of this, of how the clouds and stars and moon and sun are evidence that there is more to life than his schedule.

At one point Beau ceased paddling and looked over the edge of the canoe. He could see clearly his reflection looking back at him through the gentle ripples sent from the craft. As he followed them until they were no more, he was taken back to times as a child when he would look into those deep, mysterious waters.

Times that seemed so innocent, when so much remained to be shaped.

Deep Waters

"Beau!" whispered his father. "Get up, its time to go!"

On most mornings Beau would groan and pout at the sound of such words, though not on ones like this. Not on mornings when he was going fishing with his dad.

Beau loved those weekends—getting up in the pre-dawn hours when all was quiet, still, and dark, leaving the house and jumping into the large brown and tan Plymouth station wagon, all his siblings still in bed and out of the way where they could cause no distractions. Off they would go with the boat hooked on back, the destination some far-off land where a spacious lake with deep waters awaited them.

Such adventure and excitement existed while driving through the dark mornings of their Wisconsin homeland. Often times they would stop at some remote, brightly lit, cozy diner, where the aroma of coffee filled the air. Beau would order pigs in a blanket—sausage links wrapped inside fluffy pancakes that tasted the best when smothered with enough thick maple syrup to make them float on the plate.

Afterward they would stop at one of many bait shops along the way to choose the weapons they would wield against the elusive fish. When Beau walked into those shops at his father's side, the blood within him surged like a warrior preparing for battle. His eyes opened wide at the tackle and gear, hooks and knives, and the mighty displays of huge mounted muskellunge, walleye, and bass that once swam unfettered through the lakes.

Carl would usually go directly to the supplies they needed, while

Beau would drift off to other areas, which usually led him directly to the live wells. Minutes would pass while he examined the assortment of minnows, very aware of their unpleasant destiny and wondering if a few might somehow escape and grow into big fish. Sometimes he would grab the small net next to the tank and plunge it into the water to see how many he could gather at one time, a slight sense of amusement derived from the chaos and terror he inflicted upon them.

"Beau, time to go," he heard his father speak loudly from the other side of the shop. He'd hurry to the checkout counter, where a stick of beef jerky awaited him.

"You going to catch some big ones today?" said the kind old man from behind the counter, his glasses resting low on his nose.

"Sure hope so!" Beau said with wild eyes, his usual shyness beaten down by the taste of adventure in the air.

Again they were off, gear in hand as they climbed back into the wagon. Before long they'd be at their destination, backing the boat into the quiet lake while a couple other fishermen walked about getting their boats and gear ready, few words spoken. Carl would usually make some small talk with them, arousing a bit of laughter and wishing them well. It was his secret method to pick up a few fishing secrets that the anglers would not otherwise have divulged.

Soon it was just the two of them sitting in the boat as the early morning sun rose unexpectedly from the edge of the sky, reaching over the treetops to dispel the darkness and lift the fog from the glass-like water. Yawns, usually big ones, flowed steadily from their mouths for a good hour. They were accompanied by a cooler full of sandwiches and fruit, a few sodas and Snickers bars, and more beef jerky, and all kinds of time to just talk and listen. It simply couldn't be any better.

"Beau, what are you doing over there?" Carl would ask while casting his bait into the water. Though he was always fixated on hooking the big one, he also enjoyed beyond words the water and wind and the company of his young son, who was looking over the edge of the boat as if there was a mermaid swimming below—a usual occurrence.

Those waters lured the young boy's curiosity with a power greater than magic. He lost himself in another world when staring at those rays of light that seemed to come up from the deep, making him wonder what was down there. Some kind of feeling beyond explanation nestled itself deep within his soul while leaning over the edge of the boat and peering into them. There was so much to see.

"Just lookin'," he responded without much thought, and he kept looking and daydreaming, in no hurry to change his course.

"Okay then, but you might miss the big one! I just saw a big fin surface right over there…"

"Where!?" That was all it took to propel Beau back to his seat to pick up his pole like a soldier advancing in battle, fighting to take enemy ground and rescue the helpless.

The calm morning waters would pass into the afternoon, where they transformed into wind-streaked ripples while the sun beat down mercilessly. The soft white clouds that passed overhead provided occasional relief. In a blink, the afternoon disappeared into the evening, where the waters again became calm and the skies serene, with hues of pink and orange acting like a powerful drug on their senses. Occasionally a storm would run its course over the lake, prompting them to pause their fishing to put on raingear. If lightning showed itself, they would retreat to the shoreline until the storm subsided.

On some occasions, they would fish long after sunset, when the stars or moon would continue to draw their eyes heavenward. The taste of adventure intensified in those hours, forever altering their minds.

On most nights, though, the time to return home to loving arms would put them back into the station wagon at twilight. Off they would go, driving by rolling fields, where the flickering of innumerable bright green fireflies penetrated the landscape. Beau would lean over the dashboard and peer out the passenger door window to gaze at the display. He just couldn't get enough of them.

Upon arrival, Carl would grab their catch out of the boat and give them to Beau to carry in like a trophy. Inside, Janet would still be awake, ready to congratulate her young son on the catch, regardless of how many he actually caught, and smother him with affection. In the meantime, his siblings would crowd around the fish, challenging each other to touch them. Sometimes Dean would take one of the slimy creatures off the stringer and chase Jill and Sammy around the house with it.

To his dismay, he was powerless against Anwen, for she exhibited little fear or trepidation of these creatures, or perhaps any creature for that matter. Sometimes she even gave it a little smooch, just to show Dean what she was made of.

Despite the occasional chaos and arguments that appeared in the Jamison household, it was by all means a loving one. Beau was the youngest of the five children, followed by Samantha, Jill, Anwen, and Dean. It was a lively bunch.

On a weekly basis they would climb into the station wagon and go to church on Sunday mornings and some Wednesday nights. Complaining was commonplace as Beau and his siblings sat closely beside one another in the backseat, nudging each other with their elbows, unknowingly enjoying the feeling of closeness and security it brought.

"Get your elbow out of my face!"

"It's not in your face, and stop nudging me!"

"Dad, Mom, Sammy won't leave me alone and is making faces at me!"

"I am not! And she started it!"

"No I didn't! Mom, Dad, it wasn't me! Stop it! Ma!"

Sometimes it all would become too much for Beau, and off he would go, climbing into the furthest regions of the wagon to drift away into his own little world. Dean, the oldest of all, would continue badgering young Jill and Samantha, while big sister Anwen would be watching with muse, delighted with the commotion and contentedly looking out the window while smacking her gum. Other times she would join in the battle to defend her sisters, or rally against them.

Thankfully, Beau had plenty of imagination to entertain himself while back there, and if the battle ever turned against him, an allied force usually formed quickly to fend it off. There were many perks to being the youngest.

The station wagon would remain as the trusted steed for years to come, rolling through city streets and country roads as the sun flickered through the trees and the miles passed by. The children would continue to pile in the back as Dad and Mom would get in the front, eager and excited for whatever destination lay ahead, whether it was hours or even days away.

Occasionally, when briefly opening his eyes from a nap, Beau would see his mother turned back in her seat, smiling at the lot of them. They had all fallen asleep, five heads tilted in the same direction and resting on the shoulder of the kin next to them.

So much peace and security was felt in that station wagon, at least for the children.

The wagon rolled on, carrying them to visit nearby Grandma Winnie, who fed Beau and his siblings all the favorite and usually unhealthy foods that she learned to prepare as a farm wife. There were also the visits to the more geographically distant Grandma Elizabeth and Grandpa Stanley, who also fed them well and had a candy drawer near the kitchen that constantly beckoned eager hands to come hither.

Beau thought he was sneaky and unnoticed when attacking it, though unbeknownst to him, he was nabbed from the beginning. Grandparents are not known for administering discipline upon grandchildren, despite having eyes in the back of their head.

This fact was exhibited one fine day when something clicked inside Beau's mind to shoot at the window of Grandma Winnie's next-door neighbor. Beau held no resentment against the man; he actually never even met him. However, for whatever reason, that window became a prime target in his sights.

So it came to pass on one sunny, blue-skied day. No cares in the world existed that could interfere with any plan he chose to create, and his new bb gun, gifted to him during Christmas, was primed and ready for another day of action. And action it had.

Hiding behind the steps to the house in sniper position, Beau must've shot that window ten times, never breaking the glass and too far away to see that his shots were in fact hitting the target and inflicting significant damage. He didn't think anyone would notice, though the neighbor man later confronted old Grandma Winnie, who despite all reasonableness, sensibility, and fairness, stuck up for her young grandson. For unknown reasons she didn't think too highly of her neighbor, and perhaps this gave her a slight sense of satisfaction.

"Beau, why did you shoot at his window?" she asked tenderly with her sweet, scratchy voice while fixing his dinner later that evening, shortly after her run in with the neighbor.

"Well," he thought for a moment, trying hard to tell the story right, "I saw a bird sitting on the ledge and was trying to shoot it. I didn't think I was hitting the window," he said with a pleading tone, expecting some form of rebuke.

So convincing was he at that moment, and in sub-sequent interrogations by his parents, that he even fooled himself into believing there was a bird there.

Truth be told, there was a bird there, though it was long gone after the first bb razed its beak.

"Oh, okay then," she said with concealed wisdom. "Next time try and get the birds that are in the trees or in the air."

"Okay, Grandma," he replied, then quietly excused himself to go outside.

He walked over to the edge of the lawn right before the valley, then proceeded to pace around the yard, wrestling inside with what he told his Grandma. He knew there was no bird there and had a sick feeling in his stomach about lying to her. It was eating him up inside.

He never found out for sure if she caught him in his lie or not, but in later years, upon learning that grandparents know more than they let on, he had a pretty good feeling she knew. Nonetheless, she continued to defend her little grandson over the window issue with the toughness of a stubborn farmwoman, if for nothing else to help her neighbor understand that kids are kids.

That toughness exhibited by Grandma Winnie, along with the gentleness toward her grandchildren and others, had a source. She had been through a lot in life; trials and hardships had beaten her down to the point where all she could see was a great hand that reached out to comfort. She grabbed that hand, and in doing so was lifted higher and given eyes that saw more and a soft heart that found plenty for which to be thankful. She believed blessings and afflictions made life what it is: life that is truly life, life to be lived for others.

Old Grandma Winnie lived through the Great Depression and became a widow years later. She lost her husband prematurely to villains called whiskey and ale that befriended him when all his assets, and subsequently his dignity, departed with the financial crisis. Old Grandpa Harry left this world unexpectedly while his wife was returning from the local gas station with a case of beer, which he sent her to go buy just an hour before. He was a gentle and caring man, though not when his liquid master flowed through his veins and opened doors to all sorts of malice and evil that take the man out of man.

Of course none of this was known to Beau in those early years, and he simply knew her as an ultra-loving, sweet grandma who cooked for him and his siblings whenever she had the chance. Greasy farm food and lots of sugar and heaping portions of laughter, with an endless supply of giggling, hugs, and kisses mixed in, was found in her humble little home. As the youngest of the family and the one who exhibited the greatest appreciation for food, with the ability to consume great amounts of it, it seemed Beau received a touch more attention than the others, despite an equal amount of love spread around to each.

Several inches away from reaching the five-foot-tall mark on the wall, Grandma Winnie wore glasses that significantly enlarged her cheerful eyes, with white hair that was so white that it resembled divinity. From a child's eyes, she appeared as a sort of angel—a more aged one, with wings that moved a little slower.

Her house was a child's delight, a world set apart from everything else. The kids were always so eager to get to Grandma's, riding in the backseat of the station wagon, looking out the windows into all that passed by on the journey there. Whose turn it was to go to Grandma's was but another source of contention between the children, and many fine, well-presented debates took place because of it.

Adventure and silence existed together out there—a constant tension that produced harmony, at least for Beau.

In her backyard, just behind a small shed full of rakes and hoses and other yard supplies, sat the forbidden valley. It was always the first thing to draw the attention of the Jamison kids. They were told not to get too close, which of course made them want to get as close as possible.

The forbidden valley lay at the bottom of a steep bank filled with trees and brush. In it flowed a small stream that usually could not be seen, only heard, like the wind itself. What lived down there was a mystery, though the Jamisons' cousins, who lived just up the road, informed Beau that it was filled with alligators and other intimidating creatures that made him gasp with fear and wild-eyed exhilaration.

Indoors, Grandma's rarely-visited basement was another draw. Clean and tidy, yet dark and damp like an old castle dungeon, it drew his curiosity and provoked a desire to go down there and explore the self-canned foods and other objects that hinted a time and generation long past. Often, while sitting at the kitchen table, Beau looked over with glazed eyes at the dark wood door on the other side of the room, which led down to the rarely visited concrete floors and walls. Sometimes he would open it and look down those steep wooden stairs into the dark that seemed to call to him. Grandma would never let him go down there alone, though a few times he managed to venture down a few steps to get a look around while she was napping.

Less mysterious and guarded than the basement and foreboding backyard valley was the hell-fire cuckoo clock that hung on the wall above the kitchen sink. It ticked faithfully throughout each day for years upon years. It was especially noticeable during those still afternoon naps in the humble family room, which just days before was filled with old men from church who watched with fading hope as the beloved but not so exceptional Green Bay Packers played on the screen.

The sun shone in so brightly through the large living room window during those naps, where silence spoke and daydreams soared when Beau should have been sleeping. He was never good at napping— always so much to think about.

Every hour that little blue jay came bursting out of the little trapdoors on that clock with the intensity of a freight train that screamed down the railroad tracks controlled by a renegade engineer. If Beau had been taller, that blue jay would have been quieter, or perhaps mute, or even non-existent.

When the events of the day were laid to rest and night set in, sweet sleep awaited. However, he was often awoken and drawn to the window while Grandma was fast asleep. The window was set high, forcing him to put his feet on the heat register and step up to peer out into the wide open expanse, where vast skies sparkled with stars that made him stop breathing. Something out there grabbed him so incredibly tight in those moments.

He would just stare, looking to different parts of the sky and land, its various shapes and shades taking him deeper into wonder and awe. In the winter, a white floor of snow was illuminated by the uninhibited moon that shone through a few drifting clouds. In the summer, the warm breeze made the trees sway to and fro as the sounds of crickets and rustling leaves echoed throughout the land, pouring into his soul. Those familiar fireflies always seemed to show up too.

So quiet and still were those nights at Grandma Winnie's—the voice of silence at its highest. So much lay before his eyes there, hinting at a path lying in wait for him that he could neither see nor fathom.

Back home on Blueberry Street in Sheldon, equally sweet seasons would enter through the eyes and touch the soul. The winter months brought so much snow that the children could make tunnels and igloos in the front yard of the hilltop house. Big was that front yard to their young eyes, protected by the great Maple tree that Anwen frequently climbed, displaying her zesty spirit and athletic ability. She also broke several bones because of it, though it did little to deter her.

Warm were the memories of sitting around the crackling fireplace in the cozy family room after coming in from the cold, the whole family gathered together. Hot chocolate warmed the hands that were clasped to the mug, and the steam that rose from the top of the liquid brought heat to their faces. The fragrance of the fresh Christmas tree, selected from a tree farm and cut down together, added to the sweetness of the air.

And then there was mealtime. Everything was eaten, from macaroni and cheese with ketchup to big, juicy steaks cooked medium rare and fish and potatoes, accompanied by much joy and giggling, mostly from Sammy who just, for whatever reasons, giggled so much. Young Beau occasionally would be told to stop humming at the table, though this was difficult for him to do. He just couldn't help it. He had to do something to ease the passage of all those thoughts that ran through his mind.

One summer evening following dinner, as the sky grew darker outside, some acquaintances of Beau's parents came over and sat with them in the kitchen. Beau was supposed to be in bed sleeping, though for whatever reason he rose and walked down the long, dark hallway to observe what was going on. His presence was unknown to them. They talked late into the night, the four of them sitting around the old, round, dark wood table, the oak chandelier hanging just above them, casting a soft glow upon their faces. With the familiar aroma of coffee in the air, Carl and Janet listened to Jack and Cindy talk to them about Jesus and Heaven while a thick book sat open on the table in front of them.

Oddly enough, years earlier, Carl had to help escort Jack out of a bar for starting a fight, the same Jack who now sat with his wife before the Jamisons sharing from what he called the book of life.

Though the content of the conversation could not easily be heard, Beau's curiosity was elevated. He also felt some sort of tingle in the air that night—a powerful, friendly tingle.

Like the feeling that came while listening that evening, as well as staring into those murky waters when fishing, was the feeling that sometimes came to Beau as he sat on the church pew on those Sunday mornings and Wednesday evenings. As a lad, he knew not what was going on around him, yet he sensed something more, something in the air, even while napping or playing with his siblings under the pew, to the mild frustration of his parents.

"Hush down there!" their mother would say with an intensified whisper, the sort that finds its way very clearly into the ears of destination. Other times, their father would speak, though more loudly and with widened, intense eyes that were hard to miss, like javelins. That was usually all it took for them to stop rustling about, though it would only subdue them for a time.

When not rummaging below, Beau sat in various positions atop the tan hardwood pews that toughened the buttocks, looking at the pastor as he spoke and seeing what he thought was a white glow around his head and body. Looking around, he saw others listening attentively to his words. Sometimes one or two people would break out in some unusual language that could not be understood yet was so clear and crisp, with eyes closed atop faces of deep emotion and reverence. Quite unusual, he thought.

Even more unusual were the frequent episodes of women jumping out of their pews and running around the aisles. They would pop up like toast, run up one aisle and around and down the other. They would continue running, usually completing a square or two, just like those contestants on the Price is Right show, yelling and yipping as they flailed their hands in the air. Some of them were quite large, too, and would make a thunderous boom as they galloped, huffing and puffing when they returned to their seat. For some reason Beau didn't find it too altogether strange, figuring there must be some reason for it. Still, it wasn't the most normal thing his eyes had looked upon, and he never had the urge to do it himself.

Sunday school in the mornings brought a different picture to him than the unusual language and running. Gentle, caring, and joyful women would pour affection and attention on him and the other kids and help them create things, such as gifts for their parents. One of these gifts was a wooden key holder that Beau made for his father. It showed a verse from the prophet Isaiah that spoke of receiving strength, soaring on wings like eagles, running and not growing weary, walking and not fainting. A picture of an eagle flying high in the sky above snow-capped mountains accompanied it.

The key holder would accompany his father for many years to come, hung on his office wall. One afternoon, when Beau sat with his father in his office, he watched him lean back in his chair behind his desk and look at that key holder, letting out a big sigh. It was as if he was gazing upon a beautiful sunset that overcame his anxiety that just moments before reeked havoc on his soul. As a child, Beau did not understand the significance of that moment, nor those words, though one day he would.

In that same church just a few years later, near the age of nine, Beau was baptized. Not being much for the spotlight, he was quite nervous with everyone standing around watching. Yet the procession continued. The animated, southern-accented pastor said some words and dunked him under the water, and up he came out of the basin with hands raised high in the air.

"Hallelujah!" he heard some shout. Praise from others around him could be heard, though truth be told, he had little clue as to what was going on, of what meaning lay behind being immersed in and raised out of the cool water. The only reason he raised his hands was because he saw others do it that way before.

It was refreshing, though; that he knew.

That feeling, that deep stirring in his soul that exceeded explanation that came to him when looking into the deep waters and while sitting upon the pew, would continue to strengthen through the years. There was so much to absorb. His eyes were lured by the soft white clouds passing through the blue skies and the crimson sun setting on the horizon of the northern lakes that cast a trail of fire upon the water. The skies seemed to cry out, declaring something great.

When sitting in a deer stand with his dad on an early fall or winter morning, that same sun would capture the young boy's eyes as it climbed gently from behind the forest. It cast beautiful shades of light upon life that was once dark, accompanied by a chorus of birds, who signified the beginning of a new day. He was carried by fog-drenched fields that sat below the backdrop of fiery-pink evening skies. He was spoken to by rushing rivers and gentle flowing streams that ran in the country, where skies shimmered with stars and northern lights that mysteriously danced far away on the edge of the heavens. He was entranced by snow-covered trees, the freshness of the new air brought by the changing season, and the sword-shaped icicles that hung from the gutters of houses he passed on the long walk home after grade school. If they were within reach, they would surely find their way into his hands to be wielded for the remainder of the journey.

Swords—there was something about these ancient weapons that so attracted him.

Thunderstorms and light showers amidst the green of leaves, raging winds and gentle breezes, rainbows and fireflies—they consumed him. They left him to wonder and wander in awe over the beauty, power, eloquence, and harmony that was contained in the images that stole his breath and evoked his senses in such a way that he was forced to believe that there was something much, much bigger behind it all. The big-bang theory that would soon be presented to him held no hope for survival in this child's mind. Not even for a moment.

He was forced to believe that there was something much, much bigger behind the creation of people that spawned emotions, laughter, tears, sadness, smiles, and cries. There was something more behind imagination, intellect, creativity, curiosity, life and death, and everything in between.

There was always something bigger beating deep within his soul, something placed there that was constantly casting his eyes to the horizon and deep, dark waters, as if there was something more.

Despite all this beauty and power that was put on display for him in those years, he still had room in his sights for something else that would strongly vie for his attention: women.

Yes, he was young, but there was something about them that found their way into his sights and stood as high and true as any other experience and creation.

His interest in these gentle, long-haired creatures seemed to begin in the first grade with Crystal, a popular sixth grader at his school. She was a slice of heaven to him—tall with flowing blonde hair, she cap-

Looking out the window onto all that passed by as his siblings chattered back and forth next to him, he made the decision to shed all those excess pounds that had plagued him for years. His obesity had provided him with plenty of unwanted, unfriendly criticism from classmates and others. He finally had enough of being the "fat kid."

The announcement went public.

"I'm sick of being fat." All conversation in the car ceased. "I'm going to start jogging on the land and lose this weight." Authority rode the back of his words.

The car remained silent for a moment while all pondered his remark. His parents looked at one another, then back at their youngster, offering him encouraging comments. A more critical response was given by Dean, which evoked another argument among the siblings. Beau didn't budge, however; his course had been set.

Later that day, he set out into the wooded trail on their land for his first jog, oblivious to the biting cold of winter. The mission was clear, and the climate held no power over him. Hampered by the excess pounds, he couldn't maintain a steady pace for too long, and the jog quickly turned into a walk with intermittent short runs. He reached the large, open field at the end of the trail and traveled its perimeter, then returned the way he came.

His speed and endurance would increase with each passing day. He would rise in the mornings and set out with the first crack of dawn, rousing Buck and Lady, their faithful yellow Labradors, to accompany him. Other times he would set out in the evening after school, admiring the pink western horizon that could be seen above the tall wheat that grew in the field. His pace was quickened by the fading daylight and encroaching darkness, which set in so quickly that one could never see it coming.

Due to his tenacity toward exercise, a reduction of junk food and irregular eating, the encouragement of family, and a couple inches of vertical growth, Beau eventually took on a physique closer to his original design. He could finally fit into blue jeans and discard old, worn out jogging pants, alleviating the need for his mother to try instilling confidence in him when unable to find clothing that fit his short, round body. He would never forget the first day he walked into his small country grade school wearing jeans, astonishing both peers and cohorts with his new look.

Though the emotional wounds from this physical trial would leave a small, permanent mark on his soul, it was not nearly as great as the joy that came with this victory.

His revamped health also brought a new attitude, which won the attention of some admired female classmates, one in particular.

Country living was good.

Life for Beau and his family carried on. Many summer evenings, they would all go for a walk down the trail that wove through the land, guarded by a canopy of trees. All seemed to enjoy the times, though perhaps not Sammy, whose distaste for bugs and mosquitoes sent her into twirling fits in efforts to rid them. Buck and Lady trotted ahead and behind to protect, as any good pair of dogs would. Lady frequently stopped and went to the rear to escort Janet, who always seemed to fall behind the pack. Her pace often slowed due to her daydreaming while peering into the woods, thoughts of her children's futures and other of life's intricacies circling about in her mind.

When not on foot, someone would be riding the seemingly in-destructible four wheeler through those same trails. It barreled through the terrain in all seasons, regardless of the weather or time of day, fast enough to let the mind flow as the wind and trees raced by. Other times, they'd mount the neighbor's horses and ride for hours, adding much vitality to their country living experience.

There were the late, brisk autumns and frigid white winters spent sitting with his father in those deer stands, which Carl built himself. Beau greatly admired this work of his father. Patiently, they'd await the elusive whitetail deer that would provide many meals while talking about life and all the things that go on in it.

Other mornings were spent hanging out with his mother in the kitchen as the morning sun would peer through the windows in every season. Beau's brother, Dean, could usually be found rocking away in the chair as headphones poured loud music into his ears, while in the other room, his three sisters would sit before the fireplace on quiet evenings dreaming of life, love, and romance.

Brushed in the face by a heavy gust of wind, Beau was pulled away from reflection and looked up from the water and into the distance. It had begun to cloud in the horizon, hints of a storm brewing somewhere far away. The sun still remained, though for how long it would stay was questionable. Wiping his eyes, which had moistened with the thoughts of those years, he began to paddle hard again.

For another hour and a half Beau cut through the water before having to portage. After dragging the canoe a short distance, they climbed in again and resumed course for another half hour before reaching the small, round island. It was a half-mile from shore, about fifty yards wide, covered with red pine and a few other types of trees that stood above a smooth, soft, mossy floor. He had camped there many times in the past, and it served him well.

They pulled up to the shore and quickly stepped onto land. After inspecting the island, he chose his usual spot close to the fire pit to set up camp. He unloaded the supplies from the canoe and assembled his tent. He then pulled a small tarp from one of the bags that would be used to cover firewood in case the rains came.

Beau had brought some firewood with, though only enough for a few nights. He collected some fallen branches that were scattered around the island and spent an hour hacking away at dead standing trees with a small axe. At some point he would have to venture to shore for more wood, though for now he was amply supplied.

After stacking the wood between two trees, covering it with the tarp and taking care of other loose ends, camp setup was completed. Satisfied and exhausted, he felt the desire for a nap and found no reason not to. It had been a while since he napped in the outdoors in mid-afternoon, and it took no time at all for him to drift off.

Two hours later, Beau awoke to the sound of the wind blowing through the trees. Slightly groggy but very refreshed and calmed, he rose slowly. It was just after five o'clock and time to prepare dinner. He built a fire and heated up a cup of his wife's soup, along with smoked fish that he caught earlier that week. As he was eating beside the fire, he began to scribble down all the thoughts that emerged while canoeing to the island.

After a while, Beau came to a stopping point and rose from his fireside seat and walked to the shoreline. Standing just feet from the water that gently lapped the earth, he looked west over the lake. The sun still shone brightly off in the horizon, though it was on its way down, leaving behind a sky that was being consumed by dark clouds that came in from the southwest. It seemed they had been waiting all day for the sun to depart, and now their hour of dominion had arrived.

Later that evening, the fire burned brightly in the darkness. Beau sat before it, just staring into the flame while breathing the fresh, cool air. Highway sat beside him, subdued like his master by the glimmer and crackle of the logs. As Beau sat, his thoughts returned to those earlier years in Cringle, when all seemed so simple and innocent. It did not stay that way forever.

Though much to be grateful for, time would eventually make clear the fact that, despite all the love, compassion, and desire to make things right, there existed some thorns deep within the family that would eventually puncture the skin. These thorns existed before its formation, silently passed down from previous generations, and like the withering of a garden left unattended by those who planted it, they gradually prodded the family in a direction away from the only source that can hold things together.

There was something else, too, something that seemed to encourage this change in direction. Though not clearly defined, it was like a dark shadow that had crept in, so unsuspecting and clever that no one really saw it.

Like the passing of the morning sun and autumn's quick departure into the throes of winter, Beau passed from those blue-skied days into the years of high school and beyond, where this darkness grew in might. While the beauty of life and the joy of relationships were not completely hidden from his eyes, a thick fog grew over them and seemed to increase steadily with each passing year, pushing hope and joy further and further away.

A chill went through Beau as he thought of this. He was now completely surrounded by starless night, and small drops of rain began to fall. Faint thunder could be heard in the distance, growing nearer. At that moment he remembered the cards that his wife had given him, and he pulled them from his pocket and began reading them. One spoke of light in the darkness and how the darkness could not overcome it. Comforted, he looked up from the card into the fire; it burned steadily and was the only light for miles.

As the rain began to fall harder, Beau rose to his feet, content on finishing the night in his tent. Part of him was hoping for a starry night, though another part was eager to be lying in a warm sleeping bag while rain beat on the vinyl walls. Before going in, he secured the tarp that covered the wood to keep it dry.

He unzipped the entrance and walked into the tent. Highway followed him in and plopped down on the small rug that Beau brought for him. Beau then lay down on his stomach in his sleeping bag and lit a small lantern.

"Now, where to go from here," he thought as he looked over his current journal and some older ones he brought with, unsure where his journey into the past would now lead him. "So much to cover; so many memories…"

Just then, far in the distance, he could faintly hear the hum of an engine chugging back on the mainland, growing louder and louder, then growing distant, and soon out of earshot. Though he was far removed from the normal goings on of everyday life, there were some desolate, hilly roads that meandered through the land, and going by the sounds of this engine, it was giving everything it had to push on through them.

"Hmm…" The sound sparked a memory. Soon after, his pen began to move, and piece by piece, as seen through his eyes, the story began to unfold.

Highway to Hillary's

Tuesday, September 21, 1998, 6:15 a.m.
Sitting by the window, waiting for Ranger to pick me up and head north. Dad made a quick breakfast of toast with honey and eggs over easy before leaving for work. The sky is growing brighter, covered in gray with some light blue mixed in. There are even a few patches where stars can still be seen, though they are diminishing quickly. Daylight is fading too, summer traveling further and further away as autumn runs her course.

A year ago I would not have imagined being in this situation; yet I am here, with no place else to go.

Just as Beau was diving into deeper thought, the sounds of the deep-breathing engine could be heard drawing near. "Let's do it..." he said with a sigh, grabbing his day's belongings. He took one last look into the fall sky before getting up from his seat at the kitchen table that sat alongside a large window, slipping on his jacket, and walking out the front door.

Moments later, Ranger pulled up to the curb in front of the house in a big, black cube van. He was wearing his cowboy hat, as usual, with a look on his face giving indication that he was indeed ready to take on the day.

"You ready, hombre? Let's go earn a living!" he hollered while sitting behind the wheel, a smirk coming over his face when he saw the groggy look on his young temporary assistant.

"As ready as I'm going to be," replied Beau with a touch of subdued optimism.

A friend of the family, Ranger had done carpentry work for Beau's grandpa and father, along with other people in the area. He was an energetic sort, like an open book with a likeable and entertaining character that one didn't run across every day. He also had a reputation for quality work, slightly shadowed by the challenge of pinning him down; he was a sort of a lone wanderer at times, on the move. Yet he knew how to work, and people kept asking for it.

Upon discovering·that Beau was in need of some temporary labor, Ranger offered him some seasonal work with a client of his, if one would call her that. She was preparing to sell her lake house in Silver Creek, a small tourist town in the far north of Wisconsin, and needed help getting it ready. Little did Beau know what was in store for him.

He climbed into the van, immediately catching the smell of coffee that filled the vehicle, along with some old-school rock and roll that screamed through the speakers. Before Beau shut the door, Ranger, who appeared as if he had drunk extra coffee that morning, hammered on the accelerator, sending Beau's head back into the headrest with a thump. Partly oblivious and completely amused, Ranger continued to accelerate down the road.

And they were off.

Through the town they drove, eventually veering onto old Highway 15 heading due north, destination Silver Creek. Once on the highway, the speed picked up, and the sound of the engine roared so loudly that they had to holler to hear one another. At times Beau would glance over at Ranger and see him bobbing his head up and down to the beat of the music, bouncing in his seat with one arm on the huge steering wheel while the other hung outside, banging on the door like a drum. Occasionally he would look over at Beau, yell something of mild significance, then turn back again to resume his worship.

"Something tells me this experience will not be forgotten," Beau thought to himself with an amused smile. He sat reclined in his seat, occasionally turning his head to look out the window to stare longingly at the passing scenery, which had now turned to woods and long, stretching highway with few cars.

Just how Beau ended up in that black cube van was something he couldn't help but ponder, and it forced him to peer back into earlier times that seemed a little fuzzy and unclear. Yet the simple truth was quite plain and required little pondering and a measure of honest reflection. The years had caught up with him. The beer-soaked weekends, which began with his first experience with alcohol at a party down the road at the ripe age of ten, followed him throughout middle and high school and into college, intensifying and morphing along the way. Those weekends finally paid their dues by getting him kicked out of college for a semester due to bad grades, along with getting him fired from his job for being late or "sick" one too many times.

The memory of it was one he'd rather forget. Carved in his mind was the fear and dread of sitting before the review board that summer day just a few months earlier with several other students who were faced with the same daunting consequence. So many thoughts poured through his mind afterward. "What am I going to do? How am I going to tell the others? What will they think? Will I ever really come back?" along with a myriad of other questions and concerns.

It wasn't long after that when he was forced to make the temporary yet humbling move back to Sheldon. The Jamison family moved back there after leaving Cringle, for somber reasons, shortly after Beau graduated high school. Sheldon was several hours from college, far away from all he wanted to be a part of. Doors just seemed to be shut all over to any other option.

At the time, he was living with Ed, an old friend from high school who had been his roommate for years. They had just moved into a nice two-bedroom apartment located in a lively, central part of town. Unlike previous places they lived, this was one that a person could actually enjoy coming home to at the end of the day. He wasn't looking forward to stepping away, especially with all the energy that existed around the campus in the summer months.

He got in his car that early evening in late June and drove away from Bluff View University for an undetermined amount of time, thoughts so heavy. He always loved the highway, though he knew the miles would pass with less elation on this particular trip. "What lies ahead?" he wondered silently, the light at the end of the tunnel obscured, daylight fading as summer neared its end.

As he drove along one of the narrow country highways, he noticed the bright sun in his driver's side rearview mirror setting in the horizon behind him. The beauty of it caught his attention, evoking a desire from deep within to turn around and drive toward it. Yet that wasn't an option now, and he drove on.

Adding to the heaviness of it all was an acquaintance with Autumn, a southern-accented girl he had met not too long ago. With deep brown eyes, long auburn hair, and gentleness like a quiet summer evening, she appeared one Saturday afternoon while he was sitting at the beach reading a novel. It had something to do with bridges and love. In later years he would come to realize that it was actually about home-wrecking adultery disguised as heart-warming romance. Subtle deception, he would reckon.

She laid her towel on the sand not far from where he sat, and shortly after, he mustered up the courage to initiate communication. She received him warmly, and they subsequently shared a delightful conversation that resulted in a couple short dates. She had a boyfriend at the time, though it was long distance and seemed to be drifting long before Beau's arrival. He also sensed what seemed to be a searching for something within her. Perhaps he might be the one to fulfill that, he thought.

On one of their dates, Beau took her up to a pub in the bluffs where they sat on a huge deck overlooking a valley of green treetops. Uninterrupted, they talked of the past and what was to come, with both laughter and some seriousness mixed in. She shared a regrettable experience of giving herself away to a guy within the last year during a time when she and her boyfriend were broken up. It was not like her to do such a thing, though she was weak and vulnerable at the time. Though Beau did not know her well, she was sweet and tender, and it stung his heart to see the guilt and shame she carried from it.

Needless to say, he regrettably had to step away from the acquaintance prematurely due to his departure. He planned on keeping in touch with her, knowing that she was leaving at the end of summer. Unfortunately, he accidentally left her telephone number behind when leaving for the semester, and when he called Ed to get it, it couldn't be found.

"You sure it's not there? I had it on the refrigerator, though I may have set it on the coffee table..."

"Dude, it ain't here. I've looked everywhere."

"Alright, but if you happen to run across it, *please* call me right away," replied Beau with a strained, exhortative voice. He knew that Ed, despite his admirable integrity and responsibility, wasn't very lofty in the area of cleanliness and organization and could have easily overlooked the small piece of paper that had this girl's name and telephone number.

"You have my word, buddy. I'll look again, and if I find it, I'll call a.s.a.p. Keep in touch; we're looking forward to having you back here."

"Thanks, Ed. You'll see me soon."

Months later, after Autumn had moved away to begin working, Ed informed Beau that he found the number. It was sitting behind the lamp on one of the end tables. Beau did his best to hide the overwhelming frustration that could have been avoided had Ed decided to clean once in a while. By now the number was disconnected, and though Beau made some attempts to find information as to her whereabouts, he came up short. It looked as if Autumn was gone for good.

Confused and frustrated that someone so seemingly sweet and special slipped away, again, Beau took a look into the skies for explanation. Though taken down by the loss, he kept moving, as if something was pulling him along.

The reality of everything stung, though he did his best to push on and do what he had to do. He would get through this time, get back to college, and finish another year and a half and get on with things. Yet he knew it wouldn't be so easy and that there would be obstacles, and sometimes he did wonder what lay ahead and if he'd really make it.

As the landscape rolled by that one summer evening while driving away, he looked deep into the sky again, seeing those soft clouds pass. "One day at a time," he often reminded himself.

"Beau!" yelled Ranger above the noise, knocking Beau out of his trance. "Take the wheel for a minute."

"Got it." Beau reached over and took hold of the big wheel like a helm, while Ranger used both hands to dig in his pocket to find a lighter for his cigarette.

"Okay," Ranger took the wheel again, to Beau's relief. The steering was not so responsive. On they drove, barreling down the road in the thunderous cube van, which housed all kinds of carpentry equipment and other supplies, to where Ranger's client, Hillary, and so much more awaited.

As they drew nearer to Hillary's lake house, the roads began to climb up and down, snaking to the right and left as they passed by the deep woods on both sides that lured the eyes into the dark unknown within them. The quiet hum of the engine could be heard as they raced down a hill, turning into a roar as it went up. This procession went on over and over again as they traversed the narrow lakeside road, the fallen leaves that still displayed color blowing in the draft behind them.

Ranger, as one would expect, took these roads as a challenge and proceeded to drive faster than what the cube van manufacturer might have recommended. Yet he knew his steed well, accurately manning the wheel and gas pedal, exerting control over the road. He had a healthy fear of it that kept him in balance with the twists and turns. A couple times Beau looked over at him, a smirk coming over his face with the sight of the intensified, boyish gleam on Ranger's face as he took on the hills.

"The key is easing up right before the turns and accelerating into them. Never ever brake when you're in one! You'll end up with a tree in your engine or drinking lake water. If a deer jumps out in the middle of the road, you just have to take it head on. Besides, nothing wrong with some good roadkill for dinner!"

"You got it, captain...Soon as you put me behind the wheel, I'll give 'er a shot," said Beau, half seriously. With that, Ranger looked over swiftly with a questioning glance that quickly turned into a smile, followed by an affirmed nod. He then returned his concentration to the road, apparently not ready to leave the helm just yet.

On they ventured, up, down, and all around. They passed old but well-kept houses, nearly hidden with long gravel driveways, until finally they approached their destination. As they did, the brightly shimmering blue of a lake could be seen just beyond the trees and the house, which was perched on higher elevation. The view was enough to bring a hint of peace.

"Here we are my friend—the lake house of Hillary. Now let me remind you, she is a good-hearted woman...well, sometimes she is." His voice trailed off for just a moment as he searched for just the right words. "She is tough minded, strong, and likes things done a certain way," he turned to peer at Beau, "and is accustomed to having things done *precisely* that way. A bit peculiar too, though you will find that out soon enough. Stay steady and you'll be fine."

Beau looked at Ranger with a squint in his eye. All of a sudden, he felt as if he were about to embark on some great quest that would test his already bruised manhood. He took a deep breath in, preparing for whatever was to come.

They pulled into the driveway, and there awaiting them was Hillary herself. Beau observed her demeanor, and it fit well the description that was previously given him. She was tall and slender with sharp blue eyes that were accentuated by her light gray hair and high cheekbones. Though well along in years, she retained a measure of physical beauty and strength that warranted attention. Like a hawk, she stood with a stern look on her slightly wrinkled face, examining the van as it pulled up. She began to walk toward it with her hands on her waist and elbows pointed out. Ranger adjusted the fit of his hat as if preparing to engage in battle, quickly glanced over at his assistant, and gave the nod for them to disembark.

Now it should be known that, prior to this meeting and Ranger's comments that morning, Beau had heard from another source of Hillary's occasional stern, hard-nosed side. He had even heard that she used one of Ranger's former helpers, who was fairly well known for being ruddy and a bit on the brawly side, as a mannequin to try on old, colorful, and fluffy dresses from an era long past that she was considering throwing out. The other possibility was that she just wanted to humiliate him. It was said that much manhood was sucked out of this individual in the process, slowly to be recovered, the wound never fully healing.

Prior to accepting this employment, Beau vowed he would not perform the same service, even if it meant desertion and abandonment.

"Good morning, Hillary," said Ranger with an appeasing voice.

"If you will call it that," she responded with the sharpest of tones. "Where have you been? You said you were going to be here three weeks ago to finish up the dock. I have people coming by to look at the place, and it's down there looking as if it's about to fall into the lake!"

"I know, Hillary, and I'm terribly sorry. Terribly sorry. I had some things come up that pulled me away, and I had to tend to them. Now let's go take a look, and I'll get to work on it with my assistant. Hillary, meet Beau. He's going to be helping out up here for a couple months until he goes back to college.

"Hello, Hillary," said Beau steadily as he cordially reached out his hand. She took a deep, investigative glance at him before shaking it sternly, then returned her stare to Ranger, who had smoothly stepped out of the conversation and was already walking briskly to the dock in hopes of avoiding any more heavy air.

"College, eh? What are you doing here if you have college going on?"

"It's sort of a long story," said Beau reservedly.

"Well then, what's the short of it?"

Beau thought for a moment, wanting to articulate properly. "I...I was forced to take some time away to get some things in order and need to earn a few dollars in the meantime."

"I see," she said after a moment of silence. "Well, I have plenty around here for you to do beyond what Ranger has, given you are ready to work."

"I am."

She turned and began the descent down the slope to the dock behind the lake house, Beau following close behind. The sounds of lapping waters grew louder and louder as they approached, and the minute Beau saw the dock and stood on the shoreline of the expansive lake, he knew he'd be spending an ample amount of time down there. Deep into the waters of his heart were many lakes and trees and winds from the past and much he could not see. Perhaps out there near the cool waters some understanding would come to him.

As it turned out, no modeling services were called upon from him that day, though much work was to be done. Hillary and Ranger wasted no time in putting him to the test, and they even had minor skirmishes over who had first rights to his labor for their individual projects. Hillary, being the paymaster, usually won out. This would be the case on more than one occasion.

Random tasks abounded, like tearing out old carpeting and laying down the new, rummaging through old closets and rooms, organizing boxes and files, sifting through a packed garage that housed relics from years long past, painting bathrooms, washing windows, helping Ranger make minor repairs to the dock, and numerous other to-do's that would stretch into the days to come.

The large lake house sat high over the water and was not lacking in amenities and prestige. Inside, it carried with it an air of memory that could be felt in each room. The first floor had many windows facing the lake that made it luminous in the day and soft and subtle in the evenings. Dark wood trim ran its way around the off-white walls and climbed up the open ceiling in the family room. A spiral staircase led up to several bedrooms on the second floor, where everything from wallpaper, bathroom fixtures, and bedroom linens pointed to an era long past.

Such poignancy hung in the air, provoking within Beau thoughts of his own family and the distance that seemed to penetrate the once tight-knit unit he enjoyed as a child. Now here was Hillary, an older woman seemingly all alone in this northern home, with all these pictures and mementos. Beau couldn't help but wonder of all the family times that must have taken place here.

"Beau! Stop that daydreaming and come help with this closet."

The rumors of her character would be discovered to be true as well. She was indeed quite particular, very determined, and definitely liked things done a certain way, which always happened to be her way and nothing less. She even exhorted some men who were working on the house, along with Ranger and Beau, to sit down when going to the bathroom in order to avoid the splash effect. Beau never heard this suggestion offered before and found it quite unsettling and odd. After all, he was a man, and men stand. He quietly rejected obedience to this mandate.

The end of the day eventually came, and soon Ranger and Beau climbed into the van and drove south, tired from the day's labor. Few words were spoken as the engine hummed down the highway, both men drifting in various directions with their thoughts as evening set in.

"See you at sunrise, amigo," said Ranger upon dropping Beau off, the light of sky diminishing into night. "Thanks for your help up there. You held yourself like a man."

"Thanks, Ranger. See you in the morn."

And so began the autumn days at Hillary's.

Each morning came and went in a similar fashion. Beau would hear the van coming before it was in sight, and he would rise from the table and the routine would commence again. Yet each day brought something different as well.

Though Hillary could be a challenge at times, Beau often caught glimpses of an interior side of her that was much more kind and soft than what was shown on the surface. Though he knew little of the cares of life at his young age, he noticed what seemed to be a great burden carried on her heart, pain in the soul that could be seen behind the flicker of hurried eyes.

As the weeks passed, Beau was called upon to drive to Hillary's by himself on a few occasions and more and more as time went on. This came to the dismay of Hillary, who had unfinished projects that only Ranger could complete.

"Where is that man?" she would ask after hastily and less than graciously greeting Beau as he stepped out of his car. She often waited in the driveway for him to arrive, ready to delegate duties and demands for the day.

"He said he'd be up here either today or tomorrow, though he could not say for sure…" replied Beau with little confidence, since he really didn't have a clue when Ranger would return. He was a man on the move with many obligations but with no secretarial assistance, and he rarely wrote things down in that mighty invention called a calendar.

To her dismay, even she was powerless to do anything about it; Ranger's work was top-notch and fair priced, and she knew it. So it would remain as it was.

Though Beau would come to miss those morning drives with Ranger, he quickly adjusted to the new arrangement, and it posed no challenge. He was a lover of the open road and welcomed the opportunity to let his mind wander into the distant fields and forests that grew longer and deeper the farther north he drove. Being that his time at Hillary's passed through mid and late autumn, he was able to witness the changing colors of leaves and the early morning and evening skies that spoke of life and death, of passing summer, and of the prelude to the coming of winter with all its wrath and majesty.

For now, the skies spoke peace, which was just what he needed to hear.

There was so much to see, think, and feel in these days, and though he knew he was too young to know some of the deeper truths of life and had much to experience, the current times still seemed so pivotal. The question emerged daily of where his life was taking him and how he was going to get wherever he was supposed to go. Manhood was staring him square in the face, more so than ever, yet old, irresponsible ways still beckoned him to follow. There were decisions facing him, and the consequences and challenges brought forth by those unwise ones already made, along with the burning, growing desire for a balanced life with soundness of mind and keen senses that for some reason seemed impossible to attain for more than a moment. Every time he tried to move forward, he found himself falling off the path.

However, he hoped and felt that this time would be different, that this season in his life would produce lasting change. In some strange way, there was a confidence brewing within him whose source he could not pinpoint—a strong beating in his heart each day that convinced him to keep going, as if an invisible, firm hand were gently guiding and pushing him along.

The days continued on at Hillary's, the long morning and evening drives cruising by old roadside bars with fluorescent beer signs that cried out to lonely and wandering souls at all times of the day and night with false offers of fulfillment and happiness, where memory could be suppressed by illusion. Having spent plenty of time and energy in such places, Beau grimaced at the sight of them before turning his eyes back to the road that went ever on before him, where the battle raged between solitude and an unidentified internal struggle. It was there, in that struggle, where a mysterious hope thrived despite all uncertainty.

On many occasions, Beau could be found taking a moment's rest beside the waters of Silver Creek Lake, standing on the outermost reaches of the dock. Those waters stilled his stirring soul and put him in quiet reverie as the sun danced upon the waves that lapped the shore. There were other days when fog and gray mist replaced the rays of sun, soothing his mind while he tried vigorously to make sense of things. He believed earnestly that much in life is beyond understanding and that all things happen for a reason, yet that didn't stop his pondering spirit.

Unknown to Beau, Hillary caught sight of his reflective moments. More than once she stood before the window in the house looking down toward the waters where Beau stood, staring out into it in deep thought. For reasons unknown to her at the time, this caused her to think more deeply about the things of life as well, of times and people and places lost in the abyss of a hurried life and the weariness brought by the often destructive pursuit of wealth and power.

Some of the thoughts would cause her to smile with fond recollection. Most of the time, however, it produced an unwelcome pang that echoed from deep inside, which she fought with all her might to ignore. Sometimes a tear would swell, of its origin she could not be sure, though she quickly wiped it away and made herself busy with something, justifying that she did not have time to think of such things.

Yet, with each tear that fell, she was forced to reckon with a feeling she had not felt in so long, a burning feeling in her heart that had long been chained and forgotten. Her senses were piqued, and though she would not admit it to herself, this brought her back to that window, over and over again, to peer into those waters and trees for the first time in years.

For Beau, amidst the thoughts of college and career and his lifestyle, one subject surfaced more frequently than all the others. Often, as they had since he first took notice of the creation back on the playground of George Washington Elementary, thoughts of a mate would emerge. The longing for another to walk through life with and to love and cherish confronted him with full force in those silent moments.

Though with all the obstacles lying in his path right now, this unknown, unnamed princess who Beau thought would satisfy that deep cavern in his soul was a little more distant than usual. In a strange way, this was peaceful to him. The pursuit of romance, which had followed him since childhood, could be such a heavy burden at times, such an expense of energy that often left him lifeless and numb in the end.

"Besides, I need to get my house in order before I'll be ready to take her hand," he said aloud more than once with a quiet, surrendered voice.

Perhaps that comment was carried by the passing wind and to listening ears beyond sight, for little did he know that something in this department lay not too far ahead in the distance. It would come in a way he could not have imagined or suspected, however.

When not standing lakeside or running other miscellaneous errands and to-do's for Hillary, Beau could be found in one of the little used areas of the home—a back closet, the garage, a spare bedroom, or even the old storage shed next to the house. His mission was simple: to clean and organize, yet he was so often sidetracked by the discovery of relics of times long past that gave small eavesdrops into that hard-to-see life of his employer.

One such item was a small, cherry wood candle holder that he found tucked away behind all sorts of items, which might otherwise be considered junk, in the garage. Yet as someone once said, "one man's trash is another man's treasure." The piece had four glass sides held together by wood beams in between and a small piece of wood on the top that was used to pull up the candle setting from within. On the front piece of glass was a white impression of several ducks flying out of tall grass into the sky above.

The holder immediately caught Beau's eyes, and Hillary, seeing the appreciation of it in her young helper's eyes, surprisingly aired no hesitation in giving it to him. He blew the dust off from its surface, studied it for a moment, and then set it aside in a safe place as a reward for his labors.

Later that same day, while rummaging through one of the dozens of closets, he made another significant discovery. Hidden behind pillows and cardboard boxes was a large red and gold shoebox with the words *"Family Photos"* written in black magic marker. As usual, his curiosity won the battle in determining whether he ought to peer through them or not. After peeking out the bedroom door to confirm that Hillary was not near, he pulled out the box and gently lifted the aged cover, again blowing off dust that had accumulated from lack of use.

Within a moment Beau was immersed in Hillary's past. In the box were pictures of her in earlier years, often surrounded by children: scenes of the lake, in a boat with little kids holding up fish; Christmas with presents, wrapping paper, and snow-covered trees outside; weddings with beautiful bridesmaids and flower girls; and other joyous occasions. There were also numerous pictures of Hillary in her later years, dated about fifteen years prior, with grown children and what appeared to be her husband. The demeanor on her face showed what appeared to be resignation and disappointment, contrary to the youthful exuberance and joy that appeared in some of the older pictures.

In the bottom of that shoe box he found the most revealing photo, one which left as much mystery as it did explanation. Black and white and aged, it appeared to be a wedding picture. Hillary's wedding. Looking vibrant, beautiful, and hopeful, she stood with her arms clasped together with those of a tall, handsome, and austere man who did not match the man in the pictures he previously viewed. On the frame was carved the words *"Gregory and Hillary, Today Made One."* Though intact, the photo was encased by cracked glass that streaked to all four corners of the frame, as if it had fallen face down on a hard floor. Going by its appearance, Beau could not help but wonder if the glass broke by accident or as the result of a hurting, angry heart.

Beau examined the photo, then, turning it over, discovered a piece of yellowed newspaper attached to the back. It was a small column from an obituary with a picture of what appeared to be the same man who stood next to Hillary on the other side, though with a few extra years added on. And it was, as Beau would find out when reading the obituary. *"Gregory Denari...survived by wife Hillary and children."*

"Beau!" the words came from downstairs, making Beau flinch, pulling him out of the past like one woken from a deep dream.

"Yes?" he yelled back, quietly scrambling to get all the pictures collected. He looked one more time at the wedding picture before placing it back in the shoe box. He covered it with the other pictures, put the cover back on, and carefully returned it to the rear of the closet.

"I need your help out back with the roofing guys. Please come down at once," she said with a firm yet respectful voice.

"I'm on my way," he said, grateful that she had not caught him looking through the pictures.

All the while that Beau assisted Hillary with unloading roof shingles from a truck that had recently arrived, he thought about the wedding picture and wanted to ask her about it. She never made any mention of the man in the photo, and in retrospect, it seemed odd that only a few family pictures were on display in the house.

He couldn't find the words that day to ask her, though soon enough the time would come.

"What was your husband's name?" he asked while behind the wheel of the old Chevy pickup that Hillary used sparingly for hauling junk to the dump, which happened to be what they were doing one late afternoon. A week had passed since he had discovered the picture, and finally the moment arrived when it seemed right to ask.

"So I see you've discovered some pictures during your chores," she replied with a cool, firm, yet not altogether unpleasant tone while maintaining her gaze out the windshield. Beau bit his lip and kept his mouth shut, mainly due to a lack of any worthy response. After a few moments, she sighed and continued, "He passed due to cancer. It's been many years now."

"I'm sorry…"

"Don't be. It's a part of life," she replied with a hardened voice that seemed to come from a great distance.

"What about your children?" he asked again.

"They are grown and gone," she said quickly, turning what little attention she had given the other way. "Here is the road we are to turn on. Take a right here," she said, pointing her finger in that direction. "I don't talk to or see them much. They are very busy and far away…"

Her voice trailed off after that, turning her stare to the right and peering out the window to the passing woods, a look of reverie coming over her face and a silence that indicated that the discussion had officially ended. Yet, behind it all, there was a softness and longing that showed from behind her veiled face, as if peace was breaking into her soul and warring against the thick walls surrounding her heart.

The moment quickly passed. Hillary returned her stare forward, her face now focused and fixed ahead. Again, she was ready to give orders and make arrangements as they drove the old pickup into the dump.

The dump, oddly enough, was a word that rang fondly in Beau's ears. In earlier years, it was one of his mother's favorite places to go on Saturday mornings. How she loved sitting with her two sons as they drove out to the smelly heaps of waste. It seemed strange to them at the time how she loved those times so, though in later years, when time became more fleeting and difficult to slow down and spend time with others, they would come to better understand their mother's appreciation of those simple trips to the wasteland.

That evening they sat for dinner, one of the few times Beau stayed to eat with Hillary. Though she didn't broach the subject of the day's conversation, and while much wasn't said at all beyond the surface, she did seem to have an air about her that was less rigid, almost soft and gentle.

The day would end as such, Beau thanking her for the meal before getting into his car and returning to Sheldon.

The next day at Hillary's was business as usual. Hillary could be found walking to and fro while talking on her phone, coordinating movers and painters and financiers, while Beau worked through his extensive list of chores. She had given him a lengthy one as usual.

The afternoon found him out in the front yard splitting wood. He wasn't sure why, since it was not going to be burned in the house, but it was an order, and he wasn't about to complain since he thoroughly enjoyed this particular labor, despite his inexperience with a maul. Above him, a mostly sunny sky shone down upon the earth, boasting a beautiful blue canvas accompanied by fluffy white clouds that gingerly passed by. A cool breeze blew peacefully over Beau's skin and through his hair and then continued on through a host of birch, maple, and pine trees that stood guard over the land.

The end of the day came quickly, and like every other, Beau walked briskly to his car and set out for the usual course. He felt particularly good about things, satisfied with the day's accomplishments, aided by the beauty and serenity of the hour. He turned the volume up on the stereo and rolled the windows down to let the mild October wind roll in.

Now it seems in life that certain events catch many hustling people when they least expect it, and for unknown reasons, many of these were coming across Beau's paths during these times.

On this particular day, another one of those experiences was soon to be upon him.

He planned on stopping by his mother's house that evening; she lived just a half-hour away from his father, and it had been nearly a week since he had last seen her. It was a challenge sometimes to spend time with both of them now that they lived apart. Upon arrival he pulled into the road that led to her house, and as he approached the driveway, he saw Lady, his old and faithful canine companion of fourteen years, lying in the middle of the driveway. She often took naps here and there, basically wherever she pleased, though it did seem a little odd for her to be lying where she was.

Beau pulled into the driveway and parked off to the side so that his mother could get in the garage when she returned from work. He stepped out and walked toward Lady, and as he approached her, a sinking feeling began to swell in his stomach when, less than ten feet from her body, he received no response from her.

This wasn't altogether too unusual. There were times over the years when he'd sneak up on the poor girl while she was peacefully resting in the garage and scare the wits out of her. It produced a hearty laugh from him, though not from her. She would just lay there, her body slowly recovering from the jolt, her head perched up while her body remained in sleeping position with those sad, loving eyes gazing at him as if asking "why?" Those eyes would always heap weight on him too.

This time, though, something was different with her.

When he looked for signs of breath moving into and out of her body, none could be found.

"Oh, Lady..." he said quietly. She had taken her final nap that afternoon.

He stood over her, mouth ajar and eyes squinted in submission to reality's bitter bite. He gazed steadily upon his fallen friend, who once excitedly greeted him and his siblings as children upon first introduction, when their tiny butts wiggled so frantically that it caused them to lose their footing and slide on the linoleum floor. He placed his hand upon her, still feeling warmth, the awareness slowly setting in that the breath of life had passed from her not too long ago.

There are those unplanned moments in life when the sounds of birds can be heard so clearly above all else—unsuspecting moments when the delicate passing breeze can be noticed so much more powerfully than at other times, when the blue of the sky is for some reason so much bluer and the trees, swaying in that same breeze, seem to come alive, watching over those below like a grandfather. As Beau stood over Lady with no one else near, his heart beginning to release tears that found their way to his eyes, one of those moments was upon him.

He rose from his crouched position and went to the garage to find something to transport her body, now slightly bloated, off the gravel.

that he had carefully selected upon entering the forest. He felt incomplete in the woods without a good sword, and it would remain with hm for the entire journey.

The trail gradually grew narrower, and the woods became less dense and displayed a smooth, rolling floor of moss, fallen leaves and needles that fell from the conifers. It eventually crossed down through a gulley, where a tiny brook flowed. Despite being nearly clogged with leaves, the brook's trickling water left sweet sounds as it passed over glossy stones. Just past the brook, the trail began to rise again through the ravine into the woods, which again grew thick.

After passing a short distance into the wood, a small clearing atop an incline could be seen in the distance. There, standing firm and secure, was the old cabin. Beau's heartbeat and pace quickened with the sight of it, and a smile covered his face. For the cabin was a special place, where both clock and schedule held little significance.

He stepped through the final barricade of forest and stood in the clearing facing the east side of the cabin, stopping for just a moment to admire the view. Many tired and weary souls had found safe haven in the structure that humbly displayed large, true logs and rustic windows. A modest yet vast porch faced to the north, making both sunrises and sunsets visible to one who chose to relax in one of the handcrafted chairs that sat on it.

Earl's grandmother, who owned the property and passed it on down to the family, made those chairs herself. Most of the material used to make them was taken straight from the woods that surrounded her. Young Earl and his brothers were sent out into the woods to collect the right pieces of wood, and his father would cut and sand them for his lady.

Paradise lost then found again, or so it seemed to Beau as small streams of smoke flew out of the chimney like departing spirits of men on their way to eternity. The glow of candles could be seen from several windows, slightly blurred due to the condensation that formed on the glass. The day had become grey and drizzly, though it only made the cabin more warm and inviting to the senses.

A few weeks earlier, Beau had told Earl that he hoped to come this weekend, though he never confirmed it and knew there was the risk of an empty or already visitor-occupied cabin. Yet Earl, whose memory was still very well intact, came to the door as soon as Beau began walking up the steps. It was as if he knew beyond any doubt that his young friend was coming. In earlier years, when the Jamisions lived nearby, Beau would come marching through the woods to visit without notice, sometimes dripping wet after swimming in the lake or river with his siblings or by himself. And so it remained to this day.

Earl was a large man, clearing six foot and more, fit and trim, yet with significant mass. He had a slight hunch in his posture, though showed evidence of a disciplined life in that he still had his mobility despite being well along in years. He wore an old red and gray flannel jacket, faded blue jeans, a worn black Green Bay Packers cap, and rugged boots that sang silent songs of memorable miles long since trodden and some not yet come to pass.

"Hello, my young sojourner friend!" he said in his low, humble tone with squinted eyes and crooked smile. Earl reached out and gave Beau a big hug and afterward paused for a moment to briefly study him.

"Hmm...having known you and your family all these years I'd reckon you have something pressing on your heart." He paused for another moment, then gestured for Beau to follow him inside. "Though I trust we'll get to that soon enough. Come on in; I just made a fresh pot of strong-willed coffee in case I had visitors."

The truth was that though he did have visitors from time to time, he was not overrun by them. His cabin was not accessible by car but only by a ten-minute hike down an old, well-worn trail that was a bit shorter than Beau's passage, yet long enough to deter some from coming. Crime was not unheard of in these parts, though the place was relatively safe as folk in the area knew their neighbors and, regardless of whether they fancied each other or not, looked out for one another.

Earl depicted a simple way of life, not void of what was going on in the world around him, though not downtrodden by it either. He was far from a recluse, though took in plenty of solitude and time to just sit and listen—something he saw less and less of in the lives of those around him. Through the years, perhaps out of necessity for change in his own hurried life, Earl learned a balance, a constant adjustment to tension that kept the breath of life blowing through him and into others.

Earl's dog, Jesse, came bounding out the door and greeted Beau warmly and continued to rain down affection on him as he walked up the porch. Beau bent down to receive a few kisses from her, despite what so many said about dogs licking themselves and all. Sometimes love knows no boundaries.

"You're getting older, girl," said Beau as he noticed the white hair around her nose, "but good to see you're still young at heart."

That old yellow Labrador had been such a trustworthy friend to Earl through the years, especially since his beloved wife passed beyond the gates of splendor just under twelve years ago. With each passing year, Ruth seemed to grow even closer to Earl's heart, while the memories of her in good health grew more vivid and powerful, and missed. The pain of her loss reduced at the same time, perhaps with the knowledge that with each passing day, he drew closer to where she was.

Now Jesse sat attentively between the two men, who sat together drinking coffee in the living room next to the crackling fireplace. Beau had always enjoyed the fragrance of coffee but rarely drank it in those days, though that changed whenever in the company of Earl. There was something about their times together that made it taste so good and right. So they drank, their eyes occasionally drawn to the window that looked out to the north, where a large maple, full of color, sat all alone in the clearing. Just beyond the maple lay the forest, thick and foreboding under the vast expanse of the fresh autumn sky.

"How's your Ma and Pa doing, and the rest of the clan?" asked Earl.

"They all seem to be good," responded Beau in a revealing tone, which Earl picked up on. "I don't get to spend as much time with them as I would like to. Feel a bit distant from them at times, but overall things seem alright."

"Good," said Earl after a pause, knowing deeper truths in his heart concerning the situation. He had a strong doubt in his mind that either Beau or his siblings had grasped the true effects of their parents divorce, how it sent each one off course, spiraling in different directions and searching for something to fill the vacuum left by a broken family. Painfully, Earl knew that none had found that which truly satisfies but rather much that doesn't and that leaves wider wounds in the soul than before. Though not even Earl, with all his wisdom, honor, and experience could bring them to see it.

"Your parents love you all very much, Beau, more than ever. Did their best to take care of you. I don't know much, but this I've seen and know to be true." He paused for a moment and looked out the window. Noticing that Beau was still receptive and taking these words to heart, he went on, "Sometimes people make mistakes in life and stumble, and I'm sure if they could, they would go back and do some things differently. It's a hard, hard thing to go through…for all of you."

Though he could have said more and perhaps had an open door to do so, Earl stopped. He found no more words and felt enough was said on the matter without being invited to say more. He knew of the damage that divorce can bring, how it sweeps down silently from one generation to the next if not confronted, and longed to help Beau unearth some of its wreckage in his own life. Yet he also knew that inward and outward battles over forgiveness and reconciliation would likely find the scattered Jamisons one day. Until then, he could only listen, pray, and offer his friendship and loyalty to the family.

Beau said little in response, though his expression made it clear to see that he took the comments to heart, his mind mulling over every gently spoken word.

"I know I have good parents and that they tried," he said, remembering all the years they had provided for and been there for him, unaware that much was suppressed in his own heart and secretly altering his course.

They spoke for a while, Beau eventually opening up more about current events. This opening up normally took a long time when speaking with others, but when it came to talking with Earl, it came automatically.

"Not sure what to make of these times. Some strange feeling in me, like there is something more pounding away, yet all this stuff going on with college…I've been kicked out for a semester…" he said hesitantly while shifting around in his seat, figuring that Earl may have already known but not completely sure.

"I know," he said in a comforting tone, looking directly at his young friend and pausing a moment before saying more. "Sounds like you have some housecleaning to do in this season, as well as some searching. Times like this come upon all at some point or another." Beau sat silent and motionless, taking in each word while looking forward. "And you can trust that more will come down the road and more chal-

she looked out the front window to see her daughter racing to the mailbox, her hair bouncing up and down as she went. Such were the days. Earl would pour out thoughts and descriptions of the times in his letters, doing his best to leave out details that might cause her soul to be troubled. He would write of the stars at night that seemed to watch down on them, of the rains that would often wash away fear and worry, and the sunrises that were so peaceful and almost out of place amidst the conflict. He would share his encounters with other soldiers and their stories, recalling pictures of their wives and children they shared with him, and how some wouldn't be returning home.

Never was there a letter that didn't include his desire to see and hold her, to walk and talk together down by the river and everywhere else. And never once did those words lack truth. How he missed her so, a smile coming to his face even in the darkest of hour upon thoughts of her.

With war, though, there were some days that some might wish would have never been, and those days occasionally found their way into his letters to Ruth.

My dearest Ruth,

My desire now is to share with you of days that transpired with peace and relative calm and of my sweet thoughts of you and when we shall see each other again. However, I must share other news of the kind I hoped would not come to be.

We came under heavy fire several days ago; many didn't make it—among them, my brother Tom. That I am writing of his death at this moment is something I still cannot grasp; seems like yesterday that we were wrestling out in the front yard or lying in our bunk beds at night back home, supposed to be sleeping but just talking about whatever until late. So many memories are bombarding me. I know the two of you bonded well also, and that my loss is your loss too. I am sorry to have to share this hurtful news with you. I pray I never have to write such words again.

I think back to the night I first met you, how he was standing there with me at the time and saw my eyes light up. He encouraged me immensely in my desire to get to know you and even gave me a nudge toward you that morning in church. I wanted to punch him for it, though looking back I see it was just fear and pride and am now thankful for that nudge. By the way, I was so nervous when I came up to talk to you, though I guess without fear there is no need for courage.

Just months ago we were training together for this place, talking about what we'd do when we returned home, how he hoped to ask Ann for her hand in marriage. Instead, I held his hand as he passed away from shrapnel wounds while lying in the woods far, far away from Cringle.

I can still see clearly the moment of his passing, the sounds of gunfire and bombing going on around us, and then everything went silent. I looked over and saw him lying there, wounded in the snow. Memories of riding horses together and fishing and playing in the lake and river, of burying our father together—they flashed through my mind as quickly as lightning.

I ran to him, held him in my lap, but he couldn't speak. Then he was gone. Still under fire, I was forced to move on and had to let go of his hand that still barely clung to mine. "Goodbye, big brother," I whispered, tears falling like the morning dew that drips down the blades of grass. I was unable to give him a fitting burial, yet I know and am assured, as I know you are too, in the knowledge that he had passed on to a much better place. A place where he now dwells near a mighty river that runs with power and peace forevermore. Maybe there are even some lakes and streams there for him to fish in...

I miss him, Ruth. And I miss you. Your
prayers comfort me.
With you each day, no matter how far
away,

Earl

Earl returned months later. Some scars now existed on his skin and soul that would heal but never completely disappear, yet he was fully intact physically and mentally. Upon arrival to his hometown, he went immediately to Ruth's house and embraced her, then took her father aside at an opportune time that evening and asked for his blessing in marriage. Without hesitation, he gave his future son-in-law the blessing with great joy and a big, strong, manly hug that nearly squished him. Once released, Earl hurried back to ask Ruth if she'd accompany him for a long walk beside the river.

As they walked along the water's edge, Ruth sensed something in the air due to Earl's energy. Yet she remained silent, listening so attentively to him and his many words. In a small opening that sat in the shade of a large willow tree, where they had once shared a picnic, Earl knelt on one knee and asked her to accompany him for their lifetime. Five months later they wed under the golden maple trees outside their little church and began their long journey together as one.

Years later, Earl and Ruth were sitting in the church pew one Sunday morning when in strode a young couple with two little children. They looked rushed and anxious as they entered the sanctuary several minutes after the service began. For reasons unknown by human standards, they caught Earl's attention, and after the service they made it a point to welcome the young couple and immediately connected beyond the surface. Soon a relationship followed that formed bonds not to be broken with the coming years.

The young couple, Carl and Janet, with son Dean and daughter Anwen, were new to the area and in need of caring ears and smiles, and they took to the Timmings. Over the next half-dozen years, three more children would come into the world, the final one being Beau.

The years passed quickly, each one moving faster than the next, and the era came when Beau would come rustling through the woods with no particular agenda other than to venture. Sometimes he would be accompanied by one or more of his siblings, and they would swim in the lake or river, then sit down for peanut butter and jelly sandwiches. Sometimes they would fall asleep on the couch near the fireplace as Earl and Ruth went about their daily business, enjoying the company that graced their little cabin. Earl would pull out his old guitar and strum a few melodic songs out on the porch, the sounds drifting into the cabin and sedating all. Such peace.

Beau and his siblings weren't the only ones to find refuge there. Carl and Janet would visit from time to time, either together or alone. They shared many hours together—times of joy and struggle, tears of laughter and pain. Much wisdom was passed down through that cabin in times of need.

Many years later, however, to the sorrow of Earl and Ruth, the beloved couple that came into their lives many years before parted ways. Hurts and unhealed wounds festered and dug into their marriage, pulling their eyes and hearts away from the one source that could hold it together. Finally, the strain succeeded in pulling them apart. Earl and Ruth prayed and mourned for them and for the kids, who they knew would face much hurt and confusion as a result.

> "Honey, God hates divorce, though he still fiercely loves those who go through it," Earl gently told his wife one night in front of the fireplace as she lay in his arms, struggling inside with the implications of it.
> "He will *not* leave them…"

Now, many years later, Earl drove alone with a flood of memories pouring through his soul of those now long passed, many of whom he wished he could sit down with and hear their hearts, to listen better and understand more. Above all, though, was Ruth. Despite her absence he was not without a full and grateful heart for those who still remained in his life, and knowing that his days were numbered, gleamed with anticipation of seeing his true love again one day in heaven. He wasn't sure if that was how the Almighty had it worked out, though he did know that whatever lay beyond the gates of splendor would be exceedingly sufficient to fully satisfy and relieve the ache that lingered in his heart.

Though he still had time on this earth, and with it, work to do.

What lay before him now was to do whatever he could to aid the young man who now waded in the river near his house, a young man in the midst of fighting an inner battle that he couldn't fully understand, one that involved a difficult passage into true manhood.

Near the edge of the woods behind the cabin lay the old shed where Beau's trusty fly rod sat. He swung open the old but stable shed door and was met by the usual musty smell of items that had existed for generations. Many times he opened that door, peering into it like a child would an armory. Some childlikeness must have remained in Beau, for again he looked around as if he might discover something new or some relic of the past. Satisfied with what he saw, he took the fly rod in hand, along with a set of waders and a fishing vest, and briefly inspected them before exiting the shed and shutting the door.

He marched toward the river, passing the front of the cabin before crossing over the invisible line that separated the yard from the woods. With the fly rod in one hand, waders and jacket in the other, he wove in and out of trees that hovered over the soft forest floor, stepping over fallen logs that once looked proudly down from above. Though the encroachment of winter was dangerously close, fall still held dominance and allowed for a day of sweet sun and gentle breeze that moved effervescently through the forest.

As soon as Beau entered the forest, he could faintly hear the running waters of the river. Soon the sounds became stronger as he descended the hill that led to its shore. Through the trees he could see patches of shimmering water where the sun touched down on it, radiant enough to capture the eyes and make them squint. Beau lunged forward in anticipation, eager to be in the flowing waters that had a way of washing the soul of worry.

Once at the water's edge, he set everything down except for the waders. He stepped into them, pulled the straps over his shoulders, and adjusted them to fit his height. He then put on the fishing vest, picked up the rod, and connected its three pieces and stepped into the river. The water, clear and pristine, ran stealthily on over rocks and sand that covered its floor. It came just above his ankles where he entered, though within a few steps, it was up to his knees, and in a few more, his waist was covered.

He could feel the tug of the current trying to sweep him away, though as long as he was mindful of his balance and held a firm footing, it didn't have the strength this time of year to take him down. If it was springtime, when the melting snow emptied into the river and raised the elevation of the water, it would be a different story.

He loosed the fly from the cork handle and dipped it in the water to give it weight. Letting some line out from the reel, he began the back and forth, two o'clock, ten o'clock elbow motions until enough line was released to position the fly where he wanted it. Rainbow trout, a clever and wary fish, will often gather in deep pockets or just beyond a drop off, waiting for food to come from upstream.

With each cast Beau admired his surroundings. Inside he felt lighter and lighter as the minutes passed by, intoxicated by the sounds of rushing water and the way it sparkled as it flowed over and around the rocks. On either side of the river, tall grass swayed gently back and forth in the soft wind, along with the mighty willow and oak trees whose branches bordered the water, some of which still retained their leaves.

As they often did, the elements brought thoughts of a mate to Beau. He wondered when and who she might be and why he must wait so long. Like that day not long ago when standing on Hillary's dock, though, he turned away from the thought as best he could. He was too tired inside to enter that land of romance that had so many times left him feeling all alone, and with his situation being as it was, he still felt a relationship to be so far out of reach.

"Someday," he whispered.

A good hour went by before Beau caught his first fish—a healthy rainbow trout that pounced on his fly and fought with all he had to avoid his captor's hands.

"Sorry, buddy," he said to the squirming, slimy little critter while carefully removing the hook, "but you were destined for my stomach." After ending the conversation with his victim, he placed it in the pouch that was attached to the back of the vest and returned to the hunt.

Beau fished on for a couple more hours, the elements continuing to work on his senses. After catching several more trout, he walked out of the river and removed the vest and waders and sat down next to a large willow tree near the shoreline to rest for a minute. The tree may have put a spell on him, for within minutes after leaning his head back on the bark, he dozed off into a deep sleep.

Thanks to the sound of a squirrel in the tree above him, he woke and looked around, feeling he had been out for hours. He looked at his watch—only a half-hour had gone by. Though he felt he could have rested for hours, he lurched up, grabbed the gear, and returned the way he came, marching up the hill back to the cabin to fulfill his obligation to gather and split firewood. He put all the fishing gear back in the shed and went into the cabin.

After placing the fish in the refrigerator, he walked back outside to the woodshed, which was also behind the cabin, and pulled a granola bar from his front pocket that he packed earlier. After taking a few over-sized bites, he grabbed the old maul from inside the structure and began the assault on the logs, swinging with force, splitting one after another. He hadn't cut too many logs in his years and was no expert at it, though since working up at Hillary's cabin, he had become more proficient, thanks to some guidance from Ranger.

After an hour of splitting, he retired the maul and began stacking the logs in the shed. He then gathered dry wood and returned to the cabin, setting them down next to the fireplace. He washed up and fetched his backpack, pulling out his journal and a pen, and laid down on the couch. He was tired, yet clear minded and satisfied due to the fullness of the day. With his head resting on the soft armrest, he looked about the still cabin and beyond the windows
before opening his journal.

> *Saturday afternoon at Earl's, October 24, 1998*
> Though the tranquility at Hillary's place has far
> exceeded that of the college lifestyle, it pales in comparison to
> this cabin. Seems one doesn't know how fast they are moving
> until they completely stop. Other than the brief moments stand-
> ing on her dock, it appears I have not stopped in some time. I
> hope this weekend doesn't pass too quickly...

So peaceful, so still was the air about him that his eyelids grew far too heavy for him to bear. Just a few breaths later, he set the pen and journal down on his chest and again drifted into a sweet late-afternoon nap that spanned segments of time and space too great to count or measure, all in just a couple hours.

When the light returned to Beau's eyes, it was accompanied by the gentle yet persistent lapping of Jesse's tongue over his face. She was standing with her hind legs on the floor and her front paws on the couch, one of them on Beau's chest. Her face was right over Beau's, excited to see her old friend wake and join the camaraderie. Though the amount of saliva exchanged was a little bit excessive, even for Beau, it remained to him one of the most enjoyable ways one could be awoken from a deep slumber. He pitied those unfortunate souls who thought differently.

Beau lifted his hands to Jesse's face to pet her, allowing a few more kisses from the creature before gently shoving her away and pulling himself up to a sitting position. At the same time, Earl was in the kitchen area, taking food out of brown paper bags. Outside, the sun was making its way to the edge of the horizon, its rays of light beaming into the family room from behind the trees.

"Hmmph...I must have dozed off for a while," he said groggily. "I haven't had a nap like that in ages." The words came out with a big yawn and stretch. Beau looked around in a sort of daze while waiting to regain his senses, then shook his head to try to stir it to life. The serenity was so thick that he did not want to get up, concerned that it might dissipate.

"Goin' by the way you were snoring when I came in, seems you have been needing that rest," said Earl with a grin on his face as he unpacked the bags.

"Snoring? I don't snore," replied Beau with look of deep thought and concern. "Least I don't think I do..." His voice trailed off at the end, silence following as a questioning look came over his face as he pondered the possibility that he did, in fact, snore. Earl, taking notice of this, grinned even wider. He heard no snoring when he came into the house, though he couldn't resist taking the young chap for a little ride. "It may help humble him," he thought jokingly to himself.

Beau rose from the couch, walked into the kitchen, and leaned over the counter, which acted as a divider for the family room and kitchen, with room for three stools. Earl was on the other side in front of the sink that faced the front yard, making preparations for dinner. His eyes were moist from chopping onions and peppers on an old, thick

"Warrior?" Beau thought to himself, not accustomed to the title. Yet in a way, he liked hearing it.

After writing a few more words, Earl closed his journal and pushed the open Bible to the back of the desk. He rose to get another cup of coffee, Beau following his lead, and soon they were on the porch again, taking in the brisk morning air. The day was overcast, yet pleasant and welcoming.

"Skies are suppose to clear up for a while this afternoon, then get a bit angry tonight," said Earl as he took a sip from his coffee, one foot perched on the railing while leaning back in the rocker. "I may ask you to gather more wood to get us through the evening, and to split some more logs to get me through the winter."

"Sure thing," Beau said as a big yawn enveloped his words, eyes fixed into the woods before them. His whole body and soul were invigorated by the brisk air and colors of morning, and he wished he could wake to this every morning. Soon Jesse came out, licked Beau's right hand that hung down from the rocker, and made her way to her master's side and plopped down, as if to engage in the conversation.

"Such a fine lady you are, Jesse. Always ready for the day at hand," said Earl as he pet her on the back.

For a short time, they sat on the porch as the sun, barely visible through the trees, continued to ascend in the far away horizon, dashing the grayish-blue sky with streaks of bright pink in the distance where an opening appeared. Some laughter, reflection, and talk of fishing and family ensued. There was something about the still of the morning that allowed for such open, unrushed conversation.

Earl, who had a touch more energy running through him than Beau, shared some plans he had for the cabin. There was the work on the deck and storage shed, as well as cutting down some old trees that had reached the end of the road and whose departure would create more light and room for other, younger trees to rise up.

"The circle of life continues," Earl commented before another taking a sip of coffee.

As he was pointing to one of the trees that he was talking of cutting down, an unexpected cough came over him that he couldn't subdue, despite his best efforts. The unusually harsh sound caught Beau's attention, turning his gaze from the land in front of him to his left, where Earl sat. In an instant his tiredness left him.

"You alright, Earl?" asked Beau, while quickly taking the coffee mug, which had spilled some, from Earl's hand.

"Oh, I'm fine," said Earl a moment later, a few lingering coughs coming from him as he sat forward in his seat, hands clutching the arm-rests. He caught his breath, inhaled deeply, and leaned back in his chair in a relieved fashion, noticing Beau's eyes on him as he did so.

"Just a cough that's been pestering me lately," he said reassuringly, clearing his throat some more and catching his breath, hiding discomfort behind his eyes. "Seems I'm not getting any younger these days." The cough had subsided, though a slight wheezing still accompanied his breathing. Beau handed his mug back to him and turned his eyes back to the front, a bit squinted in consternation.

Earl was always a giant of a man, more so even in character and heart than brawn, and to witness a sign of his mortality was a new, unsettling thing to Beau. He had seen him cry before, like when Ruth passed years earlier. There was another time when he walked in on him while he was on his knees praying in front of the couch, his head buried in his hands, sobbing like a child. But this was something altogether different, something Beau would have rather not experienced that morning, or ever.

Fear gripped him for a moment, trying to distort perspective and blind his vision. It fled quickly, however, as Beau looked back toward the sky and wood, as if chased off by some invisible gatekeeper.

They remained on the rockers for a short time, with relatively few words spoken. Earl eventually rose and announced that he was going to begin breakfast. He took Beau at his word to gather and split more firewood, and again Beau acquiesced and rose himself to walk to the woodshed, the whole time taking in a deep breath of the morning air that continued to revive and comfort him. A young man on an honorable mission in the morning is of great benefit to the world and all who surround him.

Back at the cabin, Earl opened the door and walked to the kitchen, with Jesse following him around for a while before going off to watch over Beau. A big, hearty, farm-style breakfast was the plan, with enough eggs, toast, ham, sausage, and orange juice to sustain them until lunch.

As he prepared breakfast amidst the sounds of logs being split in the background, he thought of his coughing episode just a short while ago and how it wasn't the first in recent times. There were other signals too: infirmities and episodes that hinted deteriorating health. He wasn't eager to give way to old age and wasn't going to go out passively, though neither did he engage in the futility of arguing with it. His plan was to simply keep moving forward with the full knowledge that he was marching on to a better place, a march that at times would be painful and heart wrenching.

Yet his march was not without purpose, nor his journey finished.

He had hoped that he could conceal any clues to this aging process from Beau during his time here at the cabin. The young man had enough confusion in his life these days, whether self-induced or not, and Earl did not want to complicate the matter. He was stirred inside with hope and anxiousness over the young man's plight toward real manhood and the road blocks set up along the way. Yes, he knew Beau would eventually come to discover his old friend's physical decline, and to try to hide that reality of life from him would be futile. Though perhaps it wouldn't have to show itself during this time.

"Lord, help him find his way..." uttered Earl as he stood in front of the kitchen sink, looking out the window in front of him into the sky, with plump strawberries in his hands, taking a shower under the lightly running faucet.

After setting several large logs in place, Beau picked up the heavy maul and began to swing. Again he was aware of his lack of proficiency with the tool, especially compared to Earl. He was quickly gaining on him, though, and with each split down the middle, he felt a surge of blood in his veins.

"Men were made for swords and axes," he said to himself after a swift blow, not yet aware of a deeper, mysterious truth behind the words that he just spoke. He oft looked into the sky that was breaking above to reveal shades of blue before setting up another log and several more after that. "One more," he kept saying, though many logs would receive the same lie as the one before.

Taking a break from the logs, he began wielding the maul as if a sword, sending it down and around, up and over, gripping it tightly with two hands on the shaft, turning to and fro, and reveling in the swooshing noises made in the process. Jesse sat nearby, but not too near, as she had some concern for her own safety. She looked on intently and inquisitively while sitting on her hind legs, and with each peculiar motion made by Beau, she would tilt her head to the right or left as if in deep wonderment, one ear twitching to make it higher than the other. She knew him a long time yet always seemed to experience something different.

This swordplay of Beau's continued for several minutes, a grin covering his face with the sight of the dog watching him like a child. "If you were just a bit bigger, Jesse, you could act as my horse and carry me to battle!" She looked at him attentively and tilted her head. "You'd like that, wouldn't you, girl!" Her tail began to wag with excitement, not understanding her friend's words but sensing it was a call to action and enjoying even more the attention and communication.

Soon the call to breakfast came through the air. Beau picked up the logs from the ground and placed them in the shed next to the other freshly cut ones, undeterred by Jesse trying several times to lick him in the face as he hunched over. When he finished he stood up and filled his arms with several dry logs, then looked around, saddened by the knowledge that this would be the last time he'd be cutting wood in the forests of Cringle for some time.

They sat to eat, the sun now broken through the clouds and delivering glorious rays of sunlight through the windows and into various parts of the cabin, including the kitchen table. There was a golden glow about the place, one that evoked a feeling of warmth and transcendence.

Earl said a short prayer before digging into the food, thanking God for another meal and his good company. Beau hung his head in respect, accustomed to the practice. Even Jesse went quiet and motionless as she hung on the outer fringes of the table, then shifted around as they began eating and talking of the day. She knew enough not to beg but confidently hoped that perhaps she may get a taste or two of her master's cooking. Being wise in her old age, she knew that with guests in the house, there was greater likelihood of that happening.

"Ah, Jesse, you have us more figured out than we know, don't you?" said Earl after catching Beau sneak her a couple bites of his hash browns.

Some things never change.

After breakfast, Beau did the dishes and wiped off the table while Earl made preparations to go fishing down by the river. The decision of whether to go to the lake or river was always a challenging one, though due to the favorable conditions for river angling, the choice was clear.

Soon they were walking north toward the descent to the river, Earl humming as he went and Beau catching himself doing the same. He remembered how he had often hummed at the dinner table as a young boy and was usually told to stop and eat his food. He hummed all the louder with a smile as the memory came to him.

Down the hill they marched, few words spoken between them and few words needed. A pleasant comfort existed among them that allowed for simple daydreaming, Beau lunging upon branches on the forest floor beneath him, Earl whistling while walking steadily with his large arms swaying back and forth. The whole time Jesse ran to and fro between them with youthful exuberance. A truth that Earl knew, and one that Beau would soon discover, was that the more the words, the less the meaning, which would do no good for either of them in their limited time together. So on they walked, just being.

"Nice fish!" said Earl as Beau pulled the trout from the water, still fighting for its freedom that was lost because of its appetite. "Just don't forget to put him back in the water." For several hours they fished, up and down the river. They spoke of this and that in between long stretches of silence, of trivial things in life and those more simple to the heart. With a soft smile, Earl fished on, as did Beau, storing up all that his old friend said.

Beau was grateful for the stillness around him and the relative peace that it brought. Yet he was very aware that it would soon be replaced by the hustle of college life, assignments and exams, late nights and the party scene, which he both missed and despised. He knew there was more to life than hangovers and risky behavior, yet for some reason, he kept going that way. "Things are going to be different this time around," he thought to himself.

Not wanting to taint the peace of the day with thoughts of the life that awaited him back at school, he shrugged them off. Right now, he set his mind on enjoying the time in the river that now poured forth speech into the lives of two men vastly separated by time and experience yet connected through far more powerful elements.

When the two anglers began to hunger, they took a break from the action for a few moments on the river's edge. They sat on the grass near an old maple tree, whose large roots extended out in every direction. Granola bars and extra thick peanut butter and jelly sandwiches were on the menu, washed down with water they had brought from the cabin in a couple of small bottles.

It wasn't long until they were back in the water, fishing and talking, talking and fishing. Jesse patrolled the bank, as usual, occasionally jumping into the river after a frog or some other critter. Life was good.

After a couple more hours they caught enough trout to appease their hunter instincts and waded back downstream to the shoreline where they entered earlier that day. After stepping out of their waders, they gathered all their gear and returned to the path that led up to the cabin.

"That was some great fishing," exclaimed Beau, fully pleased with the day.

"Good fishing, indeed," he replied. "Hopefully enough to satisfy you for a while as you go on your way back to civilization tomorrow."

"Yeah..." Beau's voice trailed off some at the end as he looked down to the ground before him while walking behind Earl, then back up again to the trail. Though part of him looked forward to the new season that was to come and the challenge of it, he wasn't all that excited about leaving. *"It just feels so right here..."*

They put their gear away, cleaned themselves up, and left to go into town to buy some flour and other ingredients for supper. They walked down the trail that led to Earl's truck, climbed in and took off down the road.

"Caught some salmon near Lake Michigan the day before you came; time to change up the recipe a bit when cooking them tonight," said Earl. That was something about Earl that Beau always admired. Unlike many who resign or give up with old age, he never quit living, serving, and trying new things and almost seemed to grow younger inside as his aged increased.

Miles passed by on the lonesome highway on the way to town. The once blue skies had now become overcast, though it was still warm enough to have the windows down. Jesse took full advantage of this, sticking her head out as far as she could while standing on Beau's lap, her front paws on the door. She loved the feeling of the wind rushing over her head and looked as if she were trying to eat it.

Not much was said other than Earl pointing out significant landmarks and the homes and land of people he knew. There were some who sadly had passed away, no more tending to the businesses or farms that had for so long sustained them and provided to others.

"A challenging life, that farming is," he commented. "Sometimes wish I was a farmer, just so I could get up and have those chores to usher me into each day." Beau wasn't sure what to make of that comment. Earl did engage in plenty of outdoor labor, and the thought of all that farm work didn't sound like something one would look forward to. Perhaps one day he would understand and even concur.

There were times during the drive when Beau couldn't help but lean his head back, close his eyes, and doze off for a minute or two, which felt more like an hour. He was so relaxed from all the fresh air they breathed in all afternoon. His mind was unfettered and peaceful, able to fend off negative thoughts of the past and future that tried to enter in when he looked upon the encroaching clouds.

Soon they reached the destination, and Beau lifted his head again from a short nap and shook himself to regain his senses.

"Let's go get our goods," said Earl, chuckling at the sight of his sleepy companion. They got out of the truck and walked into the small market, hearing the jingle of small bells when opening the door. Earl immediately greeted the attendants behind the counter, who he knew well.

"Afternoon, Earl!" said a young girl in her teens, exuberant and pleasant, her ponytail bobbing up and down as she walked down the aisle with a big smile.

"Beau, is that you?" came another voice. From behind a set of swinging wooden doors came Ethel, an old woman who Beau had all but forgotten until he saw her cheerful face. "My have you grown!" she exclaimed on her way to giving him a hug.

Beau blushed just a little and put up no defenses. This sweet little woman always made him smile and feel special when he visited the market in earlier years. Her demeanor and character splashed onto everyone who worked or shopped in the store, and she was honored and appreciated by just about everyone who came through the doors. Her endearing and magnetic countenance was reinforced by the name of her faithful husband, who passed away just under two years ago. Aside from being Earl's most infamous fishing partner, he was a well-respected man and friend to many, who even dipped into his own pocket on occasion to cover the cost of food and supplies for those in the area who couldn't afford much. Beau's parents, in their early years of marriage, were among them.

The visit warmed Beau's insides, as Earl suspected it would. Before they left, Ethel grabbed a box of granola bars and a bag of beef jerky and forced them on him. She knew they were his favorites.

"I'd give you a box of Snickers 'cause I know you like them too, though I don't want your mother knowing I was pushing sweets on you. Now go chase after life, young man, and be good and do good. Also, don't be too much of a stranger, you hear?"

"Thank you, Ethel, and I'll get back to visit soon," he said, feeling a knot in his gut from hearing her comment "be good," knowing that she probably would be disappointed if she knew all the details. *I'll do my best Ethel,*" he said to himself while walking back toward the truck, taking another quick look into the skies that grew increasingly dark.

The drive back to the cabin seemed to take less time than the drive there. After returning, they each took to doing their own thing for a while, along with taking a short nap, as they were both thoroughly exhausted.

Upon waking, Beau pulled out his journal and began to pen some of the weekend's events, beginning with the day at hand and working backward to the passing of Lady. She had come to his mind often while in the company of Jesse. Thoughts of times spent together in Cringle, lying with her in the grass under the summer sun by the pond or walking down the trail and through the woods together. A stirring began to build in him as he reflected, brief flashes of what once was vividly appearing to him.

Outside, the winds began to pick up, the tree branches now swaying more forcefully as the clouds became darker. All traces of the afternoon sunlight and blue skies had vanished, and the sky now whispered to all who would listen that a storm was coming. The wind became much cooler, as if to draw a clear line in the sands of seasons that signaled goodbye to autumn for the year.

Soon the rains came, gentle and soothing at first, producing a light tap on the roof and porch as they sat to eat. Though ominous outside, warm and secure was the cabin within, the fire now crackling and a few candles burning. Earl sat relaxed in his chair, all cleaned up and rested after the long day, and looked as if he were one of the gatekeepers to the entrance of heaven itself. Light seemed to radiate from his face.

They savored every bite of the salmon Earl prepared while enjoying the time as usual. With the last piece of desert, which happened to be fresh cherry pie with cherries picked in the summer by Ethel and her grandchildren, they cleaned up the table and dishes, put on another layer of clothing, and moved out onto the porch. With coffee in hand, they admired the thunder that had rumbled in the distance during dinner and now continued to grow closer and more intense, while the rain beat down harder due the increased strength of the winds.

"Normally, this would be the time your mother would make you and your siblings dash to the basement, wouldn't it?" said Earl with his slanted grin. Growing up, Beau and his siblings had many experiences of retreating to the basement when big storms came through or suspected tornadoes were on the loose, ready to wreak havoc. "When you head back tomorrow, don't tell her we were out here watching," he said humorously, respectively poking fun at her foul-weather emergency antics.

Earl had no issues with sitting out on the porch as the skies obeyed their master by delivering nourishment, which looked more like punishment, onto the land. However, he was ready to go into the basement in a split second if need be, especially if the sounds of trains could be heard coming near that didn't ride on tracks made by the hands of men. Tornadoes usually give indication that they are nearing via clear, eerily calm and odd-colored skies, though the skies this night were anything but clear and calm but rather wild and wrathful.

They leaned forward in their seats in awe, like excited children, feeling the rumble of crashing thunder that was so loud it made them flinch and tremble like the Israelites who heard God's voice from Mount Sinai and could not bear its power, begging with fear not to hear it anymore. Yet Earl and Beau wanted more of this display of power, and they got it, over and over again, as dashes of lightning streaked across the vast sky and illuminated all that was and could be seen. Their long bolts seemed to hang in the air for seconds, demanding attention.

Then something unexpected happened. Out of nowhere, Jesse lifted herself to all fours and looked into the woods beyond the porch. Her eyes were fixed ahead, and she growled under her breath. Many dogs get spooked during thunderstorms, but not Jesse.

Both Earl and Beau looked over at her, surprised at her reaction at what seemed to be nothing. "What is it, girl? You see something?" She looked over at Earl, as if desperately wanting to say something, then returned her gaze ahead, and in one instant, she uncharacteristically darted off into the dark forest like one of those lightning bolts.

"Jesse!" Earl shouted as he stood to his feet. "What's gotten into you, girl!"

Beau jumped to his feet seconds after Earl, surprised by the quickness of step in his old friend. He glanced in the direction of Jesse and saw what he thought might have been a pair of menacing eyes just beyond the wood. He shook his head and blinked hard, hoping it might help him see more clearly, and searched again for those eyes but saw nothing. In a manner similar to Jesse, he ran into the cabin without contemplating his actions and grabbed the fire prodder and a flashlight from below the sink and ran out after her.

"Beau! Now what's gotten into you?" yelled Earl as Beau ran past him down the steps, the calm tone usually evident in his voice now a highly intensified one. Not as quick on his feet as he once was, he hurried inside and grabbed his shotgun from his closet, made sure it was loaded, and grabbed another flashlight from below the sink. He then ran as quickly as he could out to the outer fringes of the yard, where he could see glimpses of Beau's flashlight bouncing through the woods, then disappearing in the dark and rain.

A run through the dark, wet woods was something Beau was not expecting, though something got into Jesse, and he wasn't going to leave her alone out there. In a flash, memories of Lady lying breathless on the pavement with no one there to aid or comfort her shot through his mind.

He forged through the wood, jumping over logs and doing his best to avoid low-hanging branches, with enough adrenaline running through his blood to make him oblivious to all the cuts and scrapes the woods were giving him. He followed the sound of Jesse's barking all the way down to the river, where he found her patrolling the shoreline. There was nothing foreign or unusual in sight, though the misty darkness seemed to breathe all around, which made Beau stop and peer into the darkness beyond the falling rain.

"You okay, girl?" Beau asked as he neared her, pressing through the darkness and clinching his teeth in defiance of it. Still filled with a sort of relentless pursuit after what could not be seen, Jesse marched intently up and down the river a couple more times, looking here and there but mostly into the woods on the other side of the river. Soon she came close to Beau's side, and though still glancing around, she seemed to be signaling resignation from whatever mission she had taken upon herself.

Beau leaned over and rubbed his hand along her back, talking gently to her and trying to comfort her. He was comforting himself in the process. Despite the surge that had come over him, he was grateful that she had come close, for it was intimidating out there. At that moment, he heard Earl yelling from the top of the hill, his voice growing louder and closer like a giant crashing into trees, invoking great fear into the dark pestilence that crept in the night.

"You okay down there? What's going on!"

"I don't know...we're heading up!" he yelled back, having no other explanation. "Come on, girl," he then said to Jesse, who whined some upon the words and looked around again before obediently coming alongside him.

As they began walking away from the river's edge, Beau turned his head around one more time to look back at the river. The faint sound of howling could be heard far off in the wilderness, and there was nothing in sight other than the falling rain and blowing trees, occasionally illuminated by the lightning. Yet, as he stood there, he could almost feel eyes staring upon him, along with a very unpleasant feeling. He shook it off and stepped forward, reasoning that it must just be his elevated senses playing a trick on him.

They marched up the hill, drawing closer to Earl, who was making his way down to them, rain still pouring and thunder crackling. Jesse ran out just ahead of Beau in the direction of the cabin, and just as she did, he stopped, as if a hand was placed on his shoulder, holding him back. He looked around, stricken, sensing something unkind in the darkness that overpowered reason. A deep chill crept up his spine like long, bony fingers climbing one by one. He breathed heavy in the cool air, his breath visible and coming out of him like smoke puffs from a train.

The feeling only lingered for a moment, however, and to his great delight, his eyes fell upon a small speck of light. Earl's flashlight. Moments later, Earl and Jesse were at his side, dispelling the fear that had just overtaken him. They walked back to the cabin together, their paces quickened with the anticipation of sitting in front of the fire with hot tea and dry clothes. Soon the bright glow of the cabin could be seen as they reached the top of the ridge, which lifted his heart even higher.

"What was that all about?" Beau said as they walked in the door. "I don't remember her acting like that before."

"She gets something in her once in a while, her senses picking up things far before I do. She may have seen or caught whiff of an animal, though even so, that was out of the ordinary for her to act that way," said Earl as he took off his shoes, staring inquisitively and warmly at Jesse, who now sat before the fireplace, looking back at him with endearing eyes.

"Though what about you?" he went on. "You just up and took off after her into dark woods and rain—with a fire poker! That I haven't seen before either."

"I don't know. It just seemed right to go after her," replied Beau as he dried himself off, pausing as he spoke.

Earl suspected that Beau's chasing after Jesse may have had something to do with the passing of Lady, feeling the need to protect her in a way he couldn't protect his own dog that day. It was hard to say, though, and he kept his thoughts to himself.

"I'm going to go grab some more firewood. I think we're going to need more than what I brought in earlier," said Beau before going outside for what he hoped was the final time of the night, not eager to be going outside alone. The winds were still howling about, the ferocity of the sky still unrelenting. He walked hurriedly through the wind and rain to the shed, with a flashlight pointed at the ground in front of him and a log holder in his other hand.

He reached the shed and went to the area where the dry wood was stacked. He set down the log holder and began stacking logs, hurriedly filling it to capacity, longing to be back in the cabin.

When retrieving the final log, he lost his grip and it dropped to the ground. As he bent down to pick it up, a sudden flash of lightning tore through the sky, illuminating everything, including an unusually large, ornery pine snake that sat just several feet in front of him near the side of the shed. Its body was coiled and its head raised, ready to strike.

"Whoa!" roared Beau, throwing the log at the reptile in a split second, falling back a few steps after doing so in both anger and fright. Beau was always pretty easy going when it came to various insects and animals, but one creature he could not reconcile with was snakes, venomous or not. They disgusted and roused some sort of ferocity in him.

The snake, fearing its own safety, backed away to avoid the log, then lowered itself and slithered away into the woods. Beau watched as its tail disappeared into the forest, then aggressively grabbed the handle to the wood carrier and stomped back to the cabin, talking to himself under his breath and longing to be inside.

"What's gotten into this place!" said Beau as he walked through the door, still quite shaken by the encounter. "I go to get firewood and am confronted by a mean-spirited snake that was ready to puncture my skin!" Earl, who was putting another log in the fireplace at the time, looked up with a surprised, questioning look on his face. Beau told him the brief details with an exasperated tone while setting the wood down and taking off his raincoat.

"Something in those woods tonight..." he said defiantly, fully fixed on letting the occurrence pass into memory.

"Perhaps," said Earl, a bit silent on the matter as his eyes looked at Beau carefully, then back at the fire. Deep thought was concealed by the lines on the perimeter of his eyes. "But we're safe in here..."

"And here is where I'm staying!"

And so they sat, talking some and thinking more, all a bit weary from the day's happenings.

It didn't take too long for Beau to realize that he had nothing left physically and that the time for bed had come. He could neither muster the strength to keep his eyelids open nor entertain another thought. He rose from the couch, said goodnight to Earl, who sat pensively in the old recliner, and made his way to the guest bedroom.

"Goodnight, Beau," he said pleasantly, looking at him briefly to acknowledge his departure before returning his stare to the crackling fire in front of him, his eyes transfixed on the bouncing flames. The thoughtfulness behind his eyes caused by the night's events, hidden from Beau, was now clearly seen on his face.

Earl would remain in the recliner for some time after, much longer than usual for a Saturday night. He continued to gaze deep into the fire, praying quietly but fervently under his breath. Occasionally, he glanced out the window into the darkness where the trees could be seen swaying in the wind, occasionally lit up by flashes of lightning. On he prayed, tilted forward and his hands cusped together. The fire in his soul grew hotter, perhaps burning with more intensity than the one in front of him, his spirit in tune with his surroundings and more.

He rose after a time and went to stand on the porch, all alone as Jesse had fallen fast asleep inside. Though the storm had weakened some, it remained formidable as it slowly rolled over the land. Earl paced back and forth over the old but solid wood, his mouth uttering words as his head was lifted with closed eyes, hands upon his hips. Occasionally he would open them and look out into the woods and sky, his voice growing louder with controlled anger and undaunted power.

He eventually came into the cabin and sat down at his wooden desk by the window that faced north. In front of him a candle gently burned, now the only source of light in the cabin besides the red glow of expended logs in the fireplace. Though it was a small flame, it sufficed to light the pages of his Bible that lay open before him. The window was opened slightly as well, allowing a cool breeze to filter in, causing the candle to flicker but unable to put it out.

"Even you are controlled by one mightier," said Earl softly to the wind that could be seen in the flame's motion. His gaze moved to the pages, then out the window, before he leaned back in the chair with his eyes closed and head tilted up. Some of his best times of prayer and writing came while sitting at that little wooden desk made by his father long ago, and tonight was one of them. At times he prayed hard and fast, other times slow and weak, stopping once in a while to listen. With a power that was not his own, he contended with an invisible element that seemed to be prowling through the darkness.

This went on deep into the night. Occasionally, he would get up to walk about the floor, sometimes falling to his knees. He would rise and walk out onto the porch, then return to the desk, where he would write a few words or sentences in his journal while flipping to different pages in his Bible.

And then came dawn. With the first gleam of light on the distant horizon, he felt released to lead his weary but peace-filled soul and body to bed.

There sat an old man before a window
in a small cabin deep in the northern wood.
In front of him a candle gently burned,
smooth, steady, and peaceful its flame humbly stood.

There alone in the fading light he sat,
as twilight's final hour passed nearer to night,
into dusk where the wind began to howl,
while the gentle flame still shined ever so bright.

Then like a shadow the darkness crept in,
swallowing everything in sight but the flame.
Alone it now burned, tossed 'bout by the wind
long into night, where mightier it became.

For dark's power couldn't quench the flame, and
soon it ceded to light breaking through the trees.
Sweet sounds of birds again filled the air, as
the fierce winds bowed to a gentle flowing breeze.

Like a lone star piercing the blackened sky,
or a ray of sun breaking through the gray day,
was the flame that could not be overcome,

until the wind and dark were driven away.

And so burns this flame in the souls of men,
who wake in the dawn with a hunger for life,
who must seek the light amidst storm and gloom,
until the bright morning star rises in their hearts,
chasing away all fear and strife.

Beau clumsily pushed open the door to the guest bedroom, somehow managed to take off his outer clothing, and crawled into bed. Within moments he passed from consciousness, falling deep into sleep and dream.

And of no ordinary kind of dream did he fall into...

A child he was, surrounded by some of his siblings and relatives inside a camper. The door opened, and they walked out through the dark and rain on their way to the house, which was just on the other side of the yard. They walked along, Beau somewhere near the end of the pack that moved hurriedly to avoid getting too wet. He walked slower than the others, though, enjoying the elements.

And then there appeared a great flash of lightning, revealing a sight that made everyone stop. There, in the plants and shrubs that lined the house, was a large snake in striking position, its head raised high and intimidating tongue slithering in defiance. Beau froze, a silent enmity building in him as he stood a safe distance away, staring down the creature that seemed to mock them, yet which stood alone in what seemed to be a state of fear.

The lightning flash and picture of what seemed to be an adversary lasted for just a few long moments, time standing still.

Beau woke suddenly, sitting up quickly in bed with tiny drops of sweat falling from his face. There in the dark silence, he reflected on the dream, not sure if it had really ended or if this was an extension of it. Yet just then he heard what sounded like quiet whispers coming from the living room. He turned his eyes toward the cracked door to see a gentle glow seeping in, like that of candlelight.

Though stirred within, he was so tired that he could give no more thought to anything, and back he fell into deep sleep that would carry him gently into the morning, a peace surrounding him despite the circumstances.

The first day of the week dawned with force. The sun had broken through a few remnants of clouds and shined forth as if to announce victory. Again Beau awoke to the sweet sounds of chirping robins that are so hard to hear at other times, precious melodies that ought not to be forgotten as one travels through life. The first thing to come to his mind was the dream, full of clarity and life in every detail. Usually most of the contents of his dreams were lost only moments after waking, but not this one.

"Strange how that works," he wondered, not for the first time.

He rose from the bed, threw on a pair of worn jeans, socks, a white cotton t-shirt, and his trusty blue and grey flannel, and made his way to the living room. The first gleams of morning were still refreshing the land, slowly thawing the frost from the ground, all so still. He slipped on a pair of shoes and stepped outside onto the porch, invigorated by the crisp, chilly air. The beloved warm weather of summer that passed into autumn had now begun to depart for what was likely the final time, making way for a long, grueling Midwest winter.

He walked slowly down the steps and walked about the yard and around the cabin, his arms crossed to keep in the warmth while his eyes adjusted to the light. The dream remained on his mind, and at first he figured it was simply a response to the snake episode that transpired while collecting wood the night before. After walking around for another quarter of an hour, however, he realized that there was more to it.

The dream was not just a clever creation of his mind but rather an episode that he had experienced as a child. Up north at his aunt's place, a time so long ago he couldn't remember the specifics, that exact same occurrence took place.

He continued to walk. His eyes were fixed on the ground before him, unsure of what to make of it all and how it all tied together. All other thoughts were suspended.

Getting cold, he made his way back to the cabin. After entering, he was surprised to find that he was the only one up.

"Looks like I beat Earl to the punch this morning," he said to himself, somewhat proud, for it was rare that he would ever rise earlier than Earl. Just then, his moment of glory fled with the sounds of two different sets of footsteps on the porch, followed by the door swinging open and Earl and Jesse walking in. Earl carried a bag and two cups of coffee in a cardboard holder. Jesse came straight to Beau, stood up on her hind legs, and put her front paws on his chest to say good morning.

"There is one of those new fancy coffee shops in town; just opened recently. Thought we'd indulge a bit this morning." Behind Earl's bright morning demeanor, fatigue could be seen behind his eyes. Beau thought he may have just been a bit tired, ignorant of the fact that he had been up all night conversing with his Maker amidst the darkness. Besides, at his age, a night of little sleep was easier to endure and recover from.

For a second, Beau recalled the time he briefly woke in the night, seeing the soft light visible from the crack in his bedroom door and hearing the quiet whisper-like sounds of Earl praying. Yet fleeting was the thought, quickly trodden over by the need to share his dream and its origin with Earl.

Earl stoked a fire and they sipped their coffee in front of it. Despite the brightness and beauty of the morning, the warm air that departed with the storm had left the air far too chilly to sit outside. Inside, though, the warmth grew abundantly due to both the flames and the conversation at hand. Earl was informed about the dream and the childhood memory it rekindled. He sat relaxed yet attentive in the rocker, listening closely and speaking sparingly, his eyes set on Beau the whole time as he spoke with a touch of fervency to his voice.

Beau's words were not slipping past Earl unnoticed. With squinted eyes, Earl saw and perceived more in all this than Beau did. Despite this, he kept his deeper thoughts concealed.

"What do you make of all that?" asked Beau at the end, not really expecting an answer but rather some form of acknowledgement.

"I don't know exactly, Beau," replied Earl gently, "though I know that dreams come when there is much worry on one's mind or for purposes beyond our present understanding. I expect some light may be shed on this not too far down the road. Things have a special way of unraveling in their own time."

Beau sat silent for a moment, turning his head to look out the windows. He would've preferred to skip the waiting part associated with this.

"Yet that doesn't mean you ought not search for answers. Keep listening and pursuing."

Another long moment of silence followed.

"Seems like an awful lot of searching lately." His eyes became squinted again in thought and a mild form of inner turmoil. Rarely did Beau speak of his lifestyle to Earl, knowing that he was a man of faith who lived above many of Beau's ways, though he felt comfortable enough now to do so, trusting he wouldn't get a hard response from his aged friend. He figured Earl knew as much anyway; the reputation of one who chases the wind travels far, especially in smaller towns.

"Keep your eyes fixed ahead, Beau," Earl gently said after a few moments of searching his own heart for the appropriate words, of which there were few. "You are being watched over and there is a way that is right…you might just have to put your boots on to find it. And it will involve some tough decisions."

There was so much that Earl desired to tell the young man—of how his destiny was already laid out for him and that all he had to do was reach out and take hold of the hand that guides. Yet a voice from within told him it wasn't the time for those words, that his young friend's ears and heart were not yet ready to hear them. Nor were they open to them. Though soon, he hoped, soon may be the time.

As if planned, Beau's stomach let out a long moan that called their attention to a lesser but nonetheless important matter—breakfast. After sharing in preparation duties, Beau took his seat, while Earl puttered by the sink before sitting down.

Now by this time, it would seem appropriate to say that no more surprises remained in store for them. However, in the land of Cringle, it could be said that such logical thinking did not reign. For when the big man finally sat down, the small flower in the glass jar, which sat quietly in the middle of the kitchen table, gently wilted right before their eyes. Its once erect, white petals drooped down slowly yet surely like a man bowing before a king. A few of the petals fell off as if gravity was all of a sudden increased dramatically and they could no longer bear the weight of it.

"What on earth…" Beau said without thinking as he sat looking at the flower in awe and wonder, finding no other words or explanation for what he just saw. Earl saw it too, and like Beau, was unsure what to make of it. "Hmm…" he said with an amiable and introspective tone as he slowly sat down, staring at it with confused, intrigued eyes for just a moment before feeling the need to change the subject. Some things are far beyond understanding and better off left uninvestigated, and Earl did not want to touch this one.

Beau took a few more quick, investigative glances at that flower as the meal went on, as did Earl, though no more was said of it. They already had their fill of unusual occurrences and could ponder no more.

Yet those falling petals would come to their minds in the hours to come and in future days near and far.

And so they ate: a feast of toast, pancakes, eggs, and some fried fish to make it just right, syrup spread around generously and co-mingled with everything. They talked of the weekend and other light stuff, though the day at hand didn't leave much time to linger over the food. Earl had church to prepare for, and the clock was ticking. He invited Beau to come with, and though part of Beau wanted to, he declined.

"I should get on the road back to my dad's place to get ready for the week." The truth was that though part of Beau was anxious to get back on the road, the majority of him really did not want to leave.

Without pressing the issue, Earl humbly excused himself from the table to begin getting ready, allowing Beau time to pack the few items he brought with him. Soon they were ready to leave, and with one final look around the quiet cabin, Beau bid his farewell to the place that had become a part of him before walking out the door and down the old trail toward their vehicles.

"You know you always have a place to come and get away here, Beau, and I do expect to have visits from you. Many fish remain in those waters, and Jesse will be missing you."

"I know. I'll be back."

They gave each other a hug, and afterward Beau bent down on one knee in front of Jesse, who placed her paw on his leg in her own special way.

"You be good, girl, and I'll be back to see you soon," he said while petting her. Moments later, Beau was in his car driving away, tugged by that familiar feeling that called him back to the road, as if to return to a journey that was still very foggy to him. Just a couple more weeks remained at Hillary's before resuming the college life, and he wondered if some fog would lift in that time.

Earl deliberately puttered around his truck for a few moments after Beau's departure. He wasn't the best at saying goodbye, and his heart was full and heavy as Jesse stood by his side awaiting her cue to get into the truck.

"Ah, girl, I believe he'll find his way..." he said to her. After opening the door for her to get in, he took a deep look into the woods and sky and climbed into the truck to resume his own journey toward life's edge.

And that was the weekend at Earl's.

Moving On

Beau arrived back to his father's house an hour and a half later, following the scenic drive down Route 29 and other rural roads that led him back to the small city and its more populated streets. It was a satisfying drive, one that involved high speeds, tight turns, and slow, smooth stretches, all of which resembled his emotional state. He often found it quite noteworthy how the gas pedal so closely linked to the mind.

His father was home at the time. Upon seeing Beau, he began to put a lunch together for the two of them. Shortly after he entered the house, they sat down together to eat, a relatively uncommon occurrence for them in these times. This was not because his father didn't want to, however. Carl, as well as Janet, desired to spend more time with him, to know more about his life from day to day. It wasn't easy to get inside of Beau, though, and it was difficult for him to make time for them in his hurried, late-night lifestyle.

Yet this day was different, at least for a short time. Over a healthy portion of pan-fried walleye that Carl had caught down by the river weeks earlier, Beau told him about the talks with Earl, the fishing, and even a few of the unusual events that transpired. He was more open than usual, and his father cherished this as he sat listening attentively to his son that he had seen change and grow through the years.

"Sounds like quite the weekend, and a needed one," he said with a gentle smile on his face. "Those words of Earl's, they..." he began saying, pausing for a second to check himself, not wanting to sound imposing or exhortative. "It would do you well to keep them close to you.

They've done me well many times over the years, even when I didn't want to hear 'em." As the words came out, Carl fondly remembered the frequent mornings sitting for coffee or fishing with Earl, sharing life's complexities and challenges with him in hopes of finding some light, which he often did, whether verbally or through unspoken words.

They sat together for a little while longer, Beau eating his fill of fish to the continued delight of his father. Warmth brewed from the two of them as they sat peering out the windows into the waters beyond, though Beau's need to get on with things soon brought the moment to an end.

For a long while after Beau's departure, however, Carl sat still by the window, thinking back in his mind to times spent with his own dad, who was now long passed from the earth. He didn't get to spend much time with his dad, not nearly as much as he would have liked to—not nearly as much as he had spent with Beau and the rest of the youngsters in earlier years before the shadow crept in, which he himself did not yet fully see nor identify.

Yet there were times, those special times that remained clear and dear to his heart, like sitting in the boat with his father, fishing for the mighty sturgeon or crappie when they were spawning. Young Carl lived with his mother all the years after the divorce, and on many weekends, his dad would come pick him up to go fishing. Carl would be waiting eagerly by the door while his sweet mother puttered in the kitchen, with all his tackle and necessary clothing within reach, wide eyed and ready to go.

Off they would drive for a long day or even a weekend of fishing and talking. The talk wasn't all too deep, though, as his father didn't open up too much. He had served in the war and suffered emotional wounds that kept his words few and usually surface level. Whatever amount of conversation they shared was treasured by young Carl nonetheless.

Like all childhoods, those times rapidly passed into the coming days and years, each one vanishing more quickly than the previous. Eventually, the day arrived when Carl, now a husband and father, was sitting beside his father's hospital bed, holding his hand with only moments remaining before his death, his body now old and withered, small breaths just barely escaping from his mouth.

"I love you, son..." Carl heard him say in those final moments. It was one of the very few times in his life those words were said, and they moved his son's heart with such undeniable power, evoking tears that would be shed later in the night while falling asleep.

After a long, deep sigh, accompanied by a single falling tear, Carl's thoughts returned to his own son and the other children. Memories and visions of the days gone by and those to come swirled about, days which moved so rapidly that one could not tell where things began or where they are going.

Friday morn, October 30, 1998, final drive to Silver Creek
Another goodbye to say today. Not sure how many more of these I can take. Not much good at them to begin with.
Must keep moving on, not sure where, but I believe somewhere...

Dawn faithfully arrived that Friday morning, and the cool October air greeted Beau as he went outside to check the temperature. "Winter is drawing closer," he said quietly to himself in a slightly resigned voice. It wasn't that he didn't like winter; he found all the seasons to be distinctly beautiful and inviting. Winter, however, was long and dark, and even the most enthusiastic of outdoor lovers couldn't help but occasionally lose some steam while treading through its days.

He walked back inside, took another sip of juice, and finished off his toast before slipping his boots on and making his way out to the car. It was to be his final day of working for her, and a touch of both joy and sadness moved inside of him due to the upcoming change.

"One more time," he said to himself after closing the door behind him.

Again he was on the road, driving along that familiar route that was now a bit more somber looking. There were no longer any leaves on the trees; only the conifers, numerous in that region, remained as they were. Left behind was a cool gray and brown in the woods that once sang with such brilliant colors and vibrancy. Looking out the windshield to the east, he could see the sun beginning to burst through the horizon, rising later each morning and setting earlier as daylight faded into winter.

Among the many thoughts that came to him while behind the wheel, he thought of Earl's the most. It had been weeks since he roamed about the cabin, weeks that resembled an excerpt from a novel not to be read again for a long time, poignant but brief, like pages of fine literature quickly turned, the details only sparingly remembered. For Beau, much reflection and searching filled that weekend, but no real answers had been revealed. Someday it would all make sense, he hoped.

Excitement lingered with the thought of heading back to college. However, part of him feared the distance that would likely come between him and the solitude, peace, and clarity that came to him via the woods, water, and wind of northern Wisconsin. The pace and lifestyle he entertained in college, though exhilarating at times, usually afforded little allowance to hear oneself think. There was also the risk of it pulling him far away from responsibility, regardless of intentions.

He pulled into Hillary's driveway at his usual time, stepping out of the car and making his way to the cabin to get directives for the day. He walked in through the garage door and into the house, silent except for the sound of the wind and the steady, distant hum of a motorboat on the lake. Upon entering the house, he solemnly looked around, knowing full well that he might never see the place again. People and places attached themselves quickly to him and often didn't let go. This place would do the same.

"Hillary?" he called out, expecting a firm, sharp-witted response to come shooting through the air from some unexpected location. Just as he was about to call out again, he glanced over to the kitchen island where his eyes caught sight of a note sitting next to a pen with an envelope next to it.

He walked over to the counter, picked up the note, and sat down on one of the stools as he began to read,

> *Dear Beau,*
>
> *I am sorry to say that I won't be able to see you off on your final day here. A situation arose with a client that required my presence. It is of considerable distance from the house, too far for me to return prior to your departure.*
>
> *In the envelope in front of you, you will*

find your week's pay, along with a little extra for
the days ahead due to a job well done. On the
back of this letter, you will find your list of chores
for the day, short and light but very important
nonetheless. There is some food in the refrigera-
tor for you to eat for lunch. Take it with you if
you don't finish it all now.

Young man, thank you for your hard work
up here. It was a great help to me and a pleasure
to have you. I hope your days ahead bring good
things to you, and may you find what you are
searching for.

Regards,
Hillary

Beau stood for a moment after reading the letter, turning it over to review the list. Short and light indeed. He then turned it over again to read a second time. Though some might call the letter brief and to the point, it was about the most transparent side of Hillary he had seen to date.

The air around him was still and quiet as he folded up the letter and tucked it away safely in his pocket. An indomitable yet amiable lone-liness penetrated the room.

He attended to the list while the day passed by like a thief, more quickly than all the days before. His chores included splitting wood and moving some boxes around in the garage, along with other miscellaneous jobs, which he finished by mid-afternoon. Soon the final item on the list stood before him—removing all items from the dock so that it could be taken out for the winter. Part of Beau feared this, and part of him longed for it, for he knew what was down there.

He set the paper down, locked up the house, and walked out the back door. He retrieved the key from underneath a large, empty flower pot that sat on the patio where he, Hillary, and Ranger enjoyed several lunches. He locked it and re-hid the key underneath before making his final journey down to the dock.

For reasons he couldn't understand, he rushed through the task with haste and precision, not wanting to stand idle even for a second. Fear of facing the silence had all of a sudden become so heavy and formidable. Within him was an intense desire to leave, to escape the poignant stillness and melancholy that cried out to him to both leave and stay.

"Time to get going..." he whispered, turning his body in the direction of the path that would lead to his car. As he began to walk, his determination to leave was betrayed by a longing glance to the lake. He stopped, turned around, and walked back onto the dock, where a long moment beside the waters ensued. These waters had mysteriously wooed him throughout the whole season, and they weren't about to let go so easily.

He stood motionless, looking out over the lake, completely surrounded by the gray of day. The skies allowed no sunlight to pass through but were unable to conceal the knowledge of their presence. A cool, hard-biting wind came off the expanse that made his eyes squint and his muscles tense up in an effort to keep warm.

In its own special way, the chilled wind felt so good, so alive.

The scenery and temperature would likely appear dismal to some; the grey and bitter cold did not appear that way to the young man standing there. Rather, the sounds of the water that gently lapped upon the shore and the comfort of the soft grey clouds all appeared sweet, steady, and true. For a brief moment he let the sight and sounds wash over his soul before reluctantly and eagerly turning away, denying his desire to stay and linger over what could not be kept.

And with that, the days at Hillary's lake house came to an end. His acquaintance with her would soon become a distant memory, tucked away in the cedar chest of time where it would remain and shape the days ahead. When and if he would see her again he couldn't be sure, but he did believe in his heart that this experience would leave an indelible mark upon him.

In just a few days he'd be back on the winding country roads that led to college, where thoughts of the past and stubborn old ways would collide head on with the unknowns of the future and the undying desire for change. Also, something most unexpected awaited, something that would forever alter the course of his sails.

Mississippi Waters

Thursday, February 18, 1999, late afternoon

An unseasonably pleasant February day, warm enough to allow me to sit down here by the river. The sun is slowly moving toward the western horizon on the other side of it yet still shining down with power. It's been staying out a little later these days, thank goodness. I can feel the energy in the air that comes with these warmer winds, anticipation of the cold winter months passing away.

The days at both Earl's and Hillary's are months behind me now, yet they still feel close as I sit here. Other times they seem so far away, the peace and stillness out there only a fond memory, especially when compared with these fast-paced days and nights of bars and books that allow little time to sit and feel. My soul cries for the water and wind away from all this. Sometimes I want to run back out there and even stay, but I know that I need to finish here. Haven't spoken to either of them since; been meaning to but just can't seem to get around to it.

I wonder how they're doing—Jesse too.

These times move fast; people so close yet far away...

Beau stopped writing, looked at the words for a moment, then closed his journal and set it beside him on the bench. Leaning forward, he put his elbows on his knees and looked around at other people walking in the park behind and around him. In doing so, he remembered his Grandma Margaret, Carl's mother, mention how much she loved to just sit on park benches and watch people. The thought vanished as quickly as it came, and he returned his stare to the flowing waters of the mighty Mississippi.

The Mississippi begins as a tiny brook from its source at Lake Itasca in northern Minnesota and morphs into a powerfully flowing river, fed by a watershed that extends from the Allegheny Mountains in eastern United States all the way to the Rocky Mountains. As the great river makes its way south toward Louisiana and into the Gulf of Mexico, cutting a line between Minnesota and Wisconsin and other states, it passes through a mid-sized town in southwest Wisconsin called Redstone.

It was in this town where Beau would become acquainted with the river and become a frequent visitor during his college years. Many a time he could be found sitting by these waters that brought comfort to his weary soul, as it had for many who had gone before him and many who would follow. Life is fleeting, he often heard, and always moving on like the river, whether one chooses to go with it or not. As Mark Twain once said, the Mississippi is a "wonderful book with a new story to tell every day."

And many stories there were to share.

"Did you know that my forefathers of northern Minnesota, the Ojibway Indians, called this river *'Messipi'* and *'Big River'*?" asked a large, elderly American Indian who sat down on the bench next to Beau one late, sunny afternoon in his freshman year at Bluff View University. It was one of his first visits to the riverfront and made him wonder what else he was going to encounter in his time there.

"No, I didn't, but that is interesting..." he replied with cautious enthusiasm. He immediately noticed the hardened, lonely look on the man's dark, leathery face that gazed forward with glossy, tired eyes. His skin wore the wrinkles of many hard years and miles.

"You bet it is. It was also known as the *'Mee-zee-see-bee'* or the *'Father of Waters.'* The way this river flows, unchanged in course and courage, and the way it speaks tenderly to those who come to it, makes it like a father."

Beau acknowledged the words of the old man,

who got up and walked away after wishing the young man well on his journey. For a moment, Beau pondered on those words, and though he couldn't come to see the river as a father, he did find some semblance of truth to them.

And so began the days near the river.

Years later, he now sat on that very same bench, with recent memories running through his mind. He thought of his drives to Hillary's with Ranger and the time sitting at the table with Earl, enjoying a meal with no cares while the evening sun shone in through the window. His mind wandered from the kitchen table to the pages of Earl's Bible that fluttered in the breeze and then to the coiled snake that was revealed by a bolt of lightning. Those images didn't pass as quickly as the other memories, and they produced a peculiar, unidentifiable feeling within.

After a few moments his thoughts finally traveled elsewhere, this time to the morning at his father's when they sat together, eating a plate full of fish. They then moved to the time he sat in the sunny kitchen at his mother's house, when they talked of life while frequently peering out the window into the woods. Those talks were always more valued in retrospect. He thought of the times playing with his niece and nephews and the joy they brought to him and of having to say more good-byes before getting in the car and driving away just a few months ago to resume college.

While reminiscing of all these experiences, he could feel an ache inside but could not put a finger on it. Just as he was about to get up and leave, a more fresh and recent memory came to him, one of a much different nature and substance.

Weeks ago he had walked to the bookstore on campus on a brisk, quiet Saturday morning to get some supplies. Most of the students were still sleeping or relaxing indoors, as was usual at that time on the weekend, and Beau found himself enjoying the relative solitude of it. Typically, he was one of those who were still sleeping, despite his love for the morning that severely clashed with his pursuit of the nightlife.

He entered the store, found what he was looking for, and afterward spent some unrushed time musing around with no particular purpose.

Yet purpose was about to find him.

Just as he was approaching the checkout counter, his eyes fell upon a site that would shift the tone of his early February morning and linger in his mind for many a day after. Just beyond the checkout area, working behind the customer service counter, was a young woman of significant beauty who brought him to a complete stop. She first caught his eye due to her physical attractiveness, though she also carried with her a feminine gait that spoke louder and hooked deeper.

Through some minor, perhaps tactfully sneaky interrogation of a sweet, gentle, grandmotherly woman who attended to him from behind the checkout counter, he obtained the young woman's name and made the discovery that she was not without a boyfriend. Not surprised, he was slightly let down upon hearing this, though not enough to steal all hope.

Now it just so happened that the elderly woman was having some difficulty with the scanner, which required the girl to come over to assist her. As she approached, Beau's eyes met hers for a moment, and she said a polite hello. She didn't offer any more correspondence, however, and appeared guarded and reserved amidst her cordial demeanor and quickly resolved the problem before returning to her other duties.

"Oh, thank you so much, Amber," said the older woman with a tender, loving voice.

"Amber…" Beau said the name in his mind a few times to store it while walking away. Before leaving, he took one more look back and thought he saw her glance his way, though he couldn't be sure. Regardless, he hoped he would see more of her.

A couple weeks went by, quickly as usual, and it turned out that he did see her on a few occasions. Unfortunately, no opportunity for conversation presented itself until one spring-like day in the campus commons. She was sitting at a table with a friend, and Beau decided to introduce himself despite the nervousness that tried to shake him off course.

It was a brief discussion, likely hindered by her attentive girlfriend sitting next to her, watching and listening with such acute interest. Her eyes shifted back and forth between Amber and Beau, depending on who was speaking, leaning forward in her seat the whole time so as to not miss anything. Beau, feeling like a stranger in a foreign land, held his ground long enough obtain her name, along with other pieces of information, and discovered that she was graduating in May. He said goodbye at what seemed to be a fitting time, then walked away neither dejected nor elated. The mission to communicate had been accomplished, and he felt satisfaction in that.

As before, he hoped to talk with her again.

Off in the distance, the sounds of old church bells began to sound loudly, pulling Beau's thoughts away from Amber and back to the present. Looking at his watch and noticing that the sky wasn't getting any brighter, he got up from the bench and began his ten-minute walk back to his apartment, where textbooks and homework awaited.

Upon entering his apartment, he was greeted by the sounds of heavy, testosterone-filled music blaring throughout the brightly lit apartment. Its high ceilings and numerous windows ushered in light and also gave a special view of the sunset over the river, which was so beautiful that it even overcame the music. As he gathered his books and prepared to go to the commons, his roommate emerged from the bathroom wearing a towel, toothbrush in his mouth, his hair shooting in every direction. He had just gotten out of the shower and had an energized look on his face that indicated he was preparing to go out that night.

"Beau! You gonna come out with us tonight?" he hollered over the music, which could be heard down the block by neighbors who likely didn't want to hear it.

"No!" Beau yelled back. "I have too much homework to do."

"Huh?" hollered his roommate, unable to hear over the noise.

"I can't! Too much homework to get done!"

"Dude, come on! Can't you do it in the morning? Spring fever is rolling out there, and the bars are going to be crawling with women. We have a great after bar planned too." He responded with such ardency in his tone, dancing around a little while speaking to accentuate his words, which were slightly muffled due to the toothpaste that had built up in his mouth.

Beau looked at him firmly with the slightest grin, indicating his acknowledgement of how appealing that sounded as well as the absurdity of thinking that he would get an ounce of mind-stretching homework done in the morning following a night of partying. Though he still entertained the nightlife, his time spent there had decreased in recent times, and he had come too far since being readmitted to the college and was determined to maintain the pace.

Besides, in just a few weeks, Beau would be spending an entire week of later than usual nights with his roommate and some other friends for spring break. The mere thought of it made Beau's skin want to crawl. He looked forward to the escape from books and the normal routine, yet he was also aware of what went on during that time of the year in certain places. If his desire was to continue making positive changes, that was not a wise vacation destination.

However, he reasoned in his mind that he could handle it, that he would draw boundaries in the sand and not go overboard like so many others. At least that was his intention.

Leaving that thought behind, he proceeded to gather the necessary items, including an apple for the walk and a light jacket in case the temperature dipped low. He gave a wave to his roommate, who was eagerly waiting for Beau to cave in to his temptation, which he normally would with that sort of proposal, and hurriedly made his way to the door and down the steps to the road.

"Made it..." he said to himself.

He walked on with a healthy pace to and through the campus to the commons that lay on its eastern edge. The pleasantness of the evening quickened his senses as he looked around at the landscape and into the blue skies. A light, gentle breeze passed over his skin while he bit into the apple, and it seemed to him that something was in the air. It could have been the usual response to the warm weather that greeted those in the Midwest after a long, hard winter, hinting the coming days. Or perhaps it was something else.

He walked on, passing through the tree-filled university grounds that would soon be flourishing with green leaves, grass, and an assortment of colorful flowers. In the distance, he could see the ominous bluffs that spanned many miles in that region. They always beckoned him to come and explore, though rarely did he do so. Between academics and bars, little time existed for such activity.

Upon arriving at the commons, he set his backpack down on a table before walking over to the cafeteria to buy his lunch. Tray in hand, he returned to his table and began to eat while organizing his study materials, relatively unaware of his surroundings or the people in it. He wasn't particularly excited about doing the homework—his classes in finance did little to spur on his active imagination. Yet he believed they would benefit his future and help him provide for a family of his own someday, so he pressed on. Ignoring pleas from within to do something else, such as go out with the guys and party, he stayed focused on the task, with intermittent daydreaming.

Now it is believed that each person has pivotal moments in life, some more profound than others—moments which dig deeper trenches into the field of memory due the impact on the heart and soul, some happy, some sad, some a combination of both or a different emotion altogether. Moments that keep hope alive that there is much to live for in life, hence keeping the adventure, excitement, and even romance from fading into the drudgery and monotony that can beset a person on any given day.

Such a time was again upon him.

After finishing his sandwich and pulling his books in closer, he leaned back, stretched his arms, and did his usual inhale, exhale routine before again entering an academic mindset. He looked around the large, scarcely populated room; its emptiness was fairly typical of a Thursday night, since many students were either preparing for the bars and parties or just taking a break from studies.

Just as he was turning his eyes back to the text in front of him, he saw something that would severely disrupt any good-faith attempts at studying. At a table on the other side of the hall, sitting alone with books in front of her, was Amber, the girl from the bookstore. She was facing his direction, looking as lovely as could be.

Without too much contemplating whether he should or shouldn't act, he rose from his seat with rare boldness and began to walk toward her. He was full of nervousness and without knowledge of what he was going to say, but he kept walking anyway. He approached her table, and upon stopping a few feet from it, she looked up from her books and gave him a polite, warm reception.

"Hi, Amber," he said with an earnest tone. "I just walked in shortly ago and noticed you sitting here—thought I'd say hello." He continued on, "My name is Beau; I talked with you briefly a couple weeks ago in the bookstore…" His voice trailed off some, discreetly catching his breath.

"Yes, I remember," she replied with a gentle confidence, staring up at him while delicately twirling her pencil around in her fingers. A few minutes of small talk ensued until Beau felt he had hit a wall in the conversation and was intruding on her studies. He excused himself and wished her well with her assignments, then walked away, frustrated that the time was so short and unproductive.

Very stirred and not wanting to be obvious that his attention was hijacked by her, Beau sat upright in his chair after returning to his seat and immediately looked down at his books. He did his best to focus on his studies or at least look like he was. Under the circumstances, this was a most difficult task that perhaps bordered on the impossible. He sat looking into those books like a child staring at a television screen with nothing but static, wondering if something might actually appear.

After a short time, however, while peering out from his lowered head, he noticed that she had risen from her seat and began walking in his direction. His heart began to beat faster to the point where he could hear it like thunder in the distance. Though it seemed unlikely, he wondered if she might have a destination other than his table, but to his delight she did not.

"Oh boy," he thought, taking in a deep breath and exhaling quietly. She drew closer and finally sat down across the table from him without an air of hesitation or timidity. Beau stopped pretending to be doing homework, lifted his head, and greeted his most welcome guest.

Without delay, his pencil was set down to collect dust alongside his books, which were soon forgotten along with anything and everything else. A candid and comfortable conversation emerged between the two that would last somewhere between eternity and a gush of wind, or about an hour and a half. They talked about small stuff for a short time, though her unabashed ability to ask the deep, straight-up questions with comfort and tact soon emerged. Relationships, romance, family, beliefs, dreams—much ground was covered in a short time, and she somehow managed to get inside him, breaking down walls that often slowed or stopped others.

"So, why are you still single?" she asked with a calm, soft voice that he found easy to listen to.

Squinting in thought, somewhat surprised by her directness, he responded after a short moment of silence, "I...don't really know how to answer that, though I suppose it's because I haven't met the right one yet."

"Hmm," she responded thoughtfully, "what would make the right one? What are you looking for in a girl?"

Beau took another long pause and deep breath before answering. It was a question he had often thought about, but whenever it came up, he seemed to fumble with the answer. It seemed to pose as much difficulty as the "So, tell me about yourself" question does to unsuspecting college graduates sitting in front of a recruiter who they believe holds the ticket to their future and even a genuine interest in it. Perhaps he looked for a lot in a girl or for something he didn't yet have the words for.

"She would have to have morals, be the family type, a bit on the wild side..." His voice trailed off as he pondered the question, slightly perplexed by it, then in an effort to shift the current off of his slow moving river of thought, he turned the question to her. "What do you look for in a guy?"

"Well," she said in a dreamy tone, "someone who is faithful, kind, and sweet, who will protect me. Someone like who I am with right now...he is a good guy, and he loves me!" she said in an elongated voice, lifting her hands into the air like a child in a triumphant manner. Beau listened and watched with amusement, both intrigued and energized, not without envy, questioning in his mind the authenticity of this comment and why in the world she just said that to him. After all, why was she sitting across the table from him, sharing such things? He kept his tongue, though, remembering Earl's words on such a matter spoken years earlier out on the porch:

> "Women are a mysterious creation...to determine the cause of certain actions would be a most futile undertaking. However, Beau, a real man should still seek to know the lady in his life, all of his days."

Beau would come to learn this fact of life more relevantly in the years to follow. Now, however, all he could do was apply it with very limited understanding, quite ignorant of its depths.

The conversation eventually reached its summit with Amber needing to leave. She had to rise early in the morning and confessed her need for good sleep. She stood for a moment in front of the table where she just spent an unexpectedly large amount of time with this guy she barely knew, then respectively turned away and walked a few blocks to her off-campus apartment. Beau left shortly afterward, following a few uninterrupted moments to revel in the encounter as well as strategize how on earth he was going to get his homework done, considering his mind was now cruising the skies far above and beyond finance.

The encounter with Amber continued to whirl through his mind as he walked home. He felt he was in a daydream, feeling a gentle, peculiar rush in his veins over what just transpired. Yet a touch of confusion circled about, for he had just been approached, mildly interrogated, and dazzled by a girl with whom he felt he could say anything to after just ten minutes. A girl who seemed much more like a woman than any he had previously met. A girl who made the chase, the pursuit of women for non-chivalrous reasons, seem like a complete waste of time and energy.

However, she had a boyfriend, one who she spoke of highly. "Does she *really* love this guy?" he wondered, recalling the way she said the words, almost as if she had to convince herself of their truth. There are times when some things are just beyond understanding, and this was definitely one of them.

"Just wait and see," he told himself as he walked down the dimly lit sidewalk towards his apartment, his guts telling him he would be seeing more of her.

Later that same night, Amber lay still in bed. Lying on her side, she was covered by flannel sheets and a large, thick quilt that was knit for her birthday years ago by a special woman who knew her family well. Her eyes remained open in the dark as the sound of wind could be heard through the cracked window.

Amber was in her final semester, and her heart was full of anticipation, expectation, and uncertainty. Thoughts of her future and where her life was heading accentuated, along with her desire for marriage and family. She thought about her current relationship and how it seemed to be missing something and about this guy Beau, whom she just spoke to, who kept crossing her path. Though she wouldn't admit it yet, he roused something inside her soul. With a silent prayer, she closed her eyes and drifted into sound sleep.

The Fire Inside

Friday, March 5, 1999

A break from the books and exams has arrived. Time to ride the wind...

"All passengers please buckle your seatbelts." The sounds of clicks could be heard throughout the plane following the flight attendant's announcement. Among the people strapping up were Beau and a few of his friends. They were about to embark on the spring break trip they had all been eagerly anticipating—free from homework and responsibility at last.

Moments later, the engines fired up, reducing the amount of conversation in the plane as people's hearts began beating faster. Soon the huge flying metal machine thrust forward and took off into the sky, rising gradually until it finally leveled off and flew smoothly onward.

Beau, not particularly fond of flying, couldn't help but peer out the window to see the clouds passing underneath the plane. On they flew toward the white, sandy beaches and late nights of Cancun, Mexico—a beautiful land that is turned upside down for several weeks when college students come from all over the country, and beyond, to spend their spring vacation.

The truth of the matter is that this type of vacation is one that good parents would not want their sons or daughters to go on. For one week, many young men and women let go of responsibility, prudence and any other trait that signifies wise living.

"I won't go overboard here," Beau had said to himself over and over prior to leaving. His desire to live a life with good morals was perhaps at its peak, and he was unwilling to confront the realization that the environment would threaten to overtake him. Deep within, a part of him wanted it to.

A strange feeling lingered in him, though, one that wasn't completely new but was now more acute than before. Beyond his simple dislike and slightly strained relationship with airplanes, there lingered in him an intensified fear of death and what comes after it, of where he'd be going if this plane went down. Despite his resistance to much of the religious talk he sometimes heard, he believed that there was only one of two places a person went upon saying goodbye to earth. "Knock it off," he thought to himself, shifting his head and mentally swatting away the unwanted thoughts like he would a vigilant mosquito. "You'll be fine...you're just going to have a little fun...nothing wrong with that; *you deserve it.*" Yet even as he dismissed the afterlife thoughts as unnecessary, he had little confidence that his destination would be his preferred choice had the plane for some reason crashed.

While these thoughts teeter-tottered back and forth, Amber came to his mind and brought with her a pleasing feeling. There was something different about her. Though she didn't seem like one of those over-the-top "religious types," she did embody a sense of purity and life, and this sparked in him a desire to know more about her. He wanted to have more of what she had, more life in life.

Whether or not he'd see her and talk to her again he couldn't be sure. For some reason, though, he believed he would, and part of him felt he was doing a disservice to the potential of getting to know her by going to Mexico. He strongly doubted that a girl like herself would think too highly of a trip such as this.

As soon as the plane landed, however, Beau's caution and concerns subsided and were whisked away by the warm tropical breeze. Though he clung tightly to his loosely established convictions, which were strengthened in the respite at Hillary's and Earl's, he felt them ease up a bit as the warm wind and intoxicating energy consumed him. It was as if there was something in the air—a questionable yet enticing voice begging him and the others to just let go, to indulge.

They checked into their extravagant, bustling hotel, which was filled with virtually all college students. Here and there a family could be seen, though the looks on their faces indicated their feeling that they were in the wrong place. They took their belongings to the room on the fourth floor, changed into the appropriate attire, and walked down to the beach, lured by the sounds of multitudes of voices and thumping music that grew louder and louder as they drew near.

Upon arrival, they were met by euphoria as bikini-clad women, most of whom bore little or no shyness but rather prowess and aggressiveness, roamed alongside the bars, pools, and the white sand beach that separated them from the deep blue waters. Soon each of the guys had a drink in their hand to inaugurate the true beginning of the week. Another one followed quickly and more after that. It was there that Beau's clutch on morals was, for the most part, released, the wind itself acting like a drug trying to carry them away.

Evening came quickly. After eating a hasty meal, they left the hotel and went straight to the clubs, dressed for the night and carried by the momentum that began down at the beach. Again they were greeted by thunderously loud sounds of electronica that echoed throughout the streets and roared within the darkly lit clubs filled with hundreds upon hundreds of people vigilantly chasing all that the night had to offer. The music and the scenery reached into the inmost parts, causing a constant alteration in their minds that was assisted by a steady flow of alcohol, which wasn't the only drug on demand. Beau and a few of the guys took a small dose of ecstasy that a girl at the hotel had given them prior to going out. Before the trip, he told himself he wouldn't touch the stuff, that those days were past. Yet amidst the pulsing music, flashing lights and beautiful women so far away from home, he just couldn't resist and convinced himself that this one time was worth it. The voice inside him, which had been telling him to turn away from all this, was growing harder and harder to hear. It kept shouting, though, and would continue to do so all week, perhaps even influencing him in some way.

And so the night went on, deep into the dark where those who pursued its fruit became increasingly emboldened and daring. Beau was the last of his company to leave, engulfed by the surroundings and the evolving, intoxicating sounds produced by the DJ. When he finally decided to leave, completely unaware of the time, he and a girl who he had danced with much of the night walked through the club doors and were met by the blazing, defiant light of the early morning sun. That light was usually most welcome to Beau, and though a part of him wanted to embrace it, it now made him want to hide. It was just too bright and powerful for his altered, spent mind.

He walked the girl back to her hotel, pulled her in close, and gave her a long kiss goodnight, with full knowledge he wouldn't see her again. He had hoped for more, though she made it clear through a mixture of provocation and restraint that he'd have to invest more time and energy in her to obtain the physical. Since Beau wasn't interested in knowing her beyond the night, and for some reason was unable to lie to her to get what he wanted, he released her and walked away to return to his hotel. Besides, it was only the first night, and much of the week remained.

As he walked down the sidewalk, lulled by the soft, warm breeze, he felt a sense of pride in obtaining the kiss and desire of this girl. With this pride, however, came a lingering emptiness that he couldn't explain away. Strangely, a part of him was relieved that he didn't step over the edge with her. Shortly afterward, he noticed another girl walking alone up a palm tree lined sidewalk toward a hotel. She was very beautiful, with long, dark hair and a tall, slender figure. Yet on her face, which was bowed low, there was shown an unmistakable look of shame and frustration. It made Beau think for a moment, a slight tug of pity and compassion for her felt in his heart. He knew what most guys are about and what went on there and hence the situation she was likely coming from. The thought scattered quickly, though, and he continued his journey back to the hotel with a slight stagger in his step.

He finally arrived to the hotel room after riding up the elevator with a few other late-night thrill seekers who had come to the end of their ropes. After fumbling with his keys for several minutes, he gently unlocked the door and stepped in. The sound of his entrance made a couple ears twitch, but that was about all it did. Upon entering the darkened, stale-aired room, he was greeted by the sight of the others spread about on the floor and beds, with loud troll-like snoring coming from a few. From the edge of the curtains he could see the light of morning trying to break through. Once again he felt dismay at his inability to enjoy the light of morning that he loved so much but embraced so infrequently.

He walked over to his spot on one of the double beds and thought about changing into more comfortable clothes, but lacking the energy, he simply fell face first into his pillow.

It didn't take long for sleep to overtake him, though it was to be short. Just a few hours later, they all awoke and soon began the procession all over again.

The week carried on as such, each day passing into night and night into morning. Blurriness and fatigue increased with every hour. Occasionally there was a peaceful moment to revel in the sight of the setting sun from the balcony or beach, though the moments were few and fleeting, obscured and short lived due the non-stop nature of the trip. They, like many others, left their inhibitions at home and hoped to find freedom and excitement in this land of hedonism, a land far away from the normalcy and drudgery of everyday life, which, unknown to them, wasn't really true life at all.

For one week, many abandoned reason and responsibility, embracing temporary satisfaction that left them with permanent regrets and unmet expectations. For many, the sting of shame, debt, depression, and possibly much worse was taken home as well. It seemed they didn't fully understand how fleeting pleasure could be, turning hopeful, longing hearts into stone in such a short amount of time.

Though Beau kept from falling too far off course while there, perhaps not intentionally, his immunity from the allure that existed all around him continued to weaken. It stood little chance due to the late nights, alcohol, and other popular substances, as well as the multitude of girls who wore next to nothing and wore it daringly, with inviting black-lined eyes that were hungry and sometimes desperate to lure in the lust-filled male eyes, eyes that always wanted more.

These same men, in turn, sought to fulfill their cravings through any attractive, willing, or seducible young woman that stood before them. Most of them paid little or no attention to the hearts of their prey, consumed by their physical appetites and desire for conquest, power, and respect that they so intensely craved.

In this land far from home, few people with morals exercised them, and those who tried would find that those morals held little power, if any.

By week's end, Beau himself was near crazy in his mind. Sleep deprived, depleted of natural energy, and running out of time to live the "wild life," fatigue began to reign. Despite this, he and the others still harbored a continual, growing craving for more of the indulgences that wrecked them and hence didn't stop going until the very end. Beau would have a couple more physical encounters with women, never crossing over the line entirely but drawing dangerously close each time.

The pleasing feeling that began just a week earlier with the first taste of wine-like wind had now evolved into a raging, reckless, and out-of-control fire inside that secretly sought to char the skin, a fire that could never be satisfied. Never.

Friday, March 12, 1999
        Back on the plane, heading home. I can't feel anything inside; senses seem dead. So tired and weary...
        This trip was not supposed to go as it did, though I guess I shouldn't be surprised. When will this way end...

"May I have your attention, please. It's now time to fasten your seat belts." As if it were all a dream, Beau and his friends were again sitting on the plane back to Wisconsin. The week of fun and sun was now gone forever, to be replaced by the pressures of college and life that would antagonize him the entire flight back. Not an ounce of endorphins remained within him to produce the smallest speckle of joy. He was completely spent and exhausted, dreading the reality that awaited back home. Even the fear of death from flying had drowned, as his senses were all but numbed.

The feeling that came upon him while there, the freedom from all forms of responsibility, would follow him and remain for some time, casting a shadow of gloom and dissipation over each day. He believed there was more to life than what he experienced there, but he just couldn't seem to find it. The memory of attractive women, the care-free feeling of lying on the beach in the afternoon with a drink in hand with anticipation of the energy-filled nightlife just hours away, and the frivolous spending of money, which he really didn't have, all produced an immense desire to go back. This desire, however, was pounded down into submission by merciless reality that said "no way." The deep trenches of lust and materialism dug deep into his soul, producing a battle that raged within.

Darkness poured into areas once lit by a false light.

Despite Beau's inability to see, however, a different light remained.

Temporary Shelters

On a cool Sunday afternoon in mid-April, Earl sat contentedly with Jesse on the porch. He rocked slowly in the chair, graciously allowing the elements to soothe his weary soul while admiring the skies and the swaying branches of the evergreens. It had been a long day filled with church and spending time with others, including the eldest of his three sons and his daughter-in-law, who lived just over an hour away. The time for quietness had come, and his inner battery was in dire need of recharging. Though he loved people and was energized by them, all the socializing often left him exhausted.

It seemed to him that moderation applies to all things, including time spent with others.

The sun was beginning its descent in the west. He looked over to it fondly, as he had so many times for so many years, whether surrounded by company or just himself and Ruth, or in more recent years, just himself and Jesse. Something about it always pulled in his eyes, making him squint in reverie. Strange thing it was, how he looked into the beauty before him like it was the first time he'd seen it.

Sometimes in his earlier years, and even sometimes these days, it forced him to reckon with the captivity of activity that can beset a traveler if he or she is not paying attention to the road, even if the road is filled with doing good things.

"Son, if you can't enjoy a sunset, you're *moving too fast...*" Earl remembered his father telling him many years ago while fishing from shore one evening. It was hard to believe that he was now a grandpa while rekindling that distant memory. "Time sure moves quickly, old friend," he said to Jesse, who lay next to him on the right side of the rocker. "So many people who have come and gone and who are no more." She turned her eyes to him without moving a muscle and wagged her tail just a little at the sound of his voice, comforted by the feel of his hand petting her back.

After a while he decided it was time to begin making supper. Just as he began to rise from the rocking chair, a sharp pain shot through his chest like a dagger, forcing him to sit back down before he ever really got up.

A deep, painful groan sounded from him while sitting back in the chair. His demeanor immediately shifted to unpleasant surprise, unaccustomed to the feeling he just experienced. He had been through a war, seen those close to him suffer and die, and experienced serious injury himself, yet this was something altogether different, a far more helpless feeling with no adversary to battle.

Though perhaps there was one adversary, that being fear, which attempted to break in and take over. It was thwarted, though, by a quick, earnest prayer for strength and courage as he sat motionlessly. Other than the slow, methodical rise and fall of his chest, he was unable to move. His lungs felt as if they might burst as he sat clenching the rails of the rocker, and he did his best to breathe steadily to fend off a mounting cough that wanted to come and stir up trouble in him.

The tension eventually subsided, and he continued to just sit and finish watching the sun set in the horizon. Earl journeyed through many seasons of life, though this one was new to him. It came with a voice that echoed an unmistakable message that his days on earth were drawing closer to the end. How close he couldn't be sure, but nearer than the day before.

"Lord, I know my days are in your hands, and though I look forward to seeing heaven...it seems I ought to stay here a little longer to finish some work," he spoke into the air. His words were followed by a gentle laugh, due to both gratitude for his gift of breath and resignation of his control over it, as well as to ease his own tension. "Not yet, God..."

As he continued to sit still, his mind was opened to various thoughts, including his young fishing companion who he hadn't heard from in some time. Beau had been on his heart often lately, and he felt there must be some reason for it. He had heard from Beau's mother that he was doing well in his studies, though at the same time living quite a fast-paced life. He was also going off on some trip for college break that wouldn't do much to bring out the real man in him.

This troubled Earl some, and after feeling steady enough to get up and move around, he retrieved his journal and began to write a letter to the lad.

"I've been crawling, walking, and running on this earth for nearly eighty years, and now I'm left with so much to share in what seems to be so little time," he said as he began to paint the pages before him with words from deep in his heart.

Nearly two-hundred miles away to the southwest, at the very same time, Beau sat somberly on the edge of the mighty river. His eyes were transfixed on the steady flowing water that cast a glare upon his face from the early evening sun. As was frequent in these times, he was weary and burdened, and his mind was cluttered, heavy, and held captive by an unruly hangover—a gift from the night before.

Earl had entered into his mind briefly. The thought of being out there at his cabin in the country was an incredibly pleasing daydream at that moment, one that superseded all others.

He strode into the pages of his journal, hoping to find something in days that had since gone by...

Saturday, late March, 1999
      A moment beside the water. Much to think about as always.
      I am caught in a fog; life seems to be moving so fast, almost out of control. Some things that seem sweetly impure are within reach, while others of greater value, such as family and friends, seem to be distant. A rollercoaster ride, I presume, and probably nothing to be worried about. Seems I always manage to find my way back home, wherever that is. Must keep riding the wind, yet slowing down to let it pass through me.
      Right now, though, it's not passing through me very well.
      The fog grew thicker after a surreal trip to the white-

sand beaches and late nights of Mexico. I cannot explain the effect that it had on me, though one who lives life with the taste for adventure would understand.

I can remember the feeling of euphoria from dancing until dawn at the sleek, pulsating clubs, while women of appeal moved seductively about the floors, the inviting look of hunger behind their blackened eyes calling out.

I remember she who fell asleep in my arms on the beach as the sun rose over the ocean, waves tumbling and wind blowing thoughts through my soul. I held her to keep her warm, close yet miles apart inside. She was strong inside, respectable, and stopped me from doing what I am now grateful I did not. We just lay there and dreamed...

The trip became a part of me; its fast, uncontrolled nature sparked a desire within me. There is another desire within me, however, one that I cannot ignore...

...The desire to be sitting in a boat on a northern lake, feeling the fresh air blowing through my hair as the evening sun bounces slightly off the soft ripples, fishing pole in hand, serenity in mind.

...The desire to go for a long walk in the woods where I grew up and to stroll in the forest where the grave of my canine companion, who accompanied me with unconditional love through many of those years, lies protected by the trees.

...The desire to chase my niece and nephews around the yard and notice new things about them, things that I miss from being away. They are so perceptive despite their young age, and they grow so fast.

...The desire to be lying in a hammock on a quiet summer evening, watching with barely opened eyes as the trees sway back and forth in the warm, gentle breeze as if they have no cares in the world. Or maybe they just don't let those cares get to them. How I would love to be those trees at times. Sometimes, when my eyes would close, I would see that beautiful woman who stole my heart and soul and filled them with the colors of morning, day, and night. Someday I'd like to see her when my eyes open.

I obviously want to run wild and free yet at the same time walk with the breeze. Someday I may have to give all of myself to one of those sides, maybe not. Perhaps a balance exists that can satisfy both.

> Seems like I'm caught in a clear fog, not really
> knowing where the highway leads yet believing that it's
> going somewhere good...

Beau sighed heavily. Forcefully, if not angrily, he closed his journal and set it beside him. At that moment, he was having a difficult time seeing the good that he saw just a few weeks before when he wrote those words, or any good for that matter. Exhausting his thoughts, he looked back to the waters, which usually comforted him when under attack from the depression and despair that pervaded his being when the partying was over. Unfortunately, they offered little comfort now.

It had been several weeks since he arrived back from Mexico, yet the polluting effects of the trip still lingered. It seemed as if he and his friends had gone out to the bars more than usual lately, consuming more alcohol as well, perhaps in an attempt to hang onto that week in the sun that had long passed—caught in a fog, chasing a mirage, running from reality.

Now Beau could run no more and was completely vulnerable to every downcast thought, emotionless and unable to produce a smile. He longed for peace of mind but found little more than an ounce of it despite the power of the "father of rivers" before him.

"How did I get here?" he asked himself silently while lowering his head as one defeated and hoping for some kind of an answer.

As he sat staring into the waters, he for some reason noticed, from the corner of his eye, two middle-aged men walking toward the bench where he sat. He was not sure if they were coming to talk with him, though it seemed likely. His senses served him right.

They approached gently and courteously, briefly introducing themselves as being from a church in the area. At the sound of that word, Beau's defenses were alerted, though they were so weakened that he just went along with it. He offered no enthusiasm, however. They made a little small talk at first, mindful and cautious in their selection of words, and after a little while gently asked him if he had any thoughts on faith and heaven, and Jesus.

Despite believing in God, Beau didn't have many thoughts regarding Jesus and usually avoided the subject, not really understanding much about him and not particularly interested in knowing. He was usually turned off, offended, by these sorts who tried pushing their religion on him. However, there was something different about these guys. There was nothing imposing nor threatening about them whatsoever.

Perhaps for that reason, Beau gave them an ounce of attention and responded calmly in a steady, polite, and distant tone, "I believe in God, but I'm really not interested in hearing more about it right now," and firmly turned his head back toward the waters, indicating that he had no more words to say. He could sense that the men desired to say more after his response, for just before he turned his eyes back to the water, he caught the man standing to his right exchange a concerned look to the other, who stood just behind the bench on the same side. It was as if they could see the turmoil behind his eyes and were, for some reason, in anguish over it themselves.

Wisely, they refrained from speaking all that they would have liked to say and simply handed Beau a small, folded piece of paper. It spoke of living water and truth and light, accompanied by a painting of a stream flowing down from a huge mountain.

After doing so, they wished him well and humbly walked away, never to be seen again.

Beau stared at the picture and the words for a few moments. Then out of respect to those men, he folded it and put it in his pocket, with no actual intentions of reading it again. However, sometimes intentions are overcome, and the pamphlet would be opened and remain with him for some time deep in his dresser drawer. Like the Bible that had been handed down to him, something within prevented him from throwing this little gift away.

Slightly roused from the encounter and unable to sit any longer, Beau eventually rose from the bench. He began to walk along the river's edge, hoping to find some semblance of serenity and clear thought.

Just before he reached the end of the park's edge, a minivan came tearing around the corner on the concrete drive that separated the park from the riverfront. Music blared out of its open windows, loud enough to be heard throughout the park. There must have been seven teenagers in there, their ecstatic conversation and singing heard even above the music, carefree smiles visible on some of their faces.

As the van passed within ten feet of Beau, the teenage boy who sat in the front passenger seat looked toward the river and caught him square in the eyes. A large puff of smoke rolled out of his mouth simultaneously. Beau studied him for a brief moment, catching the look of whimsicalness and freedom from responsibility on the young man's face. He appeared lost in the music and moment together with his friends, high on life and likely other less edifying substances, going by the scent of marijuana that Beau caught a whiff of as the vehicle went by. He knew the scent well. He didn't appreciate the substance himself, for no other reason than that it made him and those he knew become slow, stupid, annoying and short of breath.

"Well, that would explain some things," he said after the van squealed by him, finding part of the answer to his question of how he got to where he now was. Taking another look at the van, he recollected earlier times of being in a similar position, riding in a similar vehicle: the Strider van.

The infamous Strider van—an emblem of reckless, irresponsible, adolescent pursuit of what appeared to be life and adventure in the young eyes of its inhabitants. For Beau, it entertained many of his weekends for a period of time in earlier years.

It was just before entering high school when he was inducted into it.

"Beau, you want to come out with us tonight?" asked his sister warily. She wasn't sure if it would be a good thing to have him come along, but she felt sorry for him sitting home with nothing to do.

"Sure!" he responded, and soon thereafter he climbed into the smoke-filled, deep-blue Chevy minivan owned by the parents of one of Sammy's guy friends. The vehicle, once used by his parents for groceries and picking up the kids from soccer, had evolved, or perhaps digressed, into a party on wheels for a rather large group of wind-chasing youth gone wild.

Beau fit right in.

Beau would ride with them weekend after weekend for more than one season, and in the process, grew close to a host of different faces who he befriended and connected with despite a significant age difference. They were an eclectic bunch with likeable personalities all unique from one another. Yet, as always, good people aren't always so good and often do not so good things. Drinking, getting high, and occasionally indulging in psychedelic drugs were commonplace while Zeppelin, Metallica, the Grateful Dead and a host of other venerable bands of yesteryear and the current day blared forth from the over-worked speakers. They roamed from party to party and from campfire to campfire, as well as road trips to rock concerts and other such venues. If there was a worthy destination, they found a way to get there.

Life was good, carefree, and exciting. Or so it seemed.

Many a weekend the van would carry its patrons to a well-known party spot deep in the woods that lay at the end of a long gravel road. This gravel road, in turn, was accessible only by an obscure country highway out in the middle of nowhere. Loud cheers and chants could be heard from onlookers as the van drove in, and all its patrons enjoyed a sort of celebrity status as they climbed out one by one, like rock stars getting out of a limo. They hooted and hollered with all their might with their beers lifted high in the air as they approached the blazing campfire that resembled the liquor burnt blood that ran like lava through their veins.

The night would pass in usual fashion. Beginning with relatively friendly conversation and laughter, it progressed quickly to rambling talk void of inhibition to a clouded state of half-consciousness mixed with aggressive behavior that either manifested in bold pursuit of the opposite sex, punches thrown at the same sex, or heavier than normal drinking to compensate for the absence of the previous two manifestations, which often led to vomiting and passing out somewhere in the bushes. This was somehow viewed as comical the next morning upon reviewing the night's events, which most couldn't remember all too well anyway.

The group, which had been together long before Beau came along, resonated deeply with the seventies. Beau found himself forming a romance with the free-spirited feeling himself. This fascination was aided by such activities as watching the "Yellow Submarine" by the Beatles under the influence of psychedelic mushrooms. That feeling that came with eating that rather nasty tasting fungus was cherished.

Within an hour of swallowing it down, everything that wasn't funny became funny, and that which was funny became hysterically funny. The laughter was accompanied by a pleasant feeling underneath the skin and throughout the whole body, the head floating in the air.

Of course this elation didn't last forever, and despite all efforts to retain it, usually by just eating more, the end of the euphoria soon came. And it came with vengeance, leaving behind a very stale and depressed reality where clear thought was not an option, and all unwanted thoughts ran rampantly like pollen in the summer wind. Reality was painfully distorted, and the only excitement that could be mustered up came with the thoughts of when the next wild night would come along. Until then, however, life had little to offer, a sort of drab, mundane process without much, if any, purpose, hope, and joy.

The Strider van inhabitants lived outside of their generation, perhaps in an effort to flee the mundane that was void of those three great treasures. Beau often pondered over how some people form nostalgia over places, times, and events that they know little or nothing about, other than from what is seen and heard through questionable media, which tends to portray things through an altered lens or perspective. Woodstock, for instance—a hyped-up event in its time that turned into an ugly, unfortunate scene full of mud, drug overdose and withdrawal, and violence. Yet it was seen with awe and adoration by those who viewed it on television decades later.

Those who rolled in the Strider van worshipped and chased after Woodstock weekend after weekend, month after month, for years on end. Though they may have come close a time or two, they never really found it.

The most anticipated ventures they had, even more than the midnight runs to the famous party spot, came on Memorial Day weekend at Two River's Mound.

Each year a caravan of cars, led by the Strider van, would venture a couple hours north to a secluded campsite. And it was no ordinary camp spot. Perched high on a mound, like a castle of old, with a forest floor covered with pine needles that fell from the tamarack pines towering above, it was worthy of appreciation. On all sides but the entrance, it was guarded by a river that, on one side, ran with rushing white-water rapids that filled the air with lush sounds. On the other side, it flowed with soothing, soft-flowing currents that whispered ever so tenderly. It was as if there were two different rivers in one.

The days would begin seemingly innocently, with a small campfire burning as everyone set up their tents and settled in. Some light fishing, a few drinks and joints mixed with just the right music, easy-going conversation, and good food followed. What kept the excitement throughout the day, though, was the mounting anticipation for the sky to darken and the partying to begin. Drunkenness and drug-altered minds would soon be upon them, leading right up to the rising of the sun the next morning.

Despite the alteration of minds, Beau recalled a few special, even peaceful moments that took place in between the darkness of the night and the light of morning. He remembered a time sitting out on a huge boulder, perhaps the size of a small car in diameter, which sat out just twenty feet from shore, a quarter way into the fast-moving river. It rose several feet above the water and could only be reached by several smaller rocks that rose out of the river to form a special, magical-like path to the shore.

There were about six of them sitting out there on that rock, their legs dangling down with feet dipped in the water. They were all caught in a daydream as water rushed by on the sides, filling their ears with solitude while the moon dipped its hands into the water and splashed their faces with its reflection. On the perimeter of the moon, the stars, though slightly obscured by its dominance, shone brightly as they always did when far away from the lights of any city or town. A fleeting sense of tranquility was in the air, accentuated by the psychedelic drugs that were beginning to take effect.

Unfortunately, the moment passed by quicker than the flowing water, and soon the debauchery accelerated into the deep of night. Eventually, after hours of wandering to and fro and hanging by the fire, after smoking countless cigarettes and consuming beer after beer that didn't seem to do anything until the drugs wore off, the sun rose and met their weary and depraved minds. They would rest some that Saturday, then resume the partying come nighttime, though their pace and intensity were a bit slowed down from the night before.

Sunday morning came like a quiet assassin, armed with the hard-biting reality that they would again have to face the life that they attempted to drive away from. Again they would be thrown into the arduous search for truth and fulfillment that they didn't know they were on, seeking to fill empty spaces within that they didn't know they had.

And those were the days of the van.

The days of the van didn't completely die, as they served as a mentor for future years. Beau would forge new friendships later in high school that led to raucous weekend evenings of piling into vehicles with anticipation, excited for the unknown of what the night might have in store. Many of the faces and friends of yesterday were replaced, by no one's choice, yet the new friendships were held together by a similar bond with a foundation made of sand. Along the highway they would drive, hungry for women, wine, and song.

Bonfires raged at remote party spots, becoming increasingly blurry as the night went on while the pursuit of women increasingly consumed them, temporarily covering up the deeper desire to have something real and true, searching, longing, running, chasing after those things that temporarily sheltered them from the confusion and emptiness of life that was all around them. This tape was played over and over again, yet for some reason they thought they were going to hear something new each time.

They entertained hangovers that lasted for days, putting their bodies through unnecessary hardship that was masked as fun. Many times Beau woke up and was unable to recall how he got home or from where he came until he looked out his bedroom window and saw his car parked in the driveway. "That was not smart..." he would say, determined it wouldn't happen again, until it did.

As Beau continued to walk along the river, the flashing memories of the Strider van and its offspring vanished as quickly as the look from the youth that just passed by. His thoughts then carried him beyond the wild times of the past to the calmer, less visible moments that existed from time to time.

Amidst the debauchery and raucousness, there were quieter moments when the music wasn't blaring or the alcohol and drugs flowing. There were moments beside quiet waters when the mind was given the chance to wander some, like the time on the boulder at Two River's Mound or driving along the highway on a clear summer day—moments when the warm sun flickered through the trees and the moon cast light upon that which would otherwise be unseen, causing daydreams to be lifted to fond places once thought lost. However, those fond places soon scattered, and the daydreams were pulled back down by the unfriendly hands of a false reality that, together with an unseen darkness, penetrated the air and secretly wreaked havoc on the soul and sought to extinguish all traces of hope.

There were the quieter times with friends when few words needed to be spoken, times when, for just a moment, that person was accepted for who they were and allowed to sit in a sort of reverie, in the comfort and security of one another, while searching silently within, asking questions of oneself that had no source for answers or truth. Aimless wandering.

There were the late nights when Beau would stroll away from the party scene and the blazing fire, as if led away by some quiet whisper into the quiet of the woods where crickets and fireflies abounded. Away from the noise, random fights, and people trying to impress each other, he forgot about what was behind him and wondered earnestly about what lay ahead. The silence allowed that voice within him to cry out, *"Isn't there something more?"* while believing, hoping, there was but not knowing where to look or how to find it as his eyes frantically searched the starry skies overhead. *"Isn't there more to all this?"*

Soon the search would continue, driving him back into the noise and chaos disguised as life. The confusion and sense of hopelessness that ran deep through his blood and the blood of his comrades would again be suppressed, for a time.

Those nights would often last into the light of the morning, when the sunrise would intensify the secret longings of the heart. By that time their minds had grown immensely weary from lack of sleep and abundance of substances, which always robbed the joy in the end and replaced it with a touch of despair—always, and deeper each time.

To the disappointment of many, the morning never failed to arrive on time, when it would find eyes transfixed on the smoldering campfire. Only a memory now lingered of how it blazed the night before. Loud voices, excitement, and haughty laughter were now reduced to murmurs and sighs that acknowledged unmet expectations and merciless head and body aches. Façade warriors of the night were reduced to quivering, insecure captives.

The inevitability of Monday would heavily set in during those

Heart Dancing in the Sky

August 29, 2006, first gleam of dawn
  I saw them. With only a few days left on this island before returning to the cabin and my family, I finally saw them. It
has been years since I witnessed the display.
  My soul felt on fire while lying next to Highway and
the quietly burning logs and glowing embers. I will never forget these times.

Beau woke from a long nap to the soothing sound of raindrops tapping
gently on the vinyl tent. It was late afternoon, and natural light poured
in. Thanks to the cover of the trees and the overcast skies, it was not too
bright.

  He was lying on his back, still as could be, not a muscle of his
body being exerted. His eyes, still half-asleep, were fixed on the ceiling.
He was tranquilized by the serenity of it all. It was the type of nap he
often dreamed of, and the clarity of thought and mind he now possessed
was beyond measure.

  Of course he had to reach a point in his island adventure to take
such a deep slumber. His brain had grown weary from days of introspection and writing, of searching the annals of life late into the night and
early morning. These particular annals weren't always the easiest to
delve into, either, and he found himself needing a break from it all. He
and Highway had escaped the confines of the island several times to give
his mind a rest, venturing onto the water to fish or to the shore to gather
firewood. Eventually, sleep was the only thing that could help.

Beau decided to lie there until the rain stopped, which it did a half-hour later. He rose from the bed, stretched hard and long, then exited the tent and walked about the island to gather small pieces of wood, Highway following close behind. Afterward, they canoed to shore to collect some larger pieces of wood. While fishing the other day, Beau had spotted a fallen oak branch, great for burning—hot and long lasting.

After an hour of rigorous chopping with a small hand axe, they loaded the canoe with the wood and returned to the island. After stacking it, Beau retrieved his fishing gear, and again they set out onto the water. He caught three decent-sized bass and one walleye—more than enough for a hearty meal.

Before returning to camp, Beau filleted the fish on the aluminum seat of the canoe and threw the remains into the water, a treat for the birds of the air. He wanted to avoid giving a bear any reason to swim to the island, however unlikely that would be. The scent of fresh fish could cause a bear to go out of his way to appease his appetite.

As daylight faded, Beau began preparations for dinner. He stirred the coals in the fire pit, which were still hot from the morning despite the rain, thanks in part to the trees overhead. He placed a handful of small sticks onto it, followed by several logs, and ignited it by kneeling down low and blowing on it.

Once lit, he rinsed and sliced up a potato and wrapped the pieces in aluminum foil, along with some butter and onions, and immediately placed it on the coals. It would take longer to cook than the fish.

While the potatoes cooked, he began prepping the fish. He took another piece of tinfoil and folded its edges, buttered it, and arranged the fillets on it. Next he shook a generous amount of lemon pepper seasoning over them and threw in a few onions for good measure.

"You'll still kiss me if I eat these, wontcha, Highway?" No response other than a blank stare.

Taking three sticks of equal size, he created a teepee about four-feet high and hung a small grill from its top using steel wire, then set it over the fire. He waited a little while for the fire to grow good and hot before placing the fish on it, just inches above the tip of the flames.

Soon dinner was ready. He sat on a log beside the fire and gave thanks before enjoying the meat of the land, which always seemed to taste better when cooked over a campfire. There was just something about it.

Though rested and content, he felt a touch of loneliness that had confronted him more than once during the week. He missed his wife and kids and the often lively exchange that occurred between them while sitting around the dinner table.

He recalled all those years being single, often spending large amounts of time alone despite being gifted with plenty of good friends. Though he believed there was a season for everything, and that his seasons of singleness were necessary and not void of purpose, he could not fathom going back to that way of life now, given the choice was his. After experiencing all the thrills and challenges inherent with marriage and fatherhood, he believed it just wouldn't be the same. It was made abundantly clear to him that man was not made to spend his days in isolation and that those who mocked marriage were twisted in their thinking, disillusioned.

It was these thoughts of family that helped him remember why he was out here. For others. This in turn triggered a sense of gratitude— gratitude for the experiences he'd been given in life, even those that hurt.

Beau finished his dinner and walked around some before returning to the fireside, where he spent the evening with a good poetry book. Dusk set in quietly and passed quickly into night. On a couple of occasions, he could hear the sounds of coyotes in the distance, the howls that evolved into a yipping and yapping they made when pursuing their prey. Then the noise just stopped, which usually indicated a successful hunt. Beau stopped reading for a moment to envision the chase, feeling a touch sorry for the victim, though understanding that that's just the way it is. That's life in the wild.

When the weight of his eyelids signaled bedtime, he jotted a few thoughts in his journal, then lay down to sleep next to the campfire. He didn't fall asleep right away but rather lay looking up at the stars as the fire softly crackled, savoring the voice of the wind moving through the trees along with the other sounds of the night. Highway rested by his feet, both calm and alert, though his eyes were growing heavy too.

"I wonder if you enjoy all this," he said to the dog. The way Highway slowly rolled his eyes to look at his master and then returned them forward gave Beau the strong feeling that the he truly did.

Every now and then, a shooting star could be seen streaking across the sky. A friend of his, credible in the area of astronomy, once surprised him with a bit of knowledge relating to those late-night delights.

"Shooting stars are actually grit, generally pulverized rock, from space that are usually no larger than a grain of sand. Some of the more spectacular ones are pea-sized, and the really wild ones are the size of an orange or larger. Traveling at very high speeds, they collide high up in the sky above the earth's surface with air molecules." Beau grinned as his friend explained this with such ardor, with arms stretched out toward the sky to add drama to the words. "Due to this speed, they begin to glow white hot. Hence we see a streak of light as they burn up. The scientific name for them is 'meteor,' but shooting star will do just fine." He paused and looked at Beau with a smile. "If your kids ask, just tell them they are not really stars."

He didn't stop there.

In response to Beau's comment that the stars looked so close together, even though he knew they weren't, his friend continued:

"Relative stars and objects in the universe are as close to one another as three frozen peas scattered in the Georgia Dome. To count all the stars in our Milky Way galaxy at one per second, it would take twenty-five hundred years. And the Milky Way Galaxy, the home of our sun and earth, is just one galaxy amidst *hundreds of billions* of galaxies in the *known* universe!" He paused, catching his breath and giving Beau a chance to process it all. "The size of Milky Way, relative to the known universe," he couldn't help but emphasize the word "known" again, "is equivalent to a quarter in an area the size of North America."

As many times as Beau revisited these facts, it never ceased to blow him away. It was beyond the grasp of the human mind and made him feel quite small.

"Significant insignificance," as one well known speaker of his day coined it.

Beau's eyelids soon grew too heavy to bear, and he slowly turned to his side and drifted asleep just a few feet from the fire. Physically and emotionally, he felt surrounded by warmth and security.

Later that night, when all was dark and silent, Beau awoke. He was lying on his side, staring into the brightly burning embers that were still producing good heat. Instinctively, he grabbed another log lying near him and set it on the fire. Then, as if compelled, he rolled over onto his back and caught sight of something high above that stole his breath.

The elusive Northern Lights.

It was as if they had beckoned him to wake.

Breathtaking as ever before, rays of brilliant colors danced with great vibrancy in the northern portion of the sky. It had been so long since he saw them, and he silently hoped to see them this week, even though summer was not the most likely time to see them.

As he watched, it felt as if his heart was dancing within him and that he was caught in a moment void of time and space. Few things could produce the feeling of euphoria he felt inside at that moment, a reminder to him that slices of heaven dwell on earth.

He watched them until they faded away, blinking sparingly, simultaneously drifting back into sleep as they parted. Several hours later, he would awake to the morning and resume the journey into the past, picking up at a place where another lesser, though still dazzling, display of lights would forever mark his life.

Small Windows and Big City Lights

"Denver omelet with cheese and two pancakes, please, and a large orange juice." Beau could taste the food while giving the order, and within a few minutes it was on his tray that was securely locked in his hands. He walked into the commons and selected a small table near a window; being able to look outside was a necessary component of this particular breakfast. It enhanced daydreaming, and he had much free time and opportunity before him to do so.

The room was relatively empty, for it was early in the day as well as late in the final exam week. Many students had already progressed beyond the throes of test taking and gratefully entered into summer mode, which left the campus in a strange, almost eerie stillness. What was usually a bustling commons was now a quiet, serene room where the morning sun hung in the air to soothe the soul.

Beau ate his food leisurely, basking in the freedom from studies and pondering the upcoming summer. Many names and faces entered into his mind as he ate, some who he would see again, others he would not. Near the end of his meal, he felt the pull to get out of there, for the quietness and melancholy were almost too elevated to handle.

He pushed his chair back and rose from the table, gathered everything onto his tray, and pushed the chair in with his other hand. He began to walk toward the conveyer belt on the other side of the large dining area, looking through the windows the whole time as he walked, his mind feeling light and carefree.

And then, as if an invisible hand came down from heaven to

redirect his attention, his head shifted to his left to guide his gaze toward a familiar sight. There, sitting by herself at a small table, her posture proper and ladylike and even a little anxious, was Amber.

"Hi, Beau," she said warmly. Beau halted and began walking slowly toward her, still trying to reason with his mind that this was actually happening. A smile immediately covered his face, though he did his best to contain it from revealing the depth of his excitement, delightfully caught off guard by the sight of her.

As he approached her table, Amber shifted slightly in her seat and pushed her book aside that she was earnestly looking into just moments before. She had one test remaining, which would mark the end of her college career at Bluff View University, where Beau still had one year to finish. They talked for a short while, more comfortable and informal than previous conversations. The air around them was alive, and at that moment, Beau wanted to be nowhere else.

Knowing that she had preparations for her test and feeling it was time to move on, Beau wished her well and began walking away. His heart pounded with each step. Inside, he was wondering if he should have said more, though before he could think any more of it, his thoughts were interrupted. Just as he was about to shift into high gear toward his apartment, he heard that special voice come from behind him.

"Will I see you again?"

The words lassoed Beau like a stallion caught by the sight of an open pasture filled with lovely mares just beyond the doors of his stable. Slowing his pace, he paused, turned, and looked directly at her.

"*Yes, you will*," he said, then continued on his way. He wondered where on earth those words came from, along with the confidence and surety that was felt in his heart and displayed in his voice.

For unknown reasons, Beau never looked back a second time. He was reassured by the overwhelming feeling inside that this was not the last time he would be seeing Amber.

Several days later, Beau finished packing up his car and once again set off onto the highway. This time, his destination was the big city of Chicago. A summer internship at a construction company awaited, along with a small room in an apartment with a couple old friends who now lived and worked there. Late nights, bright lights, and a few evenings of high-energy, dusk-to-dawn dance clubs were on the horizon.

Soon, nights that were once spent looking into the starry skies would be replaced by a brilliant skyline. It deserved and received admiration, viewed from a small window in his bedroom, which happened to be the back porch of the third-floor apartment. To Beau, of course, those big buildings made by human hands and ingenuity were nothing when compared to the marvel of stars, country horizons, and ominous mountains. Yet they were still a sight to see—manmade mountains and stars.

After about a month of living together, with summer in full swing, Beau and his roommates ventured north to meet some friends in Milwaukee for a concert near the lake. Later that evening, just before sundown, they left the concert grounds and walked to a crowded sports bar before ending the night.

Immediately after entering, Beau and Dirk proceeded to the bar for a drink. They worked their way through the crowd and stood in between a couple barstools, competing with other patrons to get a bartender's attention.

"Beau!" said Dirk in an excited tone. He leaned in and talked close to Beau's ear to conceal the message, despite the high volume of the crowded place.

"Yeah?" replied Beau curiously, sensing his friends emotion.

"Isn't that the girl from college?"

Beau looked over to his left in the direction of Dirk's gaze. He wasn't expecting any surprise, likely just one of the better looking girls they had both known at school that drew attention. What he saw, however, sitting just four stools down, was Amber.

"Yes…it is." At that instant Beau forgot about anything that was previously on his mind, and his demeanor, which shifted from relaxed to intensely focused, gave Dirk a reason to laugh out loud, which he normally did anyway.

It turned out that Amber had been the first to notice Beau shortly after he entered and wasn't the least bit upset when seeing him and his friend walk up to the bar within five stools away from her. She continued to sit with her back to the bar while surrounded by a group of friends, which included her boyfriend, and wondered if and when Beau would notice her sitting there. Yet she also felt a touch of guilt because of it. She wasn't sure how to handle the situation if he was to come over, though knew that she was excited to see him again.

Beau, with the encouragement of Dirk, quickly mustered up the courage to say hello. He, too, was unsure of how to go about that, given the company she was with. Saying hello seemed innocent enough, though, and even fitting under the circumstances. *"Just be a gentleman,"* he reminded himself.

Amber's heart began to beat a little faster when noticing, from the corner of her eye, Beau working his way toward her through the crowd. As he drew closer, his eyes never left her, and she looked his way with a soft smile. Beau's feet grew lighter when seeing this, struck by the glimpse of her sparkling eyes, and from that point it seemed as if he levitated through the crowd and landed right beside her stool.

He did his best to control his response and appear collected, though excitability was evident in his tone. Amber welcomed this, finding it quite adorable in its own way.

Her greeting was warm, as would be expected, and her gentle, life-giving demeanor quickly made Beau feel at ease. Shortly into the reunion, she briefly introduced Beau to her boyfriend and friends, some of whom he had seen on campus over the years, and then gave her attention back to Beau. They conversed for a short time, talking loudly so they could hear each other above the music and multitude of voices, catching each other up on the latest changes in their lives. Under the circumstances, they did not have much time to talk. Nonetheless, Beau could feel the same energy in the air as he did in the past when in her presence.

They crossed paths a couple more times as the night carried on. Occasionally they would look each other's way, occasionally getting caught by the other when doing so. Out of respect for her boyfriend, Beau tried to restrain from this but found it most difficult. He just couldn't help but look her way a time or two. When he did, he thought he saw what looked to be a distance between Amber and her boyfriend as well as a look of insecurity on him. Not the kind of insecurity that a man feels when he isn't sure of himself but rather one where he questions whether his girl is really his girl. Beau also recalled the night they talked in the commons and the way she lifted her arms when speaking of him, though with eyes that hinted a different sort of feeling—one of uncertainty.

He couldn't be sure, though, and maintained his distance the rest of the evening. He did speak with her one last time while standing outside after the bar closed, right before they each walked away in opposite directions with their respective parties.

"Well, what's the story?" asked Dirk with a grin on his face, hopeful that some purposeful interaction took place.

"Well, I'm not sure... though I hope to see her again."

"Did you get her number?"

"No."

"What! How come?" he asked indignantly, feeling as if Beau had let a great opportunity slip away.

"It just didn't seem right to ask...though I did get her e-mail address."

"That a boy!"

Regardless of the sense of excitement that came with this, Beau did his best to keep a tight reign on his heart. Too much uncertainty surrounded the whole acquaintance. Nonetheless, it was undeniable to him that something was taking place between them that could not be explained away, something that kept hope alive.

Sparked by the encounter, Beau walked away from that night and weekend with her running through his mind. Her beauty and personality entered into his every thought. Despite the relationship she was in, he knew that he could no longer wait on time and chance to communicate with her again, even though chance did not appear to be involved here. There is a time to wait and a time to act, and he believed the time for the latter had arrived.

The following Monday, Beau again went into detective mode in order to get her contact information. He called the bookstore on campus. Fortunately, he was able to talk with that sweet old lady who took a liking to him that morning he first met Amber. He was thankful for the opportunity to talk to her again, although this step could have been avoided had Beau not forgotten Amber's e-mail address and last name that she provided him just two nights earlier in Milwaukee.

Ignoring this, Beau pressed forward and found success. Though he did not get her direct contact information, he was given her last name. The woman even made him spell it out twice before she let him off the phone. She remembered who he was, and her tone revealed that she knew of the true intentions behind his call. She had a nose for romance and could smell it as sweetly as the fudge on Mackinac Island.

Equipped with Amber's last name, Beau eventually tracked down the telephone number of her parents' house, where she was living for the summer before departing in the fall.

One late afternoon that following week, Beau returned from work to an empty apartment. Calmed by the rays of sunlight beaming in through the windows, he dialed Amber's number. It should be noted that this happened after pacing around the room for several minutes to prepare for the call and several minutes after that, including a few mock trial runs, and sitting down once in a while to catch his breath and gain courage.

After three rings, Amber picked up the phone.

"Hello?"

Her voice nearly made Beau forget what he was going to say.

Surprised at the sound of his voice, which revealed both confidence and nervousness, Amber stopped looking through some clothing magazines while standing at the kitchen counter. She walked to the kitchen table and sat down, looking out over the vast field in the backyard. A touch of elation found her.

"Beau, you called me!"

From that moment on, a new chapter to an unending story took off running, a chapter that would take Beau through every season he had ever traveled through up to that point in life and more. It would also prepare him for others to come.

Though Beau's conversations with Amber had begun long ago in the commons at college, one could argue that the story really began to unfold with the series of telephone calls that took place in that north-side Chicago neighborhood. Their conversations often lasted hours, each time going deeper. As usual, she was not afraid to ask the deeper questions, and he was obliged to answer. The walls continued to crumble— walls that had often kept him from opening himself to others.

Though he still harbored a good dose of caution, Amber began to grow more and more on his heart with each call. Most of them took place while he sat on his small, twin-sized mattress during the incredibly hot and humid nights of that summer, sweat dripping from his brow. He barely noticed the heat during those talks with Amber, though, while his small-town eyes stared through the window at the near-ominous John Hancock Building and Sears Tower that glimmered in the distance for all to admire. In earlier years he never thought he would be living so close to them, especially while gazing out the frosted windows of the bus that carried him down rural country roads to his small grade school.

In some of the conversations, Amber expressed a great care for her boyfriend, though it appeared as a care that one would show toward a brother or a friend, not a mate. Once or twice, she even made this known to Beau through soft-spoken, heavy-hearted words. This built hope within him yet also kept him at bay due to respect for this guy who apparently treated her well.

All this came together to confuse Beau, making him uncertain of how to conduct himself in light of her relationship. The signs of interest he received from her added to the confusion, very unaware of some of the deeper struggles and longings that could shake the emotions of a young woman, even one as rooted as Amber.

There were also other reasons for Beau's persistent caution: he had crossed bridges that should not have been crossed with women in the past, and he would sooner die than let that happen with a girl like her. She deserved respect, and he desired to do things right this time.

The phone conversations with Amber would continue, their depth of enjoyment steadily increasing right up to one sunny afternoon when she called Beau shortly after he arrived home from work. Beau was usually the one to call, and to receive a call from her was most welcome. Even more thrilling, though, was the proposition she put forth within that call.

"Would you like to visit me and my family for a weekend in August, in my hometown?"

Beau nearly dropped the glass of water in his hand. He didn't have to consider his response before responding "yes," and his excitement was clearly evidenced by the dancing he did around the kitchen after hanging up the phone.

"She has a boyfriend, so don't get your hopes up..." he said to himself, stopping the dancing for a moment. Though soon he started up again, more wildly than the first time, unable to hold it back.

"Life is a highway; enjoy the ride," he often said after seeing the catchy phrase on a sports car advertisement in a magazine. Little did he know of the ride that was awaiting him that weekend at Amber's near summer's end.

Before that ride to Amber's, however, stood more days in the city, as well as one week at a place unlike many others. A place where the days pass in a manner much different from that of everyday life. A place where man and nature collide with the past, present, and future, along with other, more tangible objects.

Lake Wagatogabee

Early Saturday morning, July 17, 1999
The day has finally arrived. Wind, water, walleye, and ale will be the recipe for the next week. I doubt it will be as toxic as previous years, though something tells me it will be another unusual excursion...

"Beau, you ready?" yelled Dale from his front porch as Beau got out of his car and stepped onto the driveway. The long awaited July morning of departure had come for the annual, and renowned, one-week fishing trip.

Each summer since ninth grade, Beau traveled with the Jabowskis northeast through the Midwest roadways that led to Lake Wagatogabee, a large, deep lake located in the northwest region of Minnesota, where new stories and adventures lay in wait for the Wisconsin fishermen year after year. Dale and his family had been going to this location for nearly a decade, and one year Dale asked Beau if he'd like to join them. The rest was history.

Dale was one of Beau's best friends. Their camaraderie began back in the seventh grade within the confines of boys' chorus, the infamous classroom setting where friendships were born that would bloom in the high school years not too far away. Many of these friendships would stay much longer than anyone expected, right into college and beyond.

In that class was a humorous and harmonious meshing of personalities, and Beau again connected with others who shared a tendency in a boat on the Wisconsin waters with his father and siblings. Those times now seemed so far away to him.

Beau's upcoming trip to Amber's was no small topic of conversation on this particular trip either. In fact, it was near the front burner all week, constantly swimming in his mind, and the guys could see it. With every deep look into the sunset, he saw her and wondered what was to come. His senses told him this wouldn't be an ordinary experience. Every year at Lake Wagatogabee, it seemed Beau had a girl occupying his mind. Beau recalled a time a couple years ago standing on the dock one evening after dinner while casting a line into the water, waiting for Dale to come down from the lodge where he was talking to his girlfriend on the phone. For some reason, being by the water charged Beau's romantic thoughts year after year. As he admired the deep blue skies and rays of sun bouncing onto the lake's ripples, giving the appearance of pure gold, he would wonder when his mermaid was going to come along and why he had to wait so long.

Perhaps his mermaid had now finally come. If so, she was well worth the wait.

Now with the numerous amounts of hours that they spent on the water, it would be inconceivable to not have a special story or two arise. For people who have affection for the outdoors, stories are inescapable, especially fishing stories, which often have a special way of traveling further and further from the actual, historical truth with each retelling.

One story, however, which took place on this very vacation, remains true to its origin, unscathed by time and imagination.

It was evening time when Stu, Dale, and Beau sat in the gently swaying boat, each facing west out the starboard side of the boat. Nick was fishing by himself somewhere else on the lake, trying some new strategies that he was not willing to let the others in on just yet.

It was midweek, with no particular rush to get anywhere. They had finally settled into vacation mode and were quite comforted knowing that more than half the days still remained. It always took some time to unwind and feel relaxed after arriving, a little longer each year. Several other boats were in the area of water they were fishing in, though the solitude was abundant nonetheless, aided by the blue evening sky and setting sun.

Off in the distance to their north, just twenty-five yards from the tip of the transom, they could hear the cries of a young boy in a fishing boat with his dad and what looked to be his older brother. It appeared the boy had a treble hook caught in his finger, and his dad had the daunting task of pushing the hook through the skin of his boy's finger to expose the treble and break it off with a pair of pliers. He then had to slide the hook back through the finger and out the hole it went in from. Stu understood this situation from experience and explained it to Beau and Dale. In fact, it was Dale he had to perform this operation on, though he was too young at the time to remember.

Having enough imagination to picture the scene and knowing little joy was taking place in that boat, the three men turned their gaze back to the horizon and kept on fishing. It was assumed that all was under control, and they didn't want to lose an ounce of the peacefulness they were enjoying.

Hence, they continued the pursuit of walleye, the prized fish not only of this lake, but also of anglers throughout the Midwest and beyond. Good eating too—fresh white meat pleasing to the pallet. Beau was using a small deep-diving repalla, the kind that looks like a dark, chunky minnow and swims six to eight feet below the surface. It was one of his favorite and most prosperous baits. He confidently cast and reeled it in slowly, catching a few walleye in the first hour while conversing with the other two as the boat drifted along in the gentle, warm wind.

Now the exact string of events that took place subsequent to that are not known for certain, though rumor has it that it went something very much, if not exactly, as follows:

Dale, who sat in the middle of the boat, had become a bit perturbed by the success Beau was having this particular evening. He therefore decided that an attempt to thwart Beau's attempts at catching any more fish was in order.

"What is that thing moving around in the brush over there on shore?" said Dale, looking inquisitively in the direction toward Beau's left. Beau, not giving it much thought, looked in the direction Dale pointed and continued to do so for several moments in an effort to visually locate the noise.

"I don't see it," said Beau, looking more earnestly in the direction Dale's eyes were looking. At that moment, Dale slyly leaned over to tap his buddy's line, which was within reach of the tip of his fishing pole, hoping to trick Beau into thinking he had a bite. In the process, he accidentally cut Beau's line with the hook of his bait.

Unfortunately for Dale, Beau was not fooled and immediately knew that tug was no fish and was even less amused when seeing that his line was cut.

"Now you did it!" hollered Beau. "Just because you're not catching any fish you go and mess with my line…that was my favorite bait!" A bit of laughter followed, along with some more choice remarks from Beau said with mild seriousness. He was frustrated by the loss of that near-sacred repalla, which had brought him such good fortune on the waters that night and in the past.

Grudgingly, he changed baits and fished on despite the setback, hiding his grin caused by Dale's persistent chuckling, which he just couldn't stop doing. It wasn't long before laughter came from Beau too after calming down some and assessing the situation for what it was.

Before going on with the story, one must understand Dale. Routinely, he enjoyed testing the patience of others and devised plots in his mind to ruffle feathers, not for the sake of malice or resentment but rather to evoke laughter and perhaps to display his friendship in one of the ways he best knew how. It's likely that competition was mixed in there somewhere too.

An experience years before, when the two were in high school, gave evidence to this.

It was a fresh spring morning at Evergreen High School when Beau saw Dale in the halls before school started. He had a look on his face that made it very clear that he was hiding something, a concealed snicker that proved he had done something mischievous. Beau questioned him immediately, though Dale didn't stick around long enough to have to give away any answers. He actually fled, saying he had to get to class, which only increased Beau's suspicion. He knew Dale placed little urgency on getting to class on time.

"My car…" Beau thought immediately. Their vehicles were often used as tools for trickery, likely be-

cause that was the only option available since they owned nothing else.

Led by instinct, he walked out to the parking lot to his car, and to his utter surprise, he found a dead, gutted raccoon sprawled out right on top of it for the whole world to see. The poor creature covered the entire sunroof, and its blood streaked down the windshield, windows, and doors, painting the white exterior with streaks of red, like hot fudge dripping down from atop a scoop of vanilla ice cream.

"Hmmph!" Beau nodded his head in mild disbelief. "He did good on this one...real good!"

Knowing Dale and the unexpected things that often came from him, Beau was not completely shocked, though he was a bit speechless nonetheless. Never, ever had he seen a raccoon laid, slain, on top of his car—never anything quite like it. Though Beau wasn't big on killing animals only for sport, he was quite impressed by the originality displayed in that act, however vicious it may have appeared to some.

After a few minutes of collecting himself, Beau's creativity and desire for non-malicious redemption kicked into gear. He walked back into the school, wrote a short note that he believed was appropriate for the situation, and boldly entered the administrative office. There, he handed the note to sweet, unsuspecting Jamie Hinsley, an old friend of his who happened to be reading the morning announcements over the intercom at that very time.

So, on went the morning announcements, though with a bit of a twist: "...*and the boys wrestling team took home an impressive win over the Lumberjacks of Saginaw High School, with Bobby Vinto securing the lead at 172 pounds, pinning his opponent with two seconds left in the match. Way to go, Bobby! Whew! Now they are off to the state finals! Also,*" she continued reading with a slight, discernable change in her tone, as if gripped by uncertainty, "*a reward is being offered for anyone who...has*

*information leading to the arrest and conviction of the
person responsible for placing the dead raccoon on top of
Beau Jamison's highway cruiser."*

These words, spoken through a most innocent and
unsuspecting voice, were heard over the speakers in every
room throughout the fifteen-hundred student high school.
This included the room where Dale sat. Prior to the announcement, he sat tall and boastful with a sense of victory, though now had become quite nervous, shocked and
in disbelief over what he just heard.

"Is this for real?" he whispered to himself, sweat
forming on his brow, his palms growing clammy. It
brought great laughter and joy to Beau later when he heard
of his friend's perspiration upon hearing this announcement. And poor Jamie, she just read the note he slipped
into her stack of announcements, unaware of its content
and lack of approval from the powers that be.

Speaking of the powers that be, they heard it as
well. Mr. Klondike, the former military sergeant turned
principal, leaned back in his chair and did some intense
pondering after hearing the most unusual announcement.
His mental calculations repeatedly came to the same con-
clusions—Dale Jabowski and Beau Jamison. He rose
quickly from his seat following the revelation, as if jumping out of a bunker, and hunted down Dale.

He quickly located his classroom and stepped into
the doorway, halting the lesson and stealing all attention
without remorse. Using his index finger and a pair of eyes
that could make the sun go into hiding, he ushered Dale
out of the classroom. Dale's eyes grew large at the sight
of Mr. Klondike staring him down from the doorway with
those eyes and that dreaded finger.

And so began the interrogation.

"Mr. Jabowski," he said in his deep, steady voice
while they stood in the hallway, "do you know anything
about this raccoon situation?" His question was less a
question and more of a command to release all informa-

tion or face painful exile. Though the two of them got along well, Mr. Klondike's personality and stature was one that demanded respect and received it. He always played by the books and knew when to bend, but rarely, if ever, did he passively allow them to be broken.

"Uh, well…"

"Speak up, Jabowski! I haven't got all day."

"Well…" By this time Dale was so shaken and sweaty that he knew there was no chance for smooth talk. "I did some bow hunting last night and…" This was the truth. The night before he sat in the tranquil woods, and in his blood thirst and frustration over not seeing any deer, he shot a raccoon dead. Out of nowhere, the thought entered his mind that it would be clever to decorate his buddy's car with it the following morning. *"Oh, this is going to be good!"* he thought to himself as he carried the critter out of the woods.

"I shot a raccoon last night while hunting and…" he couldn't finish the sentence, though he didn't need to. Mr. Klondike had the facts he needed.

"C'mon Dale, let's go outside."

Together they walked briskly out to the parking lot. Dale released the whereabouts of the crime scene, resembling a prisoner under guard the whole time. However, when they got to Beau's car, they saw nothing other than the blood streaked down all sides of it.

"Where is the raccoon, Jabowski!"

"I…I don't know," stuttered Dale, though in a flash he was struck with an epiphany. *"My car…"* said Dale aloud, figuring Beau turned the tables on him.

"Take me there!" ordered Mr. Klondike. As they approached Dale's car, Mr. Klondike, a pace ahead of his prisoner, who just couldn't seem to wipe the grin off his face, was the first to discover the whereabouts of the now renowned raccoon. There it was, sprawled out on the roof of Dale's tan Malibu. It was also adorned with a few items that were pulled out of his unlocked car and was now worthy of a second and third look.

"In all the years I've been here, I've never seen anything like this," came the words from the befuddled principal, spoken as if he had just seen a piece of the sky fall in front of him. For years, he kept the two young men and many others on their toes and looking over their shoulders, administering necessary and beneficial, though not always appreciated, discipline.

This time, however, he seemed more a comrade and friend as he and Dale stood chuckling side by side. They shook their heads in a mild stupor before the fallen creature, who now wore sunglasses, had a half-smoked cigarette hanging from its mouth, and had a pack of cigarettes in one paw and a tin of chewing tobacco in the other.

"You better get this thing out of here before the hippies and tree huggers see it...and get rid of that nicotine before I have to write you up." Another pause came, reserved for chuckling. "In all my years..." he said again, the laughter still lingering as he walked away.

Though their days of killing innocent animals for less than justified purposes would come to an end, that story would live on.

In lieu of this and other similar experiences, Beau was not the least bit surprised by Dale's current sabotage of his fishing pole and went on to change his bait and continue fishing.

After drifting north for an hour or so, the deep orange sun nearing its final countdown in the west, they circled back tothe location where they first began earlier in the evening. It also happened to be the area where Beau lost his bait. The fishing had been pretty good all evening, so it was no surprise that Beau had another bite after a short while.

"I can't believe it..." muttered Dale, who hadn't had a bite all night. More unbelievable things were on the way, however.

"Is it a big one?" asked Stu.

"I can't tell...yeah, it's big...well, maybe not..." his uncertainty began causing increased curiosity in the boat.

"He always says that—'*it's big, no wait, I think it's small.*'" Dale's frustration and cynicism were mounting.

As Beau was reeling in his catch, with his cohorts watching on with anticipation, something most unexpected happened. As he pulled his bait out of the water, they realized that what he caught was not a fish but rather fishing line.

"Ha!" exclaimed Dale with delight. He still watched closely, though, as if lacking confidence in his mockery. "Nice fish there, buddy!"

Beau, not saying anything and unsure of how to assess the situation, set his pole down and grabbed the line with both hands. As he began to pull it in, he could feel resistance coming from the depths of the lake, small tugs that gave evidence of possible life. By this time all eyes in the boat, as well as those from other nearby boats, were on Beau and his mysterious line that he continued to pull in like a small anchor.

After a few moments that passed like the dripping of sap down a tree, Beau pulled in the final stretch of fishing line. To everyone's amazement, including his own, there emerged his old lucky bait that had been lost in the abyss hours earlier, along with a squirming walleye of no special size held captive by its barbed hooks.

"Ha!" exclaimed Beau triumphantly, staring at the fish as if it was a rare artifact. A wide smile of unbelief beamed across his face. "Ha! What do you think of this, Dale? Ya just can't stop it!" he said, his words echoing for all the other boats to hear, along with a smile persisting on his face big enough to see from across the whole lake.

"I can't believe it!" exclaimed Dale while staring and laughing at the fish, feeling more awestruck than competitive.

"In all my days, I have never seen anything like this," remarked Stu as he nodded his head in awe, his laughter filling the boat as well.

Some things in life just seem too good to be chance.

And so the evenings went on. With them came all the camaraderie and a sizable consumption of cheap, relished beer by Dale and Beau that often came to the displeasure of Stu and Nick. It seemed the boys couldn't have too much fun without it, so they paid little attention to their peers' concern over their behavior.

Besides, Stu and Nick occasionally partook themselves and

therefore could not say too much. In fact, Nick, after enjoying a few too many the prior night, fell backward out of the boat and landed head first into the dark waters of the lake when trying to retrieve his fish from the live well. Thankfully, no harm came to him.

Often, while sitting around the cabin or out fishing with the guys, Beau would think back to earlier days when in the boat with his father or fishing down by Earl's place. Though the times at Lake Wagatogabee were special and memorable, there was an innocence and clarity lacking there when compared with the other places, a tranquility that seemed to be tainted with the passing of beer cans and talk that often swayed away from propriety and decency. Dale and Beau were not quite as reckless and juvenile on this vacation as they had been in prior years, yet remnants of those past times remained nonetheless. Perhaps there was something in the water or air up there.

Those remnants included late nights spent sitting down on the docks facing north, with a cooler of beer and beef jerky by their side. In past years, chewing tobacco and cigarettes were tucked away in their flannel shirts, ready for action, and much action they received. This year was different for Beau in that regard, however, since he had finally given that up after many failed attempts. In some strange way, getting suspended from college helped him kick the habit.

Sitting on the dock, they would stare off into the sky that seemed so huge above the vast expanse of the lake, the stars shining so bright through the darkness. The sky gradually became brighter off to the east as the clock ticked silently, reminding them that the night that stretched into morning would eventually end. A tint of fiery-red grew from the edge of the horizon into a blazing display of orange and pink that brought such brilliant and captivating light to the morning. So brilliant were those skies, which spoke with such power and gentleness, commanding the attention and respect of the onlookers regardless of their altered state.

Through all this, Dale and Beau sat on the old wooden bench just a few feet from the edge of the dock that had been there for years and years, long before they were ever born. It had names carved into it that spoke of times long past, hearts with names etched inside, some crossed out. They laughed and talked and laughed and talked some more. Slight pauses were had in between, their conversation turning to sighs acknowledging the beauty and serenity before them, along with many silent longings of the heart that cried out like the skies themselves while the sounds of loons echoed across the lake.

As usual, the conversation always had a way of returning to the subject of women. Sometimes it ran too close to the edge of appropriateness, occasionally spilling over, though the two had within a respect and appreciation for them that kept it from going too far off course. Love, marriage, fatherhood, dreams, and desires—all the thoughts came to them in that quiet hour. Inside they were searching, and doing so with such intensity, for the thing that fills yet not seeing it or grasping onto it despite how near it was. Neither were they aware of the shadow that tried to blur their vision and push them further off course.

The sunrise would soon come, bringing with it the reality that they needed to go to sleep, reality that had slipped far from them in those hours on the dock where wind, water, and sky touched their souls.

A couple more days passed with no unusual events. For Stu, this was well appreciated. Though he enjoyed a good story and the time with his sons, he also enjoyed peace and quiet, occasionally finding his own cherished time to be alone in the recliner with Roy Orbison playing on the stereo. A couple times a week, he would call home to his wife, who he thought much of when up there. Talking to her brought comfort, in lieu of occasional commotion and scuffles with Nick and Dale. Like many fathers and husbands, he carried many burdens, and this was a special week for him to recharge.

"No more adventures," he sometimes thought to himself, knowing that with these guys it was always right around the corner, always lurking, always threatening the peace.

However, being that he was a man, the taste for adventure ran through his blood, so he unknowingly looked forward to the next occurrence.

And how quickly it always seemed to come.

Thursday morning, Dale and Beau rose and made their way down to the dock to go fishing, quite tired since they were up until dawn watching the skies change colors. While prepping the boat for the day, they met some people who were in close proximity to their age. After talking for a while and finding common ground with one another, they eventually were invited to join them for a party out on an island later that evening.

The rest was history.

Around midnight, the two Wisconsinites were sitting on the faithful bench on the dock, waiting for their new acquaintances to pick them up according to plan. It was quiet and dark, and visibility was very low, though soon they could hear the sounds of a chugging motor in the distance cutting through the night. The noise was followed by the sight of a flashlight coming from around the corner of the small peninsula to their left. The boat drew closer and closer as the sound of the motor grew louder, and soon the flashlight was blaring in their eyes.

Moments later, a large, twenty-foot alumicraft boat pulled to the dock in front of them, filled with a group of seven people. Greetings were said as Dale and Beau eagerly stepped into the boat and were hastily seated as the boat motored off toward one of the many islands that dotted the huge lake. With only one strong flashlight and the light of the moon, which was slightly obscured behind the passing clouds, they maneuvered through the boulder-filled waters.

Safe passage was made to the island. Soon they were standing before a blazing campfire where others had already gathered, while others walked to and fro about the island. Just over an hour after arriving, Beau noticed that Dale was not in the vicinity. Knowing he could not have gone far, he walked around and soon found him on the far edge of the island, sitting on top of a huge rock.

As Beau approached, he immediately understood why Dale was sitting there. The moon, fully round and seemingly within arm's reach, sat gloriously in the sky before them, with no clouds to compete with or divert attention, a radiant white glow filling the earth that, by some standards, could have warranted sunglasses. It cast that familiar but always mesmerizing white trail upon the water that stretched all the way from the edge of the lake right up to the shoreline in front of them. The stars were slightly diminished by its radiance yet still glimmered on all sides as well as in the water.

"I was walking around, looking for a place to take a leak, and then I saw this…" Dale said pointing in front of him with a raised voice filled with pure excitement, like a child who walked on grass for the first time. The whole time his eyes never turned away from the intense beauty that lay before him.

"Whoa…" sighed Beau, coming up alongside Dale for a few

moments before sitting down beside him on the huge rock, the sounds of the party in the background fading out of recognition. "I can see why you decided not to come back to the fire. This is incredible."

There is something about guys having an object to focus on when sharing time together that allows them to converse better: sports, fishing, and in this case, the creation of the sky and water.

"We've seen some beautiful scenes up here, but this is right up there with the best of them...if not *the* best."

"Some of the sunsets we have seen are tough to beat, though I agree," replied Beau. There was a moment of silence, each taking a sip of their beer. "Takes the mind off of every- thing else, even women."

"Thank goodness. They consume enough of our thoughts the way it is."

"Yeah, but they are a wonderful thing."

"Yeah, they sure are..." Dale's words hung in the air for a time, tossed around in both their minds, which were held captive by the beauty of the night, other thoughts floating into and out of their view.

"You thinking about the trip to Amber's coming up?"

"All the time."

"What do you think about the most?"

"Hard to say...just not sure what to expect. I know I can't get my hopes up too much since she has a boyfriend and all, yet it's kind of hard not to with the way things have been going. Never met a girl like her before."

"Well, whatever the case, I have a feeling this one is going to be worth a story someday in the future."

Another moment of silence followed, Beau resonating with those words and feeling that many more stories would be for the writing, in-cluding the time he and Dale were spending right at that moment. Yet, he especially looked forward to living out the story with Amber, im-mensely curious on how it would go.

"How about you? Stacey coming to mind out here?" Dale had been in a relationship for some time, one that started out sweet and strong though now showed hints of weakness. Dale, earlier in the week while waiting for the tip of his fishing pole to bend, spoke of the possibility of parting with her.

"You know, I am, but I've almost run out of thoughts on it. Too confusing, and I'd rather not think of it anymore." Those were his final words on the subject, and Beau knew not to return to them that night. "I'd rather think about this moon, the beauty out here. Makes me think about God, how no accident could create this…"

The words came from Dale out of nowhere, like one of the several shooting stars they saw that night. The pondering that took place within each of their souls after his comment ran even deeper and wider than the one of women, enhanced by the soft breeze that came off the lake and touched their faces like the hand of God himself.

Their conversations often led to brief talks of faith, usually influenced by the nature that surrounded them as well as the beer. Tonight, more so than other times, they both sat with a sort of wonderment, along with a vague sense of fear that they did their best to avoid.

"I wonder what he is thinking of us right now," he went on. "Our lives, what we're doing."

"Well, I'm betting he's not too pleased with certain parts of them," said Dale with squinted eyes due to the brightness of the moon's reflection on the water.

Beau thought back for a second to the time at Earl's—those pages of the Bible fluttering in the wind. Just then it seemed a chill came over both of them, a sort of inward struggle that pushed away the deeper thoughts of heaven and hell and what lay beyond this earth. The peace they felt with the beauty around them was subdued, though not completely overcome, amidst some deeper pangs in the heart that they couldn't understand.

"You still think about Lady much?" asked Dale, attempting to change the subject. He knew the old dog well himself and perhaps missed her just as much as Beau.

"Yeah, though not as much as I used to. Been a while now…" Beau's voice trailed off. Dale was one who could relate to the loss, and it was not the first time he had asked a question like that.

There was once a book written about two dogs who became legends in the rugged Ozarks. They were a brother and sister duo, the best coon dogs in the small county located in the southern United States. Their characters seemed to match Beau's labs well—daring and adventuresome, sweet and gregarious.

Numerous times the Jamison labs daringly escaped their kennel, either by climbing on top of their doghouse and jumping over the fence or by digging a hole far down underneath it and squeezing out. They would proceed to roam the countryside, taking unannounced journeys that would leave their owners to worry. Usually they received a phone call saying the two labs were found hanging out in the yard of some farm miles upon miles into the country, sending them on a short journey to retrieve them. Other times the dogs would return after a couple of days, trotting up the gravel driveway as if they just got back from vacation. Though they received discipline, their return brought relief to the family that was now complete again.

On one of their forbidden but unstoppable journeys, Lady came back days later, trotting up the driveway one early afternoon. Buck was not at her side. They reasoned that he wasn't far behind, though as the hours, days, and weeks passed and the skies began to fade into winter, reasoning fell to pieces, along with hope for his return. Lady didn't eat too much in those weeks, and every day a sad look persisted in her eyes.

There were no clues as to what might have happened to him. He might have been shot; dogs are known to instinctively chase deer and bring them down for sport, which often placed them in the sights of rifles wielded by territorial landowners and hunters. Someone may have taken him to be their own; he was the gentle, clumsy, and brutish type that would come to anyone for a hug, lick, or piece of food. Whatever it was that took Buck, it would forever remain a mystery.

"Did you find your dog yet?" asked Dale as they sat in science class, waiting for it to begin. Dale had a dog of his own and knew well the bond that existed between a man and canine, and it was often a topic of discussion among them.

"No…and I don't think he's coming back either."

The two sat for a little while longer on the boulder before returning to the campfire. Soon the logs died down, along with the excitement, and they returned to the boat and motored back to the dock where they were dropped off, never to see those folks again.

And so the night on the island came to a close, though not to be forgotten by Dale and Beau. Neither to be forgotten were the ensuing hours, in which the classic battle of the ages was about to take place.

Man meets wildlife.

After getting dropped off on the dock, the two intoxicated young men stumbled back to the cabin. They did their best to be quiet in the pre-dawn hours, when nothing could be heard other than an occasional owl or the howling of a wolf in the distance. For some light sleepers in other cabins, Dale's and Beau's best effort to be quiet was unfortunately not very good at all.

They entered the cabin, still striving to be silent. They obviously failed again, however, for they received some negative energy from Dale's displeased, half-awake dad who yelled out from his bedroom.

"Be quiet out there, you buncha' night owls!"

They kept on moving, quickly retiring to the safety of the bedroom and climbing into their small twin beds. Once in, they fought hard to conceal their laughter that started an hour before, for no particular reason, which grew with Stu's exhortation. Their attempt failed.

The laughter erupted further when, after only a few minutes, Beau heard fluttering sounds coming from the dark above him.

"Dale!" he whispered loudly. "Do you hear that?"

"Huh?" said Dale, unable to hear anything due to his own chuckling.

"That sound coming from above in the rafters…can you hear it?"

A moment of silence passed as Beau gave Dale a chance to listen. All it took was a second of Dale holding his laughter for him to hear the sound.

"Yeah…what is it!?" he whispered loudly. The fluttering continued, growing louder, then went silent. But it quickly returned, louder than before. This went on over and over.

"I think it's a bat!" whispered Beau hoarsely, sounding more like a muffled holler. True it was. The sounds were, in fact, a bewildered bat flying in circles around the cabin's ceiling.

Moments later, the moment of reckoning was upon them. They exploded in laughter, as did Nick from the other room on the opposite side of the cabin, when the terrified roar of Stu came bellowing out of his room.

"There's a bat in here! *It's on my damn leg!"* The shrill, deep holler roared out from the room. The bat landed right on Stu's comforter, as if it were his pet, though it received no such warm welcome as one furry little puppy might enjoy. Stu used other choice words to describe his unpleasant situation as well.

Soon all the guys rushed out of their rooms, some tripping over furniture or fishing poles that leaned against the wall in the process. They gathered like clansmen in the family room in the center of the cabin where they conducted a sort of non-verbal meeting of the minds. Of course the two island hoppers were still all buzzed up, quite amused and a touch bewildered.

Nick was clueless, as anyone would be after waking at four in the morning to this set of circumstances. He was physically present but mentally still in the dream he was having prior to the battle. It was a pleasant dream too, in which he pulled up to shore with a whole stringer of big fat fish while all the others looked on in disgust after not catching anything all day. However, he quickly became alert when he saw the untamed beast flying freely, swooping low on one of its passes and razing his head.

"Whoa! That thing almost got me!" he yelled, stumbling over the recliner.

Stu, the overall tribal leader, stood strong, armed in white Fruit of the Looms and a blaze-orange hunting cap, accompanied by a befuddled look on his face. War was upon them, and there was nowhere to hide.

He offensively and defensively took up a pillow as his weapon, barking out destruction orders while his eldest son was swinging a tennis racket. Why he had a tennis racquet, and where he got it from, is a mystery that remains unknown to this day. Regardless, he swung with a combination of fury and humor, laughing uncontrollably with each failed stroke.

Dale, looking around intently for his place in the battle, climbed on top of the large dresser that sat next to the wall in the family room. With one hand clinging to the window curtain, he swung a pillow with all his might at the disrupter of peace with each deadly pass it made.

In the meantime, Beau was still struggling to climb the wall and situate himself on one of the log beams that ran the distance of the cabin. He figured the higher he was, the better chance there was for contact. *"Be the bat,"* he thought.

For the greater part of twenty minutes, the epic struggle wore on, slow and steady some moments, roaring and vivacious at other times. The poor creature eventually met its fate when colliding with Nick's ominous tennis racket. However, this didn't happen until after the curtain Dale was holding onto tore free from the wall, sending his bulky frame crashing to the floor and producing a thunderous boom that must have been heard clear across the lake, or at least by their neighbors in the next-door cabins.

Relieved, exhausted, touched by humor, and bonded by danger, they exchanged a few words and a good share of laughter before retiring to their sleeping chambers, each falling asleep with a grin before their head even hit the pillow.

Yet the adventures weren't completely over, at least for the boys.

Early the next morning they awoke, thanks to Nick, who had the joy of rousing them out of their slumber. Wearily, they threw on some clothes and went down to the docks and climbed into one of the rental boats, feeling quite tired in all respects, though still grinning and chuckling over the events that transpired just hours ago. They wished more time had transpired between now and then since they were beyond tired and dreading the long day ahead of them.

The truth of the matter, which they all knew very well, was that they had no choice but to go. Tradition held them to it. The annual hike had arrived—a ten mile trek each way through dense, wild national forest on the northern edge of the lake. The destination was a secluded body of water where big fish swam that couldn't be caught, though year after year they tried anyway. If one of them backed out, it would spell disaster for their character and reputation for years to come, not to mention a great deal of harassment for the rest of the vacation.

This lack of choice made it easier for Dale and Beau to deal with their weariness. Had they a choice in the matter, they would have had to wrestle with the decision and hence expend more energy.

So across the lake they motored, each person's senses being revitalized by the brisk morning air and the occasional splashes of cool water that came from the small waves hitting the side of the boat. In the distance the sky grew brighter, luring in all of their eyes.

They arrived at the marked southern entrance of the national forest and maneuvered the boat alongside the small, tattered dock that looked like it was ready to fall into the water and not come back up. One by one they climbed out of the boat and pulled it ashore. After some mild bickering over who was going to carry what, they located the familiar, slightly hidden trail that would lead them to no-man's land, then briefly reviewed the map before saying goodbye to the shore and the comfortable boat cushions.

"Okay, now you remember what to do in case we encounter a bear?" said Nick with a mixture of seriousness and humor as he made final preparations to his gear. The mixture was sincere; there was a good possibility of seeing one of these animals in those thick, remote woods.

"Stare it in the eyes and scream like a girl, then run away yelling and jumping?" replied Dale with a smirk, aware of the dire fallacy of his remark.

Mildly perturbed, Nick gave his younger brother a long stare. Beau watched the exchange with delight the whole time. "No! Unless you want to be tackled from behind and have your flesh torn from your back and your skull penetrated by large, yellow teeth. After you wet your pants, just stand where you are and hold your ground—make it think you're ready to fight, maybe let out a holler and wave your arms around. But do not look it square in the eyes! If it attacks you, keep fighting, otherwise it may try eating you alive. Try gouging out its eyes. In the meantime, let's be sure to make lots of noise as we walk. They get scared of humans easily and will usually run away as soon as they hear us coming." He zipped his pack and stood up, offering one final remark. "Unless it's a mother with her cubs, then we're in big trouble no matter what…"

With that being said, Nick swung his pack over his shoulder, picked up the rest of his share of the gear, grinned at his two companions,

The day quickly reached its end, and once again they returned to the trail to begin the trip home. The late-afternoon sun beamed in through the trees as they strode along in a more peaceful, steady stride, different thoughts being evoked in each hiker's mind by the elements. Simultaneously, a gentle wind, like a quiet whisper, joined forces to make them forget their tiredness. Even the fear of bears had greatly subsided, though they each took turns singing various tunes just in case.

"Girl scout camp, girl scout camp—the donuts that they give you, they say they're nice and fine, but one rolled off the table, and killed a friend of mine...oh, I don't want to go to girl scout camp...gee, Mom, I want to go, but they won't let me go; gee, Mom, I want to go home..."

"Da gonnit, Beau, why are you singing that stupid song again! Can't you at least sing about the boy scouts? Or cub scouts?" Nick, now walking behind Beau on the trail, complained as his peaceful reflection was disturbed by thoughts of murderous donuts.

"I couldn't think of any other songs, and it just came to mind. It's been stuck in my head for years, ever since my sisters sang it all the time growing up," replied Beau, taking a deep breath to take in more oxygen. He began singing a different tune, one more acceptable to his comrades. No arguing or bickering took place from that point on, and they moved forward in unison on a mission to reach safe passage back to the cabin.

They reached trail's end by early evening and began their second leg of the return journey, again in the small boat, now motoring south. They were quite tired and looking forward to dinner and the comforts of the cabin. Each gave a few glances back in the direction of the trail's entrance, which they would not see again for a long time—much longer than they would have imagined. They then returned their stares to the lake before them and the trail of fire upon the water to their right.

After arriving and getting cleaned up for dinner, they all sat down and began filling their plates with baked beans and vegetables, along with the freshly caught fish, all grilled to near perfection. A great, unusual calm existed among the guys, who by this time were drained yet soothed, satisfied by the day's adventures.

Stu was relaxed as well, thanks to a day to himself. He thoroughly enjoyed being with his sons and Beau, though every man needs his own space to think and wander here and there.

He also had an unexpected encounter of his own earlier that day.

"I had a run in with Maurice this afternoon down by the dock," he said as he spread butter on his bread, breaking the silence caused by everyone's intense attention given to the food in front of them. Maurice was the owner of the resort, who they had known for many years. Nick, Dale, and Beau all paused simultaneously with forks full of food, lifting their heads to look at one another before turning to Stu with great curiosity and attentiveness.

Enjoying the power of attention he held at that particular moment, Stu decided to leave them hanging for a minute or so as he took a big bite of his fish. He chewed slowly while looking out the window, followed by a bite of his bread.

Silence. The boys began to twitch.

"Apparently our neighbors in the other cabins had a few words to say to her about those 'guys from Wisconsin' in cabin number three," he finally continued, smacking noises coming from his mouth. "Apparently, some were kept up all night…said they heard some banging and hollering over there…"

Each looked at one another for a moment as smiles began to crawl onto their faces. They imagined tired vacationers in the neighboring cabins rolling under their covers until they could bear no more, rousing out of their beds in fury to turn on the lights due to hearing the crashing noises and war cries coming from the cabin in the wee hours of the morning, yet not up to the task of walking outside amidst the dark and cool of night to do anything about it.

"Ah, those people from Wisconsin..." said Nick with an added accent, breaking the silence. Soon a laughter that said all that could be said filled the room, and they continued to enjoy the meal together.

Apart from all the late nights, excessive drinking, occasionally crude humor, short-lived arguments and misunderstandings, as well as the joys of a good day of fishing, there stood something more in those hours that passed at Lake Wagatogabee.

Mixed into the desolate highways, deep blue skies, serene sunsets, intensely starry nights, and ominous thunderstorms was a group of guys in various stages of manhood searching for life, while often trying to escape from it at the same time. There existed a group of men with dreams, desires, hurts, and frustrations caused by family, finances, and various other obstacles that all must face at one time or another throughout life.

The two youngest men stood at a road that had not yet crossed into the real world and the confrontation of many of these obstacles. They stood at a place where manhood and youthful, sometimes foolish, ways clashed with fury.

Much lay before them, including some trials they would not expect.

The next two days moved quickly and the week eventually came to an end, to both the dismay and delight of all. Each of them had to leave something behind there as well as much that called them to return. Little did Beau know that it would be his last trip to the Minnesota northland for a long, long time. The memories would remain a part of him, though.

Yet now, Beau had much to return to. Miles away, far from the unpredictable waters of Wagatogabee, the prospect of a young lady's hand awaited.

And that was the week at Lake Wagatogabee.

Country Roads and Foggy Moonlit Fields

Tuesday evening, late August, 1999
Some experiences in life seem to linger longer and dive deeper into the soul than others. This past weekend, I believe, will be one of those.

"And I've got a peaceful, easy feeling..." The lyrics poured loudly out of the speakers of the truck that he had borrowed from his brother for the move. His heart thumped with anticipation. Just a half-hour earlier, his three summer roommates helped him clear out his back-porch room and pack up the old Chevy pickup, then saw him off as he began his journey to Amber's and his final year of college.

It was a bittersweet goodbye; they had strengthened and forged close friendships in his months there and experienced many unforgettable times together. Random, special conversations and small adventures took place that would forever remain with Beau. Pleasant evenings after work enjoying a meal together, roadtrips, concerts, jumping out of planes at thirteen-thousand feet—the normal things guys do together. Yet now it all seemed like a distant daydream, including waving to them as he drove off down the street just hours ago, the memory being wrapped up in a package to be placed with all the other life experiences.

That one could have so many special friends, so many special times, and how they all passed through the different seasons, which never slowed down, was often a profound mystery to Beau. "Hold on loosely, but keep them close to your heart," he often reminded himself. Little did he know how many more were to come with ensuing years and how they would each leave a mark as life continued to speed forward.

On he drove, the thumping in his chest growing with each passing mile. At one point along the way, he looked into his rearview mirror and could see clearly the grand Chicago skyline fading away, along with his small twin-sized mattress hanging out the back of the loaded pickup, slightly bouncing up and down. Soon, though, to his delight, he found himself far from the city and surrounded by fields and trees, where his singing rose in intensity. He sang with all his might, tapping and banging on the steering wheel like a man high on life.

His voice increased in fervency, as it often did when this particular song played. Its lyrics of a peaceful, easy feeling associated with a woman hit Beau right in the center of the heart. And the highway, that wonderful summer highway, had its way with his thoughts, as usual, especially when the trees, hills, and bodies of water that speckle Wisconsin engulfed it.

Of course this wasn't the first time he rode off to see a girl, and the wind that howled through the truck blew thoughts of earlier days of pursuit.

Back in the days of living in Cringle, romance found the young lad after many years of eluding him.

Leanne Brady was her name, strolling into view in fifth grade. She was his first country-time crush—green eyes like the forest and long, straight, sandy-blonde hair that complimented her spirited and energetic way. She took his eyes and thoughts captive by simply existing. Again, however, the feelings were not returned. He was a bit too overweight for her liking.

Beau remained a toad for some time after that until the following year when he lost the weight and accidentally became popular, getting the girl and obtaining from her his first kiss at a birthday party. The nervousness and excitement hung heavily in the air as they stood within a couple feet of each other on that cold, snowy night in early April, staring at each other as they were about to give away a kiss in the basement. Upstairs, their peers were gorging themselves on pizza and pop with full knowledge of what was going down below them. This was big-time stuff, the kind that made headlines on the gossip press at school on Monday morning, especially a school with only a hundred and fifty students.

The thrill of the kiss, which had dizzying effects on him, remained in the air afterward. Beau thoroughly enjoyed the feeling of being a prince for the first time in his life, though that was only the beginning.

The winter months that remained brought frigid evenings of riding one of their neighbor's horses down country roads and snow-covered trails that led to Leanne's house. She lived even deeper into the country than the Jamisons' house. Sweetwater was the horse's name, and the neighbors, who lived just a half-mile from the Jamisons, gave Beau the rights to take Sweetwater out at his leisure, with just a touch of advance notice. Sweet, as Beau called him, was a mature horse past his prime but who still had plenty of vigor and heart. Despite Beau's relative inexperience with riding, the powerful animal responded well to the boy's kindness and respect and even showed affection toward him. Sweet rode proud, laughing at the cold and dark while taking good care of his young master.

A great contentment surrounded Beau as he rode on. His hands, protected by thick gloves, tightly gripped the reins. His entire body was tense from the combination of excitement and chill provided by the freezing winter air that filtered in through his hat and clothing. It wasn't nearly enough to deter him from his destination, though, but rather added to the intensity and anticipation of it all. Soon he would be sitting next to his princess in a cozy, warm house, sipping hot chocolate and maybe even getting another kiss, especially if her parents weren't around. Sometimes they'd go out for a ride together on the horse, Beau feeling like a man as Leanne's arms were wrapped tightly around his waist, with her hands in his jacket pockets to keep warm and her chin resting snug on his shoulder.

The journeys on Sweetwater to see Leanne continued on into the spring and summer. The invigorating aroma and expansiveness of the country would rouse his senses to even greater heights than the bite of winter. Sometimes Beau would give the charge to Sweet to run with the wind, and off he'd go like a thunderbolt. The feeling of the warm air gushing into his face, splashing him like rain, felt something similar to what he imagined heaven to feel like. Freedom and exhilaration filled both of their souls with each pounding step.

The landscape changed faces as they traveled, winding through wooded trails and lush green forest and beside old red barns that echoed history and time that stood still. They rode by fields that stretched for what seemed to be forever, where fireflies lit up the evening landscape and drew the attention of both boy and horse. They crossed through gently flowing streams and more turbulent rivers that flowed beneath old, narrow bridges, which he prayed for safe crossing over when hearing the loose four-by-fours rattling underneath the horse's hooves.

And there were the skies, those breathtaking skies that caught his eye no matter how many times he saw them. They were so full of color and drama on the way there, filled with stars on the return. With each trip they spoke the same message: *"Look at me..."* Beau followed orders, as did Sweet. All the elements worked within him—the smell of the air and the thumping of hooves upon the gravel, the known and unknown sounds coming from the forest. They would all become a part of him.

With each departure from Leanne's, Beau felt like more of a prince while riding off into the evening fog after saying goodbye. The longing to be with her was soothed by both the stillness of the night and the knowledge that he soon would be at her house again.

Those days of first romance that stretched through winter, spring, and summer would eventually come to an end. Middle school was just on the horizon, and those seemingly sweet and innocent kisses, which opened a door in the hearts of the youthful pair that neither of them were yet ready to walk through, drifted away.

Future attempts at relationship and romance with other girls would not be as pleasant a memory. With the entrance of middle school came other, less pristine options and ways that pulled Beau away from those things that bring life and peace. The appearance of innocence that lingered in those earlier times while riding to Leanne's would gradually be replaced by a more desperate and destructive pursuit of that which alone doesn't satisfy, darkness seeping in and casting its shadow upon paths where light once shined.

The light never died completely, however. It simply could not be overcome. It may have even secretly guided him at different turns, keeping him from losing all hope, from falling too far.

Now, years later, Beau again found himself traveling to see a girl, though the sounds of hooves digging into the ground were replaced by the steady hum of the engine. Toward the country, he drove to Amber's with a touch of freshness and innocence similar to that which existed in those years long past. Amber was a girl worthy of respect, and it brought something out of him that he didn't know was there.

At times he couldn't help but evaluate himself in light of her. In some areas of his life he was rough around the edges, areas where she appeared more smooth. He had grown over recent times, though, and stood at a place that was closer to manhood. Closer, but not quite there, and he would come to discover that much ground still remained to be covered.

As the clock ticked and the skies changed in appearance, he tried futilely to keep his expectations from mounting as he closed in on Amber's residence.

"Something could come out of this," he often said to himself, "but as long as she has a boyfriend, nothing can become of us. If a relationship doesn't birth out of our friendship, I'll just move on and be a friend." Behind those words and thoughts was much that he didn't see or understand, and deep within, a much different reality existed that was far beyond the control of his will.

The soothing summer air that flew about the truck continued to thicken with daydreams of all sorts as the radio played and miles passed. As the setting sun flickered through the hovering trees and eventually found its way behind the truck, it came into view through the driver's side rearview mirror.

This unexpectedly caught Beau's eye, drawing his mind away from everything else, even Amber. He couldn't help but give it a second look, and then a third and a fourth. Finally, he was compelled to slow down and pull over to the side of the road, where he just sat in his seat, looking into that little mirror with big eyes, in awe of its beauty and mysterious allure. He had come to see the sun this way enough times lately that he almost expected it. Despite this familiarity, it seemed to capture him in with a fresh dose of poignancy each time.

"Someday I'm going to turn around and drive with all my might right at you," he thought to himself as he put the truck back in gear and motored off, longing for that day. A long sigh followed, with no words at his disposal to fit the moment. Wonderment and questions of the past, and even more of the future, collided with him as he gazed one more time into the mirror and the bright ball of orange just above the trees. Thoughts of Hillary's and Earl's, the moonlit island at Lake Wagatogabee, and so much more filtered in. Faith and heaven followed right behind, more intensely then ever before.

Looking back, those thoughts seemed to be rekindled since Earl's place last fall. The deep heart longings evoked there, which had all but died and were covered over by a shadowlike fog in the ensuing times, now returned to the surface and were again visible, likely due to the presence of Amber.

"Do you and your friends ever talk about God?" she asked him one night in a summer conversation as he was looking out the small window at the skyline.

"Sometimes we get into it," he responded after thinking for a moment. He purposely excluded the fact that it usually only took place amongst his friends late at night after they had been drinking. That seemed to be the only time anyone had the courage to make mention of it, though the topic had a special way of always coming up and brewing controversial, lively discussion.

"Sometimes my friends and I would go for hikes through the woods near the campus and stop for a while, sit down and talk about God and life. Sometimes we would pray..." she went on, a passionate, even longing tone present in her voice.

Those words Amber spoke stuck with Beau after the phone was hung up. He wasn't used to hearing or talking in depth about that, especially from a beautiful girl.

Soon Beau entered the small town of Monticello, turning his head from side to side to take in the surroundings. On each side of the street were small, well-kept storefront shops and a couple tiny creeks flowing here and there that ran under bridges. Life appeared to flow with more simplicity and a slower pace here, much different than the frenzy of the city. This was very pleasing to the young traveler, who could feel the town and all its elements seep into his very being. His breaths were deeper and longer lasting, despite the mounting nervousness that came as he drew nearer to Amber's.

Minutes later, after a few twists and turns down old gravel roads, Beau turned into the long driveway that led to her parent's house. Just a moment later his eyes widened and breath stopped at the sight of her walking out of the house to greet him, his heart picking up pace with every fleeting second.

He stopped the truck in the driveway, slowly turned off the engine, and stepped out.

"Hi, Beau..."

"Hello, Amber..."

To describe the rest of the weekend from that greeting onward would be like describing a fleeting daydream, one with both mountains and long, deep valleys. Yet to not try would be a loss.

After standing in front of each other for a few seconds, unsure of how to greet each other, they exchanged a slightly awkward but mutually enjoyable hug before walking slowly toward the house. Pleasant small talk about the drive and summer and college filled the gap between them, both lighter on their feet than usual. They walked inside, where Beau caught a glimpse of all the pictures of family and knick knacks that gave the house a very warm feeling.

Moments later, he met Amber's mother. Though very polite and welcoming, she also carried a sense of keen curiosity regarding this young man who had traveled a good distance to see her daughter. Amber likely told her all she knew of Beau, and though not one to deny approval to someone prior to knowing them, she likely had created some of her own impressions, both good and bad. Beau could feel the heat, and since he wasn't very accustomed to dating, it caused him to tread very lightly. He faired well, however, and did his best to be a gentleman.

To his surprise, Amber had a full weekend planned out, with the majority of the time being spent with her family and younger siblings. The itinerary began shortly after Beau arrived. Together they traveled to a small, quaint town not too far away to watch a romantic movie played in a humble, old-time theatre that made one feel they were living in the forties. *"Princess Bride"* was the showing that night, and Beau thoroughly enjoyed his seat next to Amber, who to him was the real version of Princess Buttercup.

Her parents bought them a large bucket of popcorn to share, and occasionally their hands touched when reaching in. This produced a slight tingling sensation in Beau's toes that made him want to eat more. Amber felt it too. Beau chivalrously surrendered the armrest to her when the movie set in, grateful he was nowhere else at that very moment, still unable to grasp the fact that he was actually there with her. He wouldn't grasp this fact all weekend.

After the movie, they all walked out of the theater toward a riverside diner just up an old cobblestone road. Along the way, Amber led Beau off of the sidewalk while motioning to her family to keep walking to the diner, the implication that they would catch up clearly made. She and her guest strolled toward a small pond across the street where they leaned against an iron fence that separated the land from water.

Several gushing waterfalls poured down from rocks thirty feet above and crashed into the pond below. The impact produced a surreal mist that hovered in the air, illuminated by hidden spotlights. As they leaned against the fence, a pair of beautiful white swans circled about elegantly and peaceably. Side by side they stood, gazing into the picturesque scene before them and occasionally at each other, while the warm summer air blew through their hair and gently brushed their faces.

Amber shared of all the times her family had come here since she was a child and how she loved this place. Beau could see why, taken back by the surroundings.

Their words were few, though joy, excitement, and some laughter filled in the gaps. Beau was a bit reserved with his words, and even a little timid, much unlike the telephone conversations between them. This mildly frustrated him, for he felt he had so much to say and share with her. Comfort existed nonetheless, and he reasoned that he had plenty more time remaining.

There was one added element that may have added to the comfort, regardless of its distracting nature. Rex, her youngest brother, managed to break free from the pack and was frolicking nearby, asking numerous questions as any seven year old would and perhaps causing their conversation to stay above the surface. Despite Rex's childish nature, though, the mood that the small town had created in the two young dreamers could not be broken. The feeling that existed was most welcome.

It wasn't long before they pulled themselves away from the fence and joined with the rest of the family at the diner. Together they enjoyed a meal, talking of this and that, Beau still adjusting to his new company. He wasn't a big fan of being under the spotlight and wasn't sure how to handle it, hence he didn't say all too much the whole time.

They finished eating and walked leisurely back to the vehicle, piling in one by one. They drove toward Monticello on the same desolate country road they came in on, the light of the moon now painting much of the landscape white. Being in the city all summer, Beau had come to greatly miss the country skies, and his reunion with it was sweet indeed. He felt relaxed, so much so that he could barely comprehend it. Perhaps the company of a woman had something to do with it.

Just over a half hour later, they arrived back at the house, which was set back off a country road. It was secluded, with only a couple other houses in view, accessible by a gravel driveway that snaked through a patch of forest and led to a wide-open clearing. The full moon continued to shine white light onto all things, including a large field that sat on the other side of the driveway. It was beautiful enough to catch everyone's attention.

In that field sat a dense fog that rose several feet above the ground, thick as smoke and as ominous as a thundercloud. Like everything else, it was lit up with such incredible brilliancy. While the rest of the family proceeded toward the house, Beau went off in the other direction toward the field, Amber following his lead close behind for protection and from curiosity at what drew him, until she too became captivated by it.

As Beau entered into its perimeter, waist-deep in the fog, he stuck out his hand like one would into a waterfall. He could feel the moistness between his fingers, swishing them around in the mist that moved about like smoke in a fairytale. In all his years of being wooed by the sky, never had he seen this. Or perhaps his eyes hadn't been open to see it for so long that it vanished from memory. Nonetheless, it continued to hold his attention after they turned back to walk toward the door, its beauty speaking incomprehensible words, perfectly contributing to the surrealism of the evening.

Amber and Beau entered the house, settled in, and drifted into the kitchen, where they began playing cards with her two brothers. The big pine dinner table they sat by was softly lit by an antique chandelier that hung directly above the table, casting a golden glow that radiated onto everything in the room. The glow was similar to that which existed throughout much of the wood-decorated house, creating such a warm feel that seeped into one's innermost parts. Many times Beau looked Amber's way and caught her eye, who returned the look with a soft smile or witty comment, especially after ousting him with a play of the cards.

A few times, Beau thought he saw in her a restless spirit. It was almost as if she had thoughts or words bottled up inside. He remained silent, though. He figured the time would come for words, which he hoped he would be prepared for. He knew that her current relationship, however weak and drifting it was, hung on both their minds, along with so much more. He couldn't be sure whether it was right or wrong to hold back words this night, though right now he just wanted to enjoy the moment.

It didn't take long before all eyes grew heavy and weary, and the time for bed came with force. Young Rex fought valiantly to hide his exhaustion and keep the game alive deep into the night, though he blew his cover each time that his head fell forward in an effort to find sleep right there on the table. This came to the amusement of the others, who felt equally as tired. It had been a long Friday for all.

Before going to the spare room where his bed was prepared, Beau went into the bathroom to wash up. Just as he began to brush his teeth, in walked Amber with a spirited bounce in her step and a smile on her face. She stood right next to him in front of the sink as if they had been in this situation many times before. She went straight for her toothbrush, reaching across the sink in front of Beau, who had to move over just a little to make room for her.

Soon they were brushing side by side, looking at each other in the mirror while talking of this and that, with toothpaste-filled mouths that caused their speech to be slightly muffled, especially as the paste grew thicker. The way they carried on made it seem as if they had known each other for years, spitting in the sink and accidentally on each other's hands without any reaction. Beau silently beamed with joy at it all.

After brushing, Amber pulled out some dental floss and went to work.

"Would you like some?" she asked while holding the small white container up to him.

"Sure," he responded obligingly, admitting to the fact that he didn't do it very often. It was that moment that the young man was first inspired to be a consistent flosser after years of good intentions, and it would remain a practice all his days to come. It was also in that bathroom moment, and more to follow over the weekend, when he was introduced to the importance and satisfaction of thoroughly washing his face before going to bed. He always thought this was more of a girl thing. Amber shared some special wash with him that made his face feel like he had just gone jogging in the warm summer rain. He even thought she looked pretty with that thick layer of white upon her and couldn't help but laugh when seeing it upon his own face.

So there they stood, both covered with white cream, taking turns splashing themselves with water to rinse off the cleanser, while continuing to talk of this and that through the mirror. As Beau would discover in later reflection, it is the simple things in life that bring the greatest joy.

That bathroom experience would find a permanent place in Beau's memory, both into the quiet of that night and far beyond.

"Will you wake me if you get up before I do?" Amber asked softly while standing in the doorway to her bedroom, which was next to the spare room where Beau would be sleeping.

"As you wish," he said, stealing a line from the movie and evoking a smile from her.

"Goodnight, Beau…" she said seconds later, her smile now complimented with that longing tone of voice, which always had a way of both rousing and calming him. She continued to stand in her doorway for a moment before slowly moving her hand to close the door.

"Goodnight, Amber…" he replied steadily, turning back to look at her one more time before going into the room, wishing they could've talked all night.

"This is all too much…" he thought to himself as he flicked off the lights and slipped into bed. Moments later, while lying on his side and staring into the dark, he turned over onto his back with the intent to call it a day and fall asleep. Something else awaited, however. Just before he was to close his eyes after settling in, they widened at the sight of numerous glow-in-the-dark stickers shaped like stars that clung to the ceiling. He sighed, caught off guard and filled with a strange delight by them. They grew brighter as his eyes continued to adjust to the darkness, and they took him back in time to prior years of starry-skied bedrooms, times seemingly forgotten until that moment.

"JB, is that you?" said young Beau, who was half asleep when JB plopped down on the carpet floor next to Beau's bed to sleep for the night.

"Yeah, Beau, it's me. Go back to sleep, little buddy; sorry for waking you."

JB was an old friend of Beau's sisters who had been living on his own for over a year after getting kicked out of his parent's house. At eighteen years old, he was a troubled soul, on a fast track to nowhere despite great potential. When Carl heard of this, he offered to provide him housing for the summer in exchange for work done around the house. It was a compassionate move on his part, though not the wisest, as JB's lifestyle would help steer the kids off course.

This especially held true for Beau, who would taste alcohol for the first time with JB and enjoy its effects.

"Whoa!" exclaimed JB in a loud whisper after lying down, quite intoxicated and still feeling the effects of the LSD he had taken earlier in the night. "I wasn't expecting this...and they're moving!" Well, to JB the fake stars may have been moving, but to Beau they were simply put up there to help him see the sky when lying upon his bed at night while in deep daydreams, or awake nightdreams, as he liked to call them.

"You okay, JB?" asked Beau. Though only ten years of age, he served as a source of stability to the embattled, mentally-altered adolescent who lay on his floor.

JB was a reckless one who womanized and drank his fill. He frequently found himself in conflict with the authorities and in fights that left either himself or his opponent in rough shape. Underneath his rough exterior, however, was a misguided young man who just wanted to be affirmed and told that he had what it took. He went to many lengths to fill the vacuum left by the absence of what he longed for, which he couldn't see or understand himself.

His parents had forced him out of the house, perhaps pushed over the edge by his behavior. Whether their actions were legitimate or not, all JB saw was parents who didn't care for him, a lie engrained in his soul that increased in power with every sip of vodka, cheap beer, or line of cocaine.

"Beau," he said after a few moments, his young buddy listening attentively like a counselor, "if God exists and cares for me, which people keep telling me, then how did I get here? How did my life get so messed up, and where is all this going?" A moment of silence followed. "Feels so *hopeless…* " His voice trailed off, sounds of sniffles coming from him. "Goodnight, little buddy," he said before Beau could reply. He turned over on his side and pretended to sleep, not even considering for a moment that he was pouring out his heart to a ten year old.

The question posed by JB lingered in Beau's mind, and he said a prayer for him before going to sleep. In the silence that followed, Beau heard what sounded like prayerful sobs coming from his big, broken-spirited friend.

Over a decade later, as Beau lay in the room next to Amber's, he thought of the safety and comfort that was found in that little room he slept in long ago. His thoughts were accentuated by the pictures he saw earlier of her family, which were displayed on the walls in the bedroom and throughout the entire house. Similar to the time looking at the pictures of his siblings on Earl's fireplace, Beau was again confronted by the distance that now existed in his family compared with those days of childhood starry bedroom skies and riding in the station wagon.

It seemed to Beau that many families had their own version of the station wagon. Earlier that day, he received a taste of Amber's family steed, which happened to be a sport utility vehicle. It was there that Beau was able to see and sense some deeper layers to her family as well as pangs caused by the past. Evidence existed, perhaps spoken in the silent moments, of trials and challenges amidst a firm foundation where they stood together, feet on the ground.

Not much was spoken of Amber's father, who Beau discovered died many years ago in a car accident. It was clear, however, that his love for his family resonated in each child despite the imperfect man that he was. Her mother remarried years later, and the strength of the family, due to her love and nobility, could clearly be seen in the genuine character of her children: the exuberance and zest found in Amber and her youngest brother and the deep and amiable nature of her other brother Tristin. Artistic like his other siblings, he seemed mature and ahead of his years, exuding great humility and gentle ruggedness. Though they had little time to spend together, Beau bonded well with Tristin, who showed appreciation at Beau's presence and conversely voiced a lack of appreciation for his older sister's current boyfriend. This encouraged Beau's pursuit.

Rex was Rex: young and full of energy with no cares in the

world other than his animal books and other natural interests. He was all boy, swinging sticks and whatever else he could get his hands on, constantly on the move like a shark, stopping abruptly once in a while to ponder something before resuming his play.

Beau never met Amber's sister, who was married and living out West, though he could sense some deeper thoughts when Amber spoke of her—differences between them amidst a longing for closeness.

Her stepdad seemed to fill the role of a father well, being the protector and provider for the family as well as a caring husband and dad. Surely he must have felt the weight of taking over a role once held by another man and faced pressures that could not easily be seen on the surface. Beau liked him and seemed to gain his respect, and his appreciation for the outdoors helped ease the gap between them. He believed he must have had the greatest challenges with Amber. He endured great criticism, however harmless and loving, from her concerning his driving, which Beau didn't think was all that bad.

"Dad! Your turning is going to make me sick...Dad, easy on the brakes!"

One day Beau would learn the challenge of being in that position and silently defended the man, despite his desire for the young woman who voiced the complaints.

Pleasant and honorable as usual, Amber's mother spoke only a few words the whole time, seemingly holding back thoughts while continuing her acute observance of her daughter's potential suitor. Rarely one to judge too soon, she was gentle and genuinely warm and respectful in her undisclosed examination. Her heart was softened toward Beau, and part of her desired to embrace him as part of the family, though she knew there was a reasonable chance that the days ahead would not bring this to pass.

A woman of integrity and wisdom, she made family a priority above all else and had experienced life in many ways—life filled with both great joy and heart-wrenching pain and loss. Consequently, she sought the best for her children. Surely she knew and saw things that the two didn't, both about her daughter and her deep, occasionally volatile emotions common to a girl her age, or any age for that matter, and also about Beau despite the short amount of time she knew him. She knew where this acquaintance of theirs might be heading, and it might not be where either of them had hoped. Yet she kept silent on these matters of the heart and spoke sparingly, waiting for opportunities to edify to present themselves, very aware that she could be wrong and that God worked in mysterious ways far beyond a mother's understanding. The two would have to experience some things for themselves; this she knew.

Though death and the many trials of family life do not hold unbreakable power over life and restoration, it does not leave one without a few bruises. Surely some must have lingered in the family that allowed Beau into their home and hearts that weekend and in the young lady who he adored.

With all the observances of Amber's family circulating in his mind, the memory of his own parents' parting broke through. Previously tucked away, they were now unearthed just enough to glimpse into, perhaps loosened in the recent trip to Cringle.

As Beau lay still on his back, looking earnestly into the glowing stickers above, he thought of that November night years ago when he received the news. He was lying upstairs in his bed, studying, when his father came walking slowly up the steps, humbly standing in his open doorway. After a brief time of small talk, Carl went silent for a few moments before telling his son that he and his mother were separating.

"I'm going to be moving out at the end of the month Beau. Things with your mother and I just haven't been working out..."

His father's words were few despite his mannerisms, which revealed he had much more to say. Carl was always one to show his feelings more than speak them, which made it difficult for him in times like this, when communication was so vital.

Beau looked down at his homework lying in front of him then back up at his dad, nodding his head in acknowledgement, though never really able to look him in the eyes. He had no words fit to say what he was feeling, his senses overloaded. That was about it. The words thereafter were few, and his father, seemingly not knowing what else to say, slowly turned around and went back downstairs, where a gushing of tears amidst utter loneliness overtook him.

"How did it come to this…?" Carl whispered quietly in the dark as he sat before the gently crackling fireplace.

Upstairs, Beau lay in the same position as he did before being given the news. A few tears fell, though they were quickly brushed away. It was time to be strong. Walls and barricades to shield the pain were being built in his heart at that very moment, and his emotional distance from both his father and mother in those years did nothing to help the matter.

He didn't talk to many people about it. Whenever the conversation came up, whether initiated by friends or their parents, he had little to say. He felt he was mature enough to handle it, and the high divorce rate among friends' parents made it seem less riveting as well, unfortunate yet almost normal. However, he often thought that his parents had a marriage that would last forever, and this news shattered that to pieces.

Though he did his best to resist the defeating feelings that were looming, the reality was that fear and disillusionment were settling in with the changes that were taking place. He was scared, plain and simple, yet he did not know it.

This held true for all of them.

"Seems a common thing to look in the wrong direction when the wind is blowing hard," he remembered someone once say in response to the news. The words would remain with him.

Months later, in the beginning of summer, Beau and his siblings were sitting around the pool in their front yard. Carl and Janet, now living under different roofs, were showing the house to some prospective buyers. Just a few weeks prior, they had decided to sell the place, for it was simply too much to maintain individually.

At the end of the showing, the people decided to

buy the house and would be moving in at the end of summer. Upon hearing this news, the Jamison children gave each other a sullen glance before looking away to the ground and sky. Somberness was heavy in the air, and soon they all rose to their feet and went their separate ways. Distance in the family was about to increase.

After all those years, labors, and experiences, their home in the woods of Cringle would be theirs no more.

August came quickly, and just days before the house was to be handed over, Beau was blindsided by the realization of the changes to come. It happened while he was driving up the long gravel driveway one night, the same driveway that he had traveled so many times, when a certain song came on the radio that ripped through his defenses, tearing open his heart.

After parking, he stepped out of his car and leaned against it. Overwhelmed by the mixture of deep, painful emotions and the intense beauty and serenity of the starry night surrounding him, he slowly slid to the ground and released a flood of tears. Lady, now well along in years, sat by his side, whining, frequently putting her paw on his arm and licking his face, as if desperate to console him. He sat there for some time into the night, leaning against the rear tire, occasionally searching the skies for answers.

For years, Beau remembered little of the evening his father stood in the doorway, as well as that anguish under the stars. Though now, and more so in the days to come, he would see and feel more of those moments.

"This is all too much…" he said to himself again. He turned over to his side, all those memories vanishing as quickly as they came, shoved down—though not as far—into the recesses of the heart. A peace now overpowered everything else and no further reflection would be had this night. Knowing that he would be waking in the morning to spend the entire day with Amber brought a smile to his face, which remained as he strode into deep sleep under the thick, heavy home-style quilt and soft pillow that happened to be much more comfortable than his college linens.

Though it all seemed overwhelming to him, it was just the beginning.

In the other room lay Amber, a beautiful young woman on the brink of entering a new stage of life. Soon she would be led far from the protection of her childhood room and the safety of her family, who now slept soundly in beds on the floor above her. Dreams, desires, and longings knocked more loudly than ever before, together with hopes and fears that intensified her desire for the arms of a provider and protector, a friend and lover.

Though she saw much potential for this in her admirer in the other room, who traveled far to get to her, there remained some uncertainties about him and his lifestyle. There was also the situation with her current boyfriend. Despite the confusion caused by all these thoughts that attempted to make her mind spin out of control, she, like most women do, fell into sound sleep more quickly than her male guest on the other side of the wall.

Like Beau, however, her heart beat strong throughout the night.

Barns and Bats

Saturday morn, August 14, 1999

Such stillness surrounds me as I wake here in Amber's spare room. Hard to believe I'm actually here. I cannot find the words to describe how peaceful I feel here, and for whatever reason, I slept better than I have in so long in this little room, like that of an ancient mariner after a long day at sea. Maybe it's due to the solitude of the country as well as the company of a woman, who now sleeps just beyond the wall, along with the closeness of her family. The cause I cannot be sure of, though it is strangely reminiscent of the peace at Hillary's lake house and the days at the river by Earl's. Life has been moving so fast and out of control up until now, yet seems to move at a healthier pace here.

Beau closed his journal and set it beside the bed, along with his pen. He then stretched long and hard before pushing himself up into a sitting position, only to sit still for a time on the edge of the bed with his feet on the cool floor, taking in the utter silence. However, he couldn't sit still for too long, especially with the knowledge that Amber was in the room next to him. He threw on a pair of jeans and a flannel and quietly opened his door and walked like a feather to her room to wake her.

Beau approached her door, which had been left open just a crack. He knocked ever so slightly and waited a few moments for a response. Hearing nothing come from the room, he slowly pushed the door open and was met by the sight of her lying on her side facing him, deep in sleep. He didn't want to fail his duty to wake her, yet she looked far too still and peaceful to do so. It was quite early too, so he quietly pulled his head back and shut the door all the way.

Turning around, with a grin of satisfaction emerging from his face, he walked to the living room and sat on the couch. He had retrieved his journal on the way and was going to do some more writing, though shortly after sitting down an unexpected guest made this impossible. Young, jubilant Rex made the discovery that his new big buddy was awake and included himself in the morning affairs. As if executing a previously thought out plan, he began sharing his books of wild animals and birds and various other creatures with Beau, who thoroughly enjoyed his young companion.

Amber awoke shortly after, hearing the sound of Rex naming off giraffes and elephants and tigers coming into her room. Normally this would warrant frustration, but under the circumstances, it brought a grin to her face, followed by a few giggles. She soon came out of the bedroom and sat on the couch next to Beau.

"Looks like you made a new friend," she said with a smirk.

"Sure did, and learning a lot too," he responded, hiding the grin from his little friend, who shared with him such important and pressing bits of knowledge.

They spoke for a brief time, pleasantness in the air, before Amber politely excused herself in order to get ready.

After eating, they began a day that would go on to become the longest and most fleeting day Beau had lived in all his previous twenty-two years.

After helping clear the table following a good, hearty breakfast, Amber and Beau scurried out the front door and drove off in her Honda to run some errands together for her parents. After picking up some groceries and doing other random tasks, the morning had vanished into early afternoon. The time for lunch came, and Amber led them to a nearby farmer's market, where they ate an unhurried meal. By now, Beau felt more adept to his surroundings, and the fact that it was just the two of them made him feel a bit more at ease.

Amber walked into the market as if she was walking into her own home. She pushed open the old-fashioned wooden doors, the bells attached to them to jingling loudly.

"Hi Edith! Hi Jessica!" she said exuberantly, along with a few other hellos to the staff, as well as customers, who she knew by name and by whom she was received warmly. They carefully observed her companion as well, and Beau could easily sense their inquisitive eyes. Amber introduced him to many people in that old country store, who all received him with warmth, so much so that he felt as if they already knew him. Several of the most trusted ones did, and now they had a face to put with the name.

They ordered a couple sandwiches and bags of chips and sat down at a bright table near the window to eat. Amber fondly shared the history of the store, the town, and its people. Beau listened on, doing his best to focus on what she was saying, though his attention span was hindered by the simple joy of sitting there with her. His ability to take in her words was further hindered by the continuing, non-threatening observation by those in the store who knew Amber.

The lunch was brief, followed by some perusing around the store at some of the items for sale. Clothing, desserts, knick knacks, candles, and just about everything else was on display that one could imagine. The place was not all that different from the country market near Earl's. It seemed to Beau that these country stores all had something in common: immense warmth and character.

The smells of candles and chocolate and the gentle tones of summer and autumn colors were abundant, acting like wine to the senses. Beau would've been content on staying there for the whole afternoon, rocking on a couple of the handmade wicker chairs that sat in the corner. They were homemade, with quality craftsmanship, though not quite as solid as the ones at Earl's.

Of all the inviting items on display, one took precedence for two different reasons. Far off in the corner, delicately lit by candlelight and a nearby table lamp, was a wooden-framed canvas oil painting that boasted a moonlit beach with rolling sand and a few tall weeds. The great waters separated the beach from the dark blue sky above, where patches of thin white clouds drifted near the large, full moon near the horizon that shined onto the ocean, which raged with tumbling waves and breakers.

Amber stood still like a young child as she gazed into the picture, her eyes and demeanor growing soft and nostalgic.

"I used to oil paint," she said in a near whisper while exhibiting such appreciation for the painting, reaching out her hand to delicately touch the canvas.

"And now?" asked Beau after a few seconds, well aware of something going on inside her caused by the painting.

"I don't know…just seemed to have gotten away from it with college and everything else." She went silent for a moment, then continued, "I'd like to get back into it, though there doesn't seem to be much time to do so…"

It was in that very moment that the desire to buy the painting for her emerged in Beau. To his frustration, however, his college income allowed barely enough money to buy lunch. In his heart, he vowed to return for it one day soon, and before he left, he secretly gave the store owner his telephone number and encouraged him to hold it for as long as he could, humbly asking him to call if anyone attempted to purchase it. With a grin, the owner read between the lines and agreed.

Back in the car they went, chasing here and there. Along the way, Amber continued to act as a tour guide for the small town, pointing to different landmarks and sharing stories of school, family, and friends, among other things.

Part of the day's itinerary required them to stop at a store to pick out some fabric for a family friend. After pulling into the parking lot, she gave Beau the option of waiting in the car. She actually encouraged him to stay back, for it would likely take some time to find all the fabric and she was concerned it would bore him.

Though he disagreed that he would get bored, for nothing that particular day could be boring to him, he did agree to stay in the car. This appeared to be a blessing in disguise, for he quickly fell into a short nap after Amber stepped out of the car. Apparently his mind and body needed to refuel if he was going to last the rest of the day and night.

Twenty minutes later, Amber emerged from the store carrying several bags of merchandise, placed them in the trunk, and roused her sleepy guest upon getting back in the car. Beau quickly came back to life, and they sped off down the road toward the family friend for whom the fabric was bought.

"Laverne is an old friend of my mother; been a part of our family for years. Growing up she'd always have us kids over, feeding us all kinds of food and letting us play on the farm…" She went on, sharing of this grandma-like woman who was obviously dear to her.

They pulled into the long gravel driveway that ran down the middle of a large but modest yard. It was several acres in size, full of thick, green grass on both sides that was bordered by deep woods. As they pulled in, Beau admired the old, well-kept farmhouse on the left, especially its porch that wrapped around the entire house. Equally well kept was the big red barn that sat a little farther up on the other side of the driveway. He had seen many run-down barns on his journeys, though this one seemed to still have the breath of life running through it.

As one would expect, the sweet smells of candles and foods at the country market were now replaced by the unavoidable smells of manure, straw, and animals that were perhaps more pleasing to the soul than the senses. For those who loved the outdoors, however, the fragrances had a distinct sweetness of their own, perhaps better than all the others combined.

Amber led Beau up to the steps and knocked firmly on the door three times before pushing it open. As Beau followed her up the steps, he took another big whiff of the country air and another look at the barn and surrounding pastures. He gazed at the endless rolling field that stretched out as far ahead as his eyes could see, flanked by the woods on both sides and growing wider the farther out it went. It seemed borderless.

"Laverne?" she said in a lifted voice. "You here, Laverne?"

"Amber, is that you dear?" came a sweet, southern-sounding voice moments later from the other room. The sound of footsteps on the hardwood floor grew closer and closer.

"Hi, Janice!" replied Amber affectionately. Janice was a long-time friend of Laverne's who helped with administrative and miscellaneous affairs in keeping up the property, hiring staff, and coordinating volunteers. She was a large, full-bodied African-American woman who wore a personality that could make any stranger feel as welcome as could be, as she did with Beau.

"Hi, honey!" she said as she rounded the corner, giving Amber a big hug. "And who is this young man?" she said with a grin and raised voice after releasing Amber, extending her hand to shake Beau's. Of course she had already heard via the grapevine that Amber was having a visitor this weekend, though she gave no indication of her knowledge on such matters.

"This is Beau," she said almost proudly. "He came to visit me for the weekend and is staying at our place."

"Nice to meet you, ma'am," said Beau cordially.

"Likewise, Beau," she courteously responded with a gentle tone.

They all stood and talked for a few minutes, Beau sharing some details about himself upon request. Janice listened attentively, as everyone seemed to do that weekend. She was easy to talk to, and her southern hospitality opened Beau up like a book.

"I wanted to introduce him to Laverne and show him around the farm. Is she here?" asked Amber after a few moments.

"I'm sorry, Amber; she waited as long as she could but promised her ladies from the church choir that they'd go out for tea and shopping today. She asked that if you two had time tomorrow to stop back. She was looking forward to seeing y'all."

"Oh shucks," said Amber, hoping to have introduced her and uncertain of whether the following day's itinerary would allow for it.

"But listen now, you know your way around, so go on ahead. I'm going to go downstairs into the office to finish up some odds and ends. If you need anything, you know where to find me."

After Janice excused herself into the basement, Amber began to lead Beau through the richly decorated farmhouse. It was filled with so much wood, which poured out such inviting smells, making one stop to sniff frequently. Beau learned that Laverne's late husband was a wood smith of sorts in his spare time, always hanging out in the barn creating tables, chairs, and other furniture, as well as knick knacks and the like. He especially enjoyed making things for his lady, the evidence of this seen throughout the house.

"He tried proposin' to me with a wooden ring, but I wasn't havin' it," Amber said in a voice imitating Laverne's, laughing gently at the memory of hearing her speak these words.

They walked up the steps that had lavish, dark-stained rails on both sides that appeared sturdy and stealthy, despite their old age. As they slowly walked up the stairs, Beau noticed some family pictures hanging on the left side of the wall. One caught his eye more than the others, encased in an oval, dark cherry oak frame that was as old as could be, yet finely preserved, its wood still polished and shiny. Within the frame, a large family of all ages was displayed, with faces that wore what appeared to be the weight of hard-lived years, yet with smiles that gleamed out of the picture itself.

"I like this picture," said Beau as they walked up. Amber turned her head around, saying nothing but smiling softly upon seeing the thoughtful reflection on his face when viewing it. She became thoughtful herself while staring at him and then at the picture.

"C'mon, Beau, more to see upstairs," she said in a low, playful tone as she continued to walk slowly up the steps. Beau's attention swiftly swayed from the picture, and he continued following her up the steps.

They gingerly walked into the different bedrooms, each of which displayed a different mood and theme amidst their simplicity. Neither Beau nor Amber was in any rush to get on to the next, as a feeling of intense calm engulfed them.

The feeling of calm mixed with pure energy was perhaps the most poignant as they walked into the final and largest bedroom of the house. The air was thick with memory and emotion as the sun gleamed into the brown, wood-stained room and aged floors that now glowed like visions of heaven. The rays of sun also shone onto the old handmade quilts that rested on the large bed, much like it did as a child at Beau's grandma's house in those late afternoons when he would be pretending to nap. Most naps were pretend for Beau; usually he was just daydreaming as the clock ticked and ticked. Silence spoke then, just as it did now.

"This is Laverne's room," Amber said in a soft voice as she strolled across the room, delicately running her fingertips over the footboard of the bed, then upon the large wood dresser that had a large oval mirror attached to it. A whimsical fashion accompanied her every move, which didn't go unnoticed by Beau.

"Many times she would send me up here to take a late-afternoon nap when she saw my eyes getting heavy from too much playing or crafting. I can remember lying here, wondering what her husband must have been like, feeling so sad for her that her true love had passed away... then I'd fall into deep sleep and dream. Safe..."

Beau stood still as she spoke, looking at the rays of sun gleaming in through the windows, feeling their warmth. His ears were fully fixed on Amber's voice, which now carried a tone that was much different than any other he heard from her.

"I'm sure he is still with her, close to her heart," said Beau after a time of silence, his thoughts suspended by the depth of Amber's reflection and the way she moved about the room like an angel, inadvertently studying her and listening closely.

Amber, whose back had been facing Beau while slowly strolling across the room, slowed down even more at his comment and lifted her head slightly. For whatever reasons, his words had penetrated, perhaps because she had heard so little from his heart until that moment. She stopped her stroll for a moment and stood ever so still, turning her head slightly in Beau's direction. A soft, gentle smile came over her face. She then lifted her eyes from the floor and looked deeply into his, then looked down again, like a child staring at the grass, as she turned and began to walk ever so slowly in his direction.

"I think you're right," she whispered, drawing closer to him with her eyes still fixed on the floor, slowing her pace to a near standstill when arriving at his side, her hand gently brushing his. Beau stood tall and still as he stared humbly at the wood floor in front of her, briefly catching her eye then moving his stare to where their hands touched, very aware of her presence that had all of a sudden become something very new and powerful, even more so than before.

As time stood still, as it seemed to be doing a lot lately, Beau felt the overwhelming desire to grab hold of that soft, delicate hand and seek the kiss of Amber's lips that were very alive to him right now. The heat felt inside his entire body and mind made him near dizzy.

Within Amber, a desire to receive that which Beau desired to give burned strong as well, so strong and with such force that everything else in her mind was removed other than this young man standing inches away, who she adored in a way she couldn't understand. She wasn't expecting this and held her breath while standing still at his side, eyes closed and head bowed, ready to turn his way at a moment's notice.

Despite the fire that burned within him, Beau resisted with

an adversary he could not see proved a difficult task indeed. This adversary's name happened to be ignorance.

Amber sighed heavily at this silence. She looked down in frustration, then up river and into the sky, then back down again at the wood dock they sat on. Beau's eyes tracked her movement, desperately wanting to say the right words but unable to find them.

Just as he was about to speak something, what exactly he wasn't sure, Amber's mom called down from the cabin.

"Are you two ready to go back to the house? We're hoping to leave shortly."

"Yes, mother, we're ready." She gave Beau a quick, blank look before rising to her feet and walking up the steps to the cabin. Beau rose slowly after sitting for a moment, frustrated that they left off like this, feeling as if the book had been closed before turning the rest of the pages. He caught up with her near the cabin, trying earnestly to hide his emotional state so that her parents wouldn't see it. They saw it quite well, however. Parents can see further, and the fact that neither Amber nor Beau were any good at hiding anything on their faces did little to help conceal the matter.

Evening came quickly. The once upbeat and exhilarating mood of the weekend had now shifted down to a lower gear and continued to descend. The end of the weekend was nearing, and the residue from the dockside conversation had substantially reduced hope for something to come from Beau's visit to Monticello. Amber had pulled back significantly from Beau since then. She was confused by the situation at hand, by her desires and his reserved pursuit of her, and especially by his words on the dock, which she knew held some validity. Yet they seemed too cut and dry, too rigid, too opposite of what she wanted to hear.

Confusion also circled in her mind of her distant boyfriend, if he was even still that in her heart despite the deep care she felt for him, and how it wasn't him with whom she was spending the weekend. There were also the rough edges around Beau that she hadn't noticed before, edges revealed through certain words, actions, and responses that didn't seem to conform to who she thought him to be inside. She desired a man of virtue and faith, and over time, not only this weekend but in previous conversations, there arose reasons to question the sincerity and depth of his spirituality.

These uncertainties were not as pressing at the moment, however, especially considering that her own devotion to God stood on shaky ground. She was also faintly aware that her actions and words might be sending him mixed signals. The confusion mounted and in turn made her want to pull far away from him.

Behind it all, deep within Amber in places beyond her sight, was the secret hope that somehow, someway, despite all the obstacles that she preferred to ignore, which she believed true love could overcome, Beau would carry her off into the sunset. It seemed, however, that a different painting was being created, one which she didn't wish to see.

Beau could sense her pulling away. He resisted acknowledging this, though, so confused himself by everything.

Yet hope, always the last to die, remained. Time remained as well, quickly waning as it was.

Before the night reached its close, Beau and Amber spent an hour hanging out in her bedroom after washing up, while her parents sat upstairs talking. Amber sat upright in her bed with her reading glasses on and looking quite sophisticated, peering through some magazines and speaking sparingly. Beau sat on the floor near the foot of her bed, his back resting against it, writing in his journal of the day's events. He couldn't help but notice that the magazine she was looking through was exclusively wedding gowns, with a bright white bride on the cover and many more within. She sat so silently, her demeanor now more stern than soft, with her glasses resting low on her nose.

Though conversation wasn't completely absent, it lacked transparency and included many awkward pauses. Walls were being built through unspoken and spoken words. Just as Beau was about to retire to the spare room, feeling slightly defeated and distraught at the mood that had replaced the excitement that dominated earlier in the day, something happened—something very unexpected, though not all too unfamiliar…

There was a fluttering in the air, and thanks to his peripheral vision, he saw a small black object out of the corner of his eye. *"It can't be…"* he thought to himself while morphing into soldier mode, still and intense.

"Amber!" Beau whispered loudly, as if they were all of a sudden under siege.

"What?" she said sharply, a bit surprised and mildly offended by his forthcoming tone.

"Get your head under the covers!" She did as he had ordered, not really sure why she obeyed him since she didn't see the varmint, though once she peeked her head out and caught a good glimpse of it, she fully understood. "Ohh!" she said in a girlish tone as she quickly scurried underneath the protection of her thick quilt, pulling it over her head and curling up into a ball.

The bat had returned, this time with even more vengeance than before.

"Seems a strange thing, these frequent run ins with the creatures of the night," thought Beau subconsciously as he prepared for yet another battle. There was the time as a child up north, the bat at Bruce and Jane's cabin, old friends of the Jamisons. Round and round it flew, up and down and all around the high-ceilinged structure, horrifying the women as the men went after it with various forms of kitchen utensils and outdoor sporting goods. The whole time, young Beau and his siblings watched on with a touch of fear and great amusement.

"Get 'em, Dad, get 'em!"

Of course the recent battle of Lake Wagatogabee, which would surely be recorded in the great annals of time, could not be forgotten either.

Now it was Beau's turn to face the menace, pitted against nature with no one else to aid him. The safety of a fair lady at stake also increased the intensity and valor of the situation. In reality, bats can be gentle and are beneficial to the environment, though they can be rabid, and for this reason, and for the sake of his manhood, it was an evil creature with cruel potential.

"Don't leave me!" cried Amber when, while peeking her head from under the covers, she saw Beau leave the room.

"I'll be right back!" he assured her and ran into the family room to grab the weapon of choice, that being a pillow, and rushed back into the room where he began swinging with ferocity in every direction at the little beast. Its passes were frequent since it was flying in a bedroom, an area much smaller than what Beau was previously used to. Tactics in war are always changing, and one must always be ready to adjust and overcome.

While swinging the pillow, to no avail, Beau could hear the muffled voice of Amber come from under the covers.

"Is it still there? Where is it? Are you okay?" she said, peeking her head out once in a while to see.

"Yes...get your head back under the covers!" he exhorted, and she did so without hesitation as the discombobulated creature soared within inches from her head.

"Ohh!" she exclaimed again, closing her eyes and darting back under the covers after feeling a slight breeze caused by the bat swooping near her.

After about twenty minutes of relentless swinging and maneuvering, the poor creature met the pillow head on and was landed, then smothered. Just as this happened, Amber's stepdad entered the scene, supposedly after hearing the commotion, and assisted Beau in getting it into a shoe-box and out the front door. Together they released it into the night and quickly re-entered the house, hastily shutting the door behind them as one would to prevent cold winter air from entering. This bat was fortunate: had the reinforcements not entered, Beau would have had to squish it to its death with the pillow.

Afterward, everyone who was awakened by the incident, which happened to be the entire household, returned to the safe havens of their bedrooms to re-enter into rest. Beau went to Amber's room and noticed that the lights were off. He hoped she would still be awake and was disappointed that she had already retired for the night.

"Beau?" he heard her speak as he walked away from her door. He quickly turned and went back to her room and stood in her doorway. The light from the hallway shined in and revealed her lying on her side, facing Beau with her eyes open, her blankets pulled tightly and securely up to her neck.

"You okay?" he asked her, relieved at the softness that now exuded from her demeanor and the longing look on her face. It seemed the bat had some positive effects.

"Yeah, I'm okay. Thank you for protecting me," she said in a soft voice that made Beau's eyes heavy.

"I have some experience with bats," he said jokingly. "I was ready for him."

A brief silence followed, Amber rustling a bit under the covers and Beau repositioning himself while leaning against the doorway, not sure what to say as his heart beat like war drums.

"Well, goodnight, Amber…" he said hesitantly with bowed head, breaking the silence as a defeated feeling swept over him.

"You're going to bed now?" she said more loudly.

Despite the recent display of courage and what appeared to be another open door to Amber, there existed within Beau discouragement, confusion, bruised confidence, and fear of losing something that was not his, all of which blocked his ability to see, think, or communicate. Therefore he did what he only knew to do in that situation. He pulled away.

"Yes…I'll see you in the morning," he said gently, a false confidence in his voice. He wished her well one last time before closing her door and walking to his room, his heart feeling like an anchor dragging along the bottom of a lake. After he crawled into bed, while lying on his back with eyes wide open, there was nothing he desired more in life than to be in the other room talking with Amber. Yet an unseen fear kept him chained to the bed. He hoped the morning would bring new tidings.

Regret over this would follow him closely in later days.

In the other room, Amber lay in the darkness, her heart aching and confused. A few tears broke free from her eyes.

"Why…why did it turn out like this?" she whispered into the air in the form of a prayer, comforted by the stillness in the air but receiving no answers. Soon she fell into sound sleep, hope for something more to come from the weekend being released. Doors to her heart, which once again had been narrowly opened to Beau just moments ago, were now being shut.

Sunday morning came all too quickly, at least for Beau, and it was a day much different than the rest. A downcast spirit was in the air that one could bitterly taste. Amber had little to say. Her mood filtrated into everyone, who spoke few words as well in order to not provoke her. The original plans to go to church with her and her family were aborted by her request. Her claim was that Beau needed to get home to see his family, said with overtones in her voice that Beau tried not to hear.

Beau, however, did not desire to leave this soon and hoped that the day would still bring new tidings and moods. To his concealed dismay, however, he soon found himself standing outside the house about to get into the truck, saying goodbye to Amber through an invisible wall that cut at his heart. She politely, yet without emotion, bid him farewell and returned to her house without looking back.

Dismayed but not completely hopeless, Beau slowly climbed into the truck and proceeded forward down the gravel driveway, away from the house that he had pulled into less than forty-eight hours earlier. He took one final look into the rearview mirror at the house before turning onto the road. His mind was running a hundred miles an hour, fleeing from the cold farewell he received from the girl who once stood standing and waiving to him like an angel upon his arrival.

He was unsure what to make of that weekend but sure that he wanted to know this girl more, sure that he had met someone quite unlike any other who could be the one he was destined for. There was something much different about her. She was spirited and full of life, zest, and wildness, yet she was also real and transparent. She lived a life guided by morals, a life that gave evidence of faith, with words voiced that said the same. She rocked his senses like no other woman had and in the process inspired him to think deeply about his own convictions, about who he was and the kind of man he wanted to be.

It was all new to him.

As he drove off, he replayed all the scenes of the weekend—the simple act of brushing their teeth together and the immense joy that came with it. The movie and the swans, the comfort and laughter had in the times spent with her family, the moonlit field, and especially the time at Laverne's farmhouse.

He was also forced to replay some of the less elating moments, like the conversation on the dock and his inability to say what was on his heart, which was so unlike all the transparent telephone conversations they had. Too many times he felt he had a tennis ball lodged in his throat.

But what plagued his mind most of all, which he fought with all he had to reason away but could not, was how she seemed to distance herself at the end, and her initiation of his early departure. It left a strange haunting in his mind that battled the hope he clung on to.

"I should have gone in there to talk to her last night," he kept saying to himself. Recalling some of his actions, some vulgar words and responses that slipped out a couple times, he wondered if she saw things in him she had not seen before and didn't see some things she hoped she would. Perhaps the confusion of her leaving for Ohio in less than a week, and what to do about her current relationship, got the better of her. He couldn't be sure. Nothing seemed clear.

Despite all this, he believed he would see her again and that the confusion would unravel and pass.

"I know I'll see you before I leave, in your hometown," he recalled her saying earlier that weekend after Beau requested her visit to Sheldon. These words of hers came before the distance did, though he clung onto them nonetheless.

Soon he turned off the country road that had led to her driveway and was on the familiar interstate. With the increasing speed of the truck, his head was flushed with longing and an overpowering lack of control over his thoughts. The song he was listening to upon arrival again played in the tape deck, though this time it grabbed him harder than before.

Like songs of the past, the lyrics spoke into the times with words about what a woman could do to a man's soul and a peaceful feeling the singer had because his feet were on the ground. It also spoke of a voice the singer heard, telling him that he might never see this woman, this potential lover and friend, again.

Beau drove on with the warm wind rushing through the truck. No peaceful, easy feeling was anywhere to be found, nor did there appear to be any solid ground under his feet. He was also unaware of the significance that some of these lyrics would hold in the days to come.

For some, the weekend might not have seemed like anything too far out of the ordinary. For Beau, however, whose romantic longings were supercharged since birth and accentuated over the years by time and circumstance, it was one of sensory overload. With the depth of a novel, it was deep and wide and long reaching, mixed with elation and a strange peace amidst grueling uncertainty as to what in the world was happening. "Surrealistic" would be a fair word to describe the experience, and it would stretch into the years ahead, revealing more and more about life along the way.

Slipping Away

Friday, September 3, 1999, Labor Day Weekend

Dad and I were out on the water at 5:30 this morning. A cool, comforting breeze met us there as we stood in the boat casting our baits, surrounded by the misty gray morning. A slight fog rose above the glassy water, the air damp and refreshing. I can still taste it.

We caught a few fish that brought some excitement to the early hour, filleted and ate them, along with homemade cornbread, for breakfast while looking out over the river below. I missed a nice musky too; felt a great tug and saw the big fin come swirling over the surface of the water just twenty yards out before it shook my bait out. I could hear dad let out an "oooh!" when he saw the wake it left. One of these years I'll catch 'em.

Today I leave for my final year of college, just four days after Amber departed for Cleveland to begin her new job in the real world. I remember well the calm, blue-skied evening she left. I was sitting on the back porch at ma's place while waiting, hoping, to receive the phone call from her letting me know she'd soon be stopping in on her way back from the visit to her grandparents' place, who live up north—the same call I thought I would receive days earlier.

The excitement gradually faded as the call came late, telling me she would be unable to come since they were running behind schedule. I didn't know what to say; wish I would have tried harder to get her to come. Not sure why I didn't.

I know she was distant when I left her house a couple weeks ago, though I wasn't expecting it to turn into this. Hopefully time will bring changes.

Strange feeling now, a sense of something slipping away.

Thank God for the water...

Weeks had passed since Beau drove out of that gravel driveway in Monticello, and in that time the memory of it had become etched in his mind. Each day he hoped to hear from her. Each day he fought to hold on to the hope, for which he had a large supply, for better or worse.

The time had now come for him to leave for college and dive back into the fast-paced life of academia, exams, and bars. Grudgingly, he had to say goodbye to that summer that had left such a big mark on him. Summers had always evoked powerful emotions in him and consistently became more fleeting than the previous, touching the deep places before disappearing. This one would be no different.

After Beau settled back into college life, there were a few short phone calls and e-mails with Amber, though an increasing distance grew with each one. Beau made a few attempts early on to visit her, driving southeast down the highway toward Cleveland. His friends called him crazy for doing so, but his ears weren't open to such advice. To his dismay, his efforts came up short as she couldn't be reached by telephone when he arrived in town and didn't return his calls, making the drive back to college long and arduous.

It seemed she had said a silent goodbye that he was not hearing or willing to hear. She continued relations with her old boyfriend too, which did little to spur hope within him. Like girls from the past, he believed he would eventually get over her and meet someone new, though for some reason it seemed this one would take longer to get over. He was never good at letting go of things to begin with, and there were some elements to his acquaintance with Amber that were much different than the others.

Beau went on many thoughtful walks beside the Mississippi in those days, more than ever before. His head was usually bowed forward, looking at the ground before him, searching for answers yet finding none. "How did it come to this..." he thought to himself time and time again. Sometimes a smile would come to his face when replaying some of the scenes that took place with her, both that weekend and in the previous encounters. The smile was soon replaced with a sigh and grimace, though, as the reality that she was far from him, both physically and emotionally, found its way back.

There came a weekend that autumn when he drove to her hometown, to the place where those swans captured them that one late summer night during his weekend visit. Beyond simply reliving the past and drowning in reverie, there was a mission behind the trip. Beau had vowed to buy the painting she admired long ago, remembering vividly the moment when she gazed into it like a young girl in a fairytale. He had planned on doing this since the moment he saw it move her, and now he had the money to do so. To Beau's relief, it was still on display, though slightly hidden by the store owner, who believed Beau might still come back to claim it.

The painting would remain in his possession for some time, reminding him of that weekend that grew further and further away. He believed anything was possible and perhaps believed too much that the day would come when they would be together and he could present it to her. However, as so many other things, it served as an indicator of a truth, which Beau could not yet see as the wind passed through his downcast soul.

Despite the sullenness that was thick following that weekend at Amber's, a peculiar thing happened that took away some of the sting caused by her mysterious flight. Within Beau, a desire awoke to go back to the pews that once acted as a playground for him as a child. The fact that his motives may have been mixed with the desire to win the favor of Amber didn't matter; he was going to church on his own will for the first time in the history of his life, and there was something more to it all than just Amber.

In the two weeks he had remaining in Sheldon prior to going back to college, he visited the small church close to his mother's house. It was there that something unplanned happened. The God that he always believed in but avoided seemed to become more real. In some unexplainable way, it was as if he was alive and breathing and near.

One of those mornings, while driving away following the morning service and feeling quite good about things, Beau recalled an experience long ago when he tasted something much different while sitting on a pew.

Around the time of boys' chorus class in middle school, Beau befriended Pat and Dylan, two of his sister's guy friends. Though they were a couple years older, an immediate connection was again made due their similar zest for deviance. Though human life and respect for adults, for the most part, were maintained, the three free-spirited travelers enjoyed their "freedom" and took it to advanced levels.

One Sunday morning, Dylan and Beau accompanied Pat to mass. Being allies, they would not let their comrade face this peril alone. Pat, a strong-willed, loyal, and witty fellow, was by no means an avid fan of going to this ritual, though he was told by his father that he had to go. It should also be known that this particular morning followed an evening in a country field under the stars, sitting in and on top of Dylan's old Chevy Impala, reveling in sophisticated conversation that was enhanced by cheap beer, plenty of cigarettes, and mind-bending hallucinogens that would come back to bite them after daybreak. Though they had their share of long nights, this one was one of the more severe. Sleepless, they walked into the church smelling and looking like road-kill with a smile.

It should also be known that Pat's dad, a deep-voiced, stout man of high intelligence, usually spent these mornings, and many other days, with his own cheap beer and fishing pole amidst his exhortation for his son to attend mass. His mother, a pleasant woman who, in Pat's terms, was a "Bible thumper," lived on the other side of town and often tried to steer him toward the God who he didn't really buy into. Dylan's parents walked a slightly different path. They were of the line of hippies and still carried relics of the sixties with no apparent affinity to faith or conservatism. They were hard-working, genuine people and provided for Dylan, who also gravitated toward the liberal path.

Pat's and Dylan's circumstances, together with Beau's loose roots in evangelical Christianity, created a unique, sometimes flammable chemistry.

This chemistry frequently revealed itself in all the times they spent together. Though sometimes toxic, there was something special in those slowly passing days and late nights that spanned all four seasons. There was something lingering in all those country drives to random destinations, road trips to party spots and rock concerts, nights of sitting under the sky on the hood of a car or around a campfire, where substance-filled conversations rolled that centered around women, God and his existence, his possible existence, his complete lack of existence, the cosmos and all those darn stars and planets, and Monty Python, among other things.

That something, that chemistry, was also revealed on this particular Sunday morning.

The three light-headed, bewildered, and somewhat obnoxious juveniles stumbled into the building that morning and did little to promote the reverence in the place. The dry, stale, lifeless organ-filled climate didn't do too much good either, and Beau couldn't help but look around as if expecting more. After all, it was a place of God, a holy place. Shouldn't there be more light? More energy? More life? Though Beau knew his own life was not "holy," he did believe in a creator of lightning bolts and thunder and felt there ought to be some hint of them in a place supposedly made for him.

As they sat with heavy heads in the darkened balcony, laughter began to emerge from deep within them for no particular reason other than that they should *not* be doing so in such a place. They tried stopping more than once, though their futile attempts only made it worse. This laughter further increased each time the nearly deceased organist accidentally knocked her music sheets onto the ground, producing an unharmonious sound through the speakers that bounced off the walls of the sanctuary. The inadvertent heckling of the three punkish youths, which grew with each catastrophic tumbling of paper, shattered the poor woman's hopes of recovering her poise and confidence.

Their laughter continued as they made their way out the door following the service, none of them recalling the message given by the priest. They heard some words, though didn't understand them—words that would one day make more sense.

Following Pat's wedding, years down the road, Beau saw that same priest sitting around the smoky, candle-lit bar area of the restaurant where the reception was held. With apathy present in his demeanor, the priest sat with what appeared to be a drink in his hand, mostly alone, talking occasionally with people while looking very inept in his black suit and white collar. Something about it all seemed quite strange to Beau, out of place.

Unlike that experience in the balcony, Beau now felt a strange closeness to that which he couldn't see. His thoughts were captured in a way that was new to him or perhaps just forgotten—captured like they were as a child, before the shadow crept in.

He shared this with the pastor, who with a discerning yet optimistic tone, gave him the contact information of a church near Beau's college. His intentions to go there were sincere, though he would never make it as the college lifestyle cunningly and systematically pulled him back into the late nights that had marked all his years there. Old influential friends did nothing to steer him clear of the night and rather aided his return to decadence. At the same time, the motivation and strength to stay on course and for purity, which was influenced by Amber, was weakening, especially as she drifted further away. The huge vacuum in his life activated by her absence grew stronger.

Though he never drifted completely off course after her departure, he would wander. In a breath, the God that Beau was feeling closer to grew distant again. However, it was not God who was stepping away.

That fall wasted no time in disappearing into the dark chill of winter, where the weeks became more and more saturated with late nights, studying, and planning for the future. The busyness took his mind further from Amber, the pain behind her absence subsiding, though never fading completely. That portion of Amber that didn't fade away continued to have an influence on him, acting as a sort of white angel on his shoulder. Many times the memory of her and what she represented prevented him from stepping through doors that he might have otherwise jumped through. Opportunities for impure interludes presented themselves time and time again, though he turned away.

Yet as Amber continued to drift from his mind and winter gave way to spring the following year in his final semester, things shifted. The knowledge that the end of college was fast approaching, together with the warming temperatures that always worked on the senses, caused the partying to intensify as much as ever. After all, each person only goes around once, or so they reasoned. With this, unlocked doors that should not have been walked through were, and one night things went too far.

It was a Saturday night when Beau and a few friends went to a party a few blocks down the street. After having a few drinks and feeling pretty good, enjoying the laughter and escape from studying and other responsibilities, he met an attractive younger girl who showed an interest in him and vulnerability toward his words. Something about this triggered welcome feelings—feelings of power and respect.

While leaning against the wall talking to one another, he had no intentions of going anywhere with her beyond conversation. However, his inhibitions faded further and further away with each drink, enhanced by the encouragement of his friends to keep after her. Before he knew it, he was being drawn in by her longing stares and mildly suggestive comments, which he also began to voice to her. Soon he was leading her by the hand out the front door of the house and walking down the dimly lit streets toward his apartment.

"This is wrong," he kept saying to himself under his breath, "Nothing is going to happen, *nothing*," while feeling a strange sense of powerlessness with each word as desire overpowered prudence.

Early the next morning, the girl was the first to wake. After sensing no affection coming from the guy who lay next to her, she left his apartment in a hurry, shamed and disgusted with herself for giving away her body and emotions. With every breath, she struggled with a sense of emptiness, guilt, and confusion that was felt deep inside. She couldn't hide from it. She wondered if Beau would call her and take away these feelings, but she had a bad feeling he wouldn't, the way it was with guys before him.

"Why did I do this?" she thought despairingly to herself, with no good answers to console. It appeared that her desire and longing for love had steered her wrong again. For a few days she would hold on to hope that he might call and dispel her worry, though the call would never come. As a result, another stone was rolled in front of her heart.

After she left, Beau lay still on his bed, hoping to fall asleep and forget about what just happened, stunned that it happened at all. Thoughts of Amber and what she would think shot into him like arrows, preventing him from obtaining an ounce of rest. He felt no feeling of victory or manliness, integrity, or honor. Rather, he was numbed and desensitized, heavy like a damp quilt with his own shame and guilt, unable to open his mouth or mind to a prayer or an illuminated thought.

A realization stared at him of how this girl would be trampled inside and brought to new depths by his selfishness. He could not look it in the eyes but tried hiding under the covers. He thought of women he cared for and how they would feel had they been used the way he used this girl. It was not the first time something like this had happened after a night out, though the guilt weighed heavier this time and would not go away with the setting of the sun that evening.

In time, the weight of guilt would pass, and the memory would be tucked away as new days were brought forth. College was winding down; a new world was awaiting him. He had no choice but to get up and move forward.

Unexposed wounds fester instead of heal, however.

Monday eve, May 8, 2000
    The final days of college are upon me. I seem to be traveling a path that is sometimes so off course, sometimes so lonely. In all these years, though, bright times exist that prevent all hope from being lost. Experiences and relationships continue to reveal goodness in life that keeps me pressing on toward something I can't quite get a handle on, a goodness that keeps me from falling completely off course.

I don't know what that something is, though I recall feeling it while sitting out on the bridge that stretched over the pond at our old house in Cringle. Whether my spirits were high or low, the fog over the calm water and the gently swaying trees produced in me a peace, regardless of any confusion within me. Other times I felt it through laughter with friends and family, appreciating the distinct character of each person.

I often felt it while spending time with my niece and nephews. They are so full of life, joy, and boundless imagination. They know how to live.

I have felt it while driving along country roads and highways, looking into the rearview mirror to see the sun shining brightly before setting. Strange how all thoughts were put on hold in those moments, as if something were pulling my heart toward the sky.

College graduation came and went like a thief. All those years walking about the campus and all the people that had crossed his path were now filed away in memory. Some he would see again, though most would be gone forever. Beau finished walking through the ceremonies, though just barely; he nearly didn't graduate due to a decline of studying toward the end of that semester, which produced some unfavorable grades. A few days later, he would again be returning to his hometown.

As he emerged onto the highway to drive that old northeast route for the last time, he looked back to see those bluffs of southwestern Wisconsin growing smaller and smaller, emotions running high and low and everywhere in between.

And those were the days of college.

Beyond the Trees

Friday, late June, 2000
On the road again. Leaving was harder this time, yet
it comes with more adventure than ever before.
The highway continues to be a home to me.

"Goodbye, Beau," said his mother after giving her son a big hug.

After all the times of packing him leftover meals to take with him back to college, she was now seeing him off as he embarked on a journey to a place that would become more than just a temporary stay away from hometown. There was a different feeling behind this departure, one that she knew promised fewer visits from her son as the pace of his life would intensify even greater than it did in college. She was excited for him and proud, yet it was hard to see him leave.

"Goodbye, Ma," he said as he began walking toward the car.

"Can you call me to let me know you made it safely?"

"Sure, but it's going to be late..."

"That's okay, I'll be up," she said quickly with a smile in her usual energetic, caring fashion, and with that he got into his car and drove off. She stood out on the porch with her hands in her sweatshirt pocket, the cool evening air producing a slight chill. After Beau's car had disappeared from sight down the road, she slowly turned around and walked back into the quiet house after glancing into the setting sun, a hundred thoughts rushing to her mind.

When inside, she walked to the sink and began to clean up the dishes from the dinner they just shared, recalling the conversation with fondness. Beau had shared thoughts of Amber, a wonderment toward it that he seemed to be finally releasing, as well as a sense of excitement and nervousness about the changes coming his way.

With a deep sigh, she looked longingly out the window above the sink while scrubbing, recalling many other times together in the past. She thought of meals shared in earlier years, of preparing food in the kitchen as the evening sunlight poured in. Beau, who wasn't the quickest to open up with his feelings, would often talk to her about the things of life in those moments. As always, she also thought of other times when all the children ran about the old house they lived in years ago. Now all was so quiet.

"Please be with him…" she whispered with a pleading tone, looking through the window into the sky. With that, a lone tear made its way out from behind her eyes, followed by several more.

"On the road again," said Beau as he sped down the highway, the music plenty loud enough to hear above the wind that rushed in through the open windows. It had only been a couple weeks after arriving back in Sheldon following graduation, and he could hardly believe that he was again behind the wheel. It seemed his destiny was to involve much time spent on the road.

Little did he know what else it would involve, which he would come to discover soon enough.

Once again he was driving south, back to Chicago, where a finance job at a construction company awaited him. The position wasn't what he would consider a dream job, though he reasoned that some good experience would be gained for the future, and it paid well. He looked forward to being a provider for a family some day, and this seemed like a step in the right direction.

The real world was upon the young graduate, and for the most part, the road was looking good. Yet he knew more was at stake: decisions that would bear more weight, with results and consequences more readily seen. Part of him feared this move—he had often stumbled in the past in pursuit of level paths, and there was much to offer in the windy city that could steer a well-intentioned young man way off course. Nonetheless, this seemed the course he was intended to travel, so on he drove as night took over the skies.

Within Beau's heart, one thing continued to beat just as loud as the changes that were upon him. Amber. After all this time, a speck of hope still remained. Whether this hope was friend or foe he could not determine.

He arrived at his new apartment just after 1:00 a.m. He parked in front of the building, and after fulfilling his duty to call home, began hauling his belongings up to his third-floor dwelling using an old, sliding-door elevator, along with a winding set of stairs for the larger items.

After an hour of fast-paced unloading, he was finished. The search for a parking spot began, which lasted longer than he wished to remember. Bad parking was one of the costs of living in a trendy, well-kept neighborhood. Exhausted, he returned to his small, two-hundred-fifty-square-foot studio, where he sat down on one of the boxes. He looked around the apartment and out the windows, taking it all in. Soon he realized he had nothing left to give and lay down on his small twin mattress for the first time in his new home.

Beau quickly settled into his new surroundings, and the days began to pass by more quickly than ever before. Each morning he walked to the train that would take him to work and bring him back at the end of the day. Whether walking downtown and looking up at the giant skyscrapers or strolling along a quiet, tree-lined street, thoughts of family, friends, and the deeper things of life now occupied more of his mind. It seemed to him that the exit from college had carried him into a new realm where life held more gravity, more meaning.

One night shortly after his arrival, he began unpacking some boxes that had been untouched since he moved in. While sitting on the floor drinking one of those fancy, high-priced coffee drinks that he bought from the Starbucks down on the corner, he reached into the box full of books next to him and began randomly pulling them out, briefly examining each before placing it in either the "keep" or "give away"pile. Some, like old textbooks on subjects that he preferred to forget, even found their way into a "throw away" pile.

On his fourth reach into the cardboard box, he pulled out a very familiar book. It was the old black Bible, with tattered leather cover and family names written inside, which had been given to his family so many years ago.

"You're still with me," he said amiably, amazed that this particular book still remained with him after all his changes in residence over the past six years. As he sat there, holding it like a pearl, the ominous memory of the pages of Earl's Bible flapping in the breeze came vividly to his mind. Along with this came the memory of those cherished talks with Amber about life and faith and those few Sunday mornings subsequently spent at the small church where he felt so close to something he could neither see nor touch.

Sparked by these memories and more, the consideration of going to a church unexpectedly entered his mind. Much time had transpired since Beau had been to one, and his heart was not where it was in those weeks following Amber's departure. He had grown a bit distant toward spiritual matters in that time, which made the mere consideration enough to make him shiver.

Regardless, the thought was planted beneath his skin, and there it would stay and grow over the ensuing days and weeks.

Days and weeks passed by quickly to a late Saturday afternoon. Beau returned home from a day at the lake, tired and relaxed from the sun and wind. He went to his mailbox, pulled out its contents, and immediately began thumbing through it all, sorting through what was usually a lot of junk mail.

Just as he reached the bottom of the stack, there appeared a trendy, eye-catching postcard. Looking closer at it, he began to read the words: "Top Ten Reasons Why People Don't Go to Church:" He looked closer still and read the top ten reasons. One stuck out: "I'm a good person and I don't want anyone to tell me differently."

Beau stared at that sentence for a moment, briefly acknowledging the fact that that particular thought had crossed his mind a time or two. He turned over the card and saw that it was advertising the opening of a new church down the road, almost walking distance from his apartment building. The opening day was set for early September.

Instead of throwing it away with the rest of the junk mail, he kept it and continued his walk up to his apartment. After entering, he went straight to the kitchen and posted it on his refrigerator with a magnet.

"Just in case," he said to himself, not yet determined in his mind to go. As time drew nearer, he'd make the decision.

For whatever reasons, the days passed more quickly than ever before, and soon the week before the grand opening of the church was upon him. That whole week he couldn't escape the thoughts that the upcoming Sunday was the one that the postcard spoke of. That Saturday, his mind was tossed to and fro as he pondered the question of whether he was going.

'I'm going, maybe…No, I'll go some other time…No, go now or you'll never go. Go!' Within him, though, deep in the unseen places, the decision to go had already been solidified. Even the anguish that collided with him on Sunday morning could not deter him from stepping out the front door, slowly yet steadily, to make his way down the road and to church.

He walked briskly down the street through the cool, gray September day. A few fallen leaves blew about his feet, separated from the trees overhead that still retained the majority of their leaves and luminosity. As Beau walked on, his eyes were fixated on the ground before his feet, while deep thoughts ruminated everywhere in his soul. Occasionally he glanced to the skies above, as if to seek comfort, the burden and anxiety he carried both lightened and intensified by them.

In a blink, he found himself approaching the building. He paused for just a moment before walking up the concrete steps that led to the main doors, taking in a deep breath of air. He proceeded to make his way up the steps and through the doors that some friendly looking people opened for him and walked stealthily toward one of the old wooden pews in the back of the large, high-ceilinged room.

Several people with friendly faces tried to engage him in conversation on his way to the pew, though he was not having it. Cordially, if not a bit harshly, he waved off their attempts with an air of brevity. One man, however, managed to somehow shake his hand just before he entered the sanctuary and give him a good look in the eye.

"Have you ever considered ministry, son?" the man asked humbly near the end of the handshake after pondering a moment, sensing something in the young man that provoked the question. Beau felt a sudden shock run through his spine at these words. With a blank look for a response, he quickly pulled his hand away and retreated to the pew near the back of the building, where he shrugged off the comment.

"*Ministry?* What's this guy thinking?" he thought to himself, shaking slightly for unknown reasons by the comment. "He obviously doesn't know me."

Occasionally Beau would glance at the bulletin that was handed to him upon entrance, both out of curiosity and to avoid making eye contact that could lead to someone wanting to speak with him. He was wary about these churchgoers. If he knew they were all like Earl it might be different, but they were all strangers to him now in a somewhat strange land. Yet as he sat there quietly in the long wooden pew next to an older couple, who were tied up with what appeared to be their granddaughter, he sensed something in the air, something both familiar and at the same time new. It gripped him.

Soon the service began. A band began to play music that he found quite appealing, with instruments and voices that produced a sound that was surprisingly melodic and current. He hadn't expected to hear this type of music in a church; though the lyrics were churchy, they also displayed both heart and life. Some hands were raised in the half-full room, and many eyes were closed in reverence with lifted or bowed heads as they sang. Unlike childhood days at church, he saw no galloping or other unusual events. There was something very real about it.

When the music faded, Beau discovered that the middle-aged man who shook his hand just moments ago was actually the pastor. After acquainting himself with the audience and sharing some history of the church, he began to preach.

And preach he did.

From his mouth came words that penetrated Beau's soul, and the whole time that familiar presence that Beau sensed grew in strength. For nearly an hour this went on, his attention bent on the words that came from the preacher, which in turn came mostly from the Bible that sat on a small podium in the center of the stage. To and fro the man walked, speaking with increasing authority, sincerity, and fervency, mixed with an appropriate touch of humility and lightheartedness that produced laughter from the listeners. All ears in the large, wood-beamed room, or sanctuary as Beau would soon discover it was called, were tuned in to this one man's voice.

And then it was over. Beau sat still for a few moments while others rose and began to walk around. He gazed at the wood ceiling that glowed softly due the light cast upon it, as if he could see the sky through it. "I am the way, the truth, and the life," was written on one of the walls, grabbing his attention again as it did a few times throughout the service. After a few moments, he rose from his seat, intent on exiting without interference.

He succeeded on getting out of the building unscathed, politely refusing any more attempts at verbal engagement. He shot out the doors, only to be met by the light of the late morning that momentarily blinded him. He wasn't expecting that, nor was he expecting in any way to go through whatever it was that he had just experienced inside.

"That was not normal..."

Beau again walked briskly down the sidewalk, his eyes going from the sky to the ground as deep breaths went in and out of his mouth. His pace quickened as both excitement and fear ran through him, not sure what to make of it all. He came to his apartment building and burst into his quiet little studio—his tiny refuge in the vast city—and sat on his couch that overlooked the narrow, tree-lined one-way street. He sat there for nearly half an hour before getting up to eat, taking in everything he had just heard and felt.

After eating some leftover lasagna, feeling over-whelmed and drained by the morning, he rose from the futon and closed all the shades to stop the onslaught of light and went to his small bed in the corner and sat down. He picked up that old, beat-up Bible that for so long was tucked away in obscurity, though never forgotten, and began looking up some of the verses he heard. He was curious to see if they were really in there. He set it back down after a short while and lay back, falling into a deep sleep after a few moments of lying with open eyes that saw so much more than the bare wall above him, deep breaths still going in and out of him.

Each Sunday, Beau could be found making the same journey down the sidewalk toward those concrete steps. Each Sunday, a touch of resistance faced him upon waking, though it was always overpowered by a fiery determination and an irresistible desire that tugged at his heart to go down the street to the small church on the corner.

Each week he left with something more—more insight into life and discoveries of things in the Bible that he didn't think could be in there. Each night he would lie awake on his bed, peering into those pages as if searching for lost treasure.

On the train in the morning, he would again be peering into those pages. While reading, occasionally looking out the windows into the sky beyond the tall buildings, his heart felt as if it was coming alive in unprecedented ways.

Yet in those ensuing times not all was peaceful and cozy. Within him, a battle of epic proportions between good and evil raged on for weeks and months, invisible to the common eye, including Beau's. If there ever really was an angel and devil that sat upon one's shoulder giving advice, they were now engaged in all out war over rights to the young man's soul.

Day in and day out, into the morning and into the night, he was bombarded by thoughts of his future and where he was going, of what he would have to leave behind in order to walk the path that was set out in these pages. There were days sitting beside the waters of Lake Michigan, looking off into the distance where no shore could be seen, thinking hard as the wind pounded against his face. He often prayed in those times, unknowingly.

Other times he'd be walking down the sidewalk, head down in deep thought, thoughts battling one another. He pondered family and old friendships and those who had come and gone, all that mattered, and how those relationships might be altered with his change of direction. He also thought of what he was living for and the man he wanted to become. So much for the mind to weigh. So much.

"There is so much going on inside me these days," he said to his mother one early evening on the phone while sitting forward on his couch, the wind blowing in softly through the living room windows. "Been thinking a lot about my faith and where things are going. Been struggling a lot inside too; don't know what to make of it…"

"Oh, Beau," she said gently with joy in her tone, "if there is a struggle going on inside you, that's a good sign. Just keep on looking up, and you will get the help you need to win." His mother knew of the recent visits to the church, and it brought great warmth to her. Yet she knew to keep her words few in these times. A man, however old or young, has to take his own steps on his way back to destiny, and she knew this full well.

They talked for a little longer of this and that before he hung up the phone. His mother's words continued to sound in his mind, though, as they would for several days and days beyond.

Along with her words, there were those spoken recently by his father as well. "Beau, you might have to step away from some of those friendships...if they're getting in the way of you growing, they may not be true friendships in the first place," said Carl after Beau commented on the challenge of resisting the night life and some old friends who found his new attraction to faith unsettling and disturbing.

That night, as usual, he laid himself down to sleep on his small mattress that was tucked away in the walk-in closet. His parents' words, together with segments from Sunday's messages and elsewhere, ran through his mind like a torrent. He also recalled many nights of lying awake in bed during college years, intoxicated after an evening of partying, compelled to speak into the dark with a trembling voice, *"God, I know you must not like the way I'm living, but I know no other way..."* It seemed he now knew of the other way.

Eventually, calm would settle in, just enough to allow him to drift off to sleep.

Yet even in his sleep, he could not find escape from all that was going on. Deep in the night, he was caught up in a dream that would not pass from his mind upon waking.

In the dream he ran, hard and fast and without looking back and without direction. Through the woods and fields he ran, crossing shallow rivers and streams and hurdling over barbwire fences, his clothes torn and tattered, blood mingled with sweat dripping down his skin. On one side there appeared fell shapes of bodies with hell-bent eyes reaching out with long, skinny, and malicious fingers, trying to grab hold of him. They were futile, though; he would swing out at them with fury and knock them down, one after the other, as he continued to run. Yet they kept coming. On the other side was a bright light and figures of gentility that exuded a quiet, undeterred power that had their hands open to him, reaching out as if urging him to take hold and escape, non-threatening, though ever so ardent and compassionate. He pulled away from them too, however, as if he couldn't accept their help, fighting incomprehensible compassion on one side and hideous malcontent on the other. On and on he ran, branches whipping him in the face while dodging trees. He soon became very tired and weary, often stumbling to the ground. On one fall it felt as if he wouldn't be able to get up, distressed when looking behind him and seeing the evil forms crowding around with delight. Overwhelmed by their numbers and their mounting grip upon him, he nearly gave up, until he lifted his head one last time to see a great white light that lay just beyond the wood...

Beau woke suddenly, launched into a sitting position with sweat beading down his skin. He flung the sheets off his bed, jumped to the floor, and walked into the living room, where the window had flung open from the late autumn wind. The curtains swayed aggressively and the noise of rustling branches outside could be heard clearly. He walked over and stood before the windows, peering out beyond the street lights into the sky, running his hands through his damp hair while trying to re-count and examine the dream.

Insight and answers into that dream would not be found anytime soon, though the weeks and months that transpired brought a peace that overcame everything else. Day after day his heart yielded to a different way of life as all his strength to resist change had gone from him.

Finally, the moment came one day when he chose to leave behind all that had slowed him down in the past, to trust in something he could not see but knew beyond any shadow of doubt had always been there. Always. Even in those early days in the fishing boat with his father and when gazing out Grandma Winnie's window into the wild night.

If one were to ask him when the moment happened, he wouldn't be able to say. It all seemed to flow together over the days and months and longer, though he would say, without question, that he didn't do it on his own.

Beau, who once unknowingly worshipped the nightlife and all that came with it, among other things, turned back to that which he ran after and dreamt of so fondly as a child, that which he ran so far from as he stepped into adolescence and beyond, yet that which always pursued him no matter how far he traveled in miles and spirit.

And then there was light and peace.

It was late spring when Beau again entered into a tub of cold water, just like he did over a decade ago. He made the decision on his own, aided via the gentle encouragement of others, this time fully aware of the significance behind the immersion. He had come to learn that freedom did not come without a sacrifice of some sort and that a great price had been paid long ago for his freedom from an empty way of life—a way that once held him down with a lesser power than what now dwelt inside him.

Aside from his friends accidentally allowing his head to hit the back of the tub on his way in, the experience was a special one, signifying a great race that had begun in his heart, mind, soul, and body that would forever change the trajectory of his life.

One crisp, refreshing morning just days later, Beau walked out the front door of his apartment, and in a way that he couldn't describe in his journals at that time and still can't to this day, he felt as if he could truly see.

As he looked into the distance, it felt as if he had for so long been blind to truths of life that were hidden behind a thick veil of dark shadow that had consumed everything. He walked along with quickening pace, nearly tripping over the cracks in the sidewalk that he wasn't paying attention to, gazing into the full green trees that flickered with rays of sweet sunlight. In them he could see beyond into more clearly defined shapes and colors that carried his thoughts deeper into life and relationships and all that came with it, both in the past and present, with visions of tomorrow, and with them, peace.

Though many things still remained a mystery and would forevermore, much was being unlocked in the depths of the young traveler and would continue to do so in the days ahead, days and years that shifted from a reckless pursuit of temporary shelters and all that doesn't satisfy to chasing even more recklessly after that which created all things and which was true and right.

✤ ✤ ✤ ✤

It wasn't long before the desire to share all the changes with Earl swelled up in Beau, and he determined in his heart to journey up to those secluded northern woods where his old, wise friend roamed. He hadn't spoken to Earl in some time—a combination of busyness coupled with a want to be surer of some things held him back from reaching out to communicate.

He longed to share everything with Earl since it all started happening, and many times he considered either picking up the phone to call or simply driving up there. He restrained each time, though, perhaps instinctively knowing that he needed his own time to chart his course before returning to the cabin.

"A man needs to find his own way, Beau." He recalled Earl's words from a time many years ago while sitting in the canoe with him. "I've given you all the thoughts I have on the matter…" Beau was deciding on whether or not to go to college, and he needed to make the decision soon. Earl cast his bait into the water as he spoke those words, then began gnawing on a thick piece of spicy beef jerky, not saying a word more on the subject. Beau sighed heavily during this silence, again not getting a direct answer from Earl, as was common. It drove him crazy at times, though one day he'd thank him for it. Though not that day.

On Thursday morning of that week, Beau awoke, stretched hard and long, and jumped out of bed with zest. He was looking forward to carrying out his plan of calling Earl that evening after work, just to make sure that he'd be around the cabin for a visit that weekend. Beau had a good feeling what the answer would be, though he wanted to confirm nonetheless.

He arrived home from work late that night. After making himself a spaghetti dinner and taking some time to settle in and let his mind unwind, he picked up the phone and called the cabin. After just a few rings, the answering machine came on, so Beau left a brief message before hanging up. He then began puttering around the house before getting ready for bed.

Several hours passed, and just as Beau was about to retire to his bed, the phone rang. He immediately looked at the clock: 11:58. It was uncommon for him to get calls this late and was mildly surprised by it. He walked over to the kitchen and looked at the caller I.D. before taking the call. *E. Timmings*. Beau quickly picked up the phone.

"Hello?"

"Beau, is that you?" said a younger sounding voice than that of Earl's.

"Yes. Is this Seth?" asked Beau upon hearing the humble voice, which carried a drained but urgent tone.

"Beau! Yes, it's me, and it is great to hear your voice."

Seth was the youngest of Earl's three sons, all of whom traveled extensively but found time to return to the Northwoods for brief stretches of time, usually just to catch their breath and spend time with their father. Beau fondly recalled times playing around and wrestling with Seth and his older brothers, as well as his own brother Dean, when growing up. They were all older boys who he always admired for their good character and sense of inner strength.

"You too! What are you doing up there?"

All went silent for a moment. Seth then began to speak after a short sigh, moving right past small talk to the heart of the matter. "Beau, my father is ill. It is beyond irony that you called tonight; I was going to be calling you shortly to tell you the news…"

Seth went on to share how he came to the cabin early in the morning, just after sunrise. He approached the front of the cabin and found his father lying on his stomach, facing the door to the cabin with his right arm stretched out in front of him and his head lying on his right cheek. He was barely breathing.

"There was firewood scattered all around him, as if he was bringing an armload of it in and fell on his way up the steps. Looks like he tried to make it into the house after falling but couldn't make it. I must have arrived not long after the heart attack." Beau gasped at the sound of those words. "I checked to see if he was still breathing and was relieved to find that he was, though barely…no other signs of life were coming from him." Seth paused for a moment to catch his own breath, with rising emotion being exuded in his explanation. "Beau, he is at the Northwood's Memorial Hospital. Great care is being given to him, but they say he may not make it through the night."

At this Seth's voice began to break up, silent, all but sniffles coming through the phone. "It would be good for you to come back as soon as you can. *Right now* if at all possible."

For a moment Beau sat speechless, not yet fully grasping the gravity of the situation. A thousand memories and emotions barraged him with every blink.

"I'll get my stuff together and leave right away."

"Drive careful, Beau, but do come quickly." Again Beau felt the weight of the situation in Seth's tone. Always a sincere and gentle-voiced man, Seth was now very serious and dire with few words. His steadiness didn't leave him completely, though—a testimony to the character of his father.

"Hey, Beau," he said just as the conversation was about to end.

"Yeah?"

"It's good to hear from you."

"You too. See you in five hours."

And so it followed on that late summer eve, Beau hung up the phone and prepared for a quick exit. He packed his backpack only with necessities and ran out the door like a gust of wind, not looking back once.

He lunged down the steps and rushed through the entrance of the building and proceeded to run down the quiet, dimly lit street to his car. On the way, he called a few good friends to let them know what he was doing and that he might be gone for a few days, or longer.

Once behind the wheel, he raced down the narrow, car-filled streets to the relatively wide-open midnight highway. He stopped once along the way to gas up and buy a cup of strong coffee to keep him company on the long, lonely drive north.

Company seemed more plentiful on the drive than he expected, however, in the form of thoughts and memories that shot through his mind. He drove on into the deep of night, where traffic dwindled near to nothing. The city lights, which once dulled the sky, vanished behind him and ceded to an ominous canopy of stars and traces of far off galaxies that whispered secret things.

On he drove, comforted by the sky and the serene lands around him and the humming of the tires on the road, warm wind gushing in through the windows. The radio in the car wasn't working, and all the better, for there was so much to hear in the quiet of that hour.

"Your will be done," he said aloud while peering up through the window. He recalled a sermon he heard a short while ago about the event at the Garden of Gethsemane. Beau still had much to learn of the will of God and the mystery behind it, though inside he knew it was the best way, regardless of contrary desires. Those words kept coming to his mind, over and over, yet he unabashedly hoped that Earl's time was not yet over, wanting more than anything at that moment to see his old friend alive.

"Not yet...but your will be done," his voice cracking this time with each word. Tears began to well in his eyes, which continued to be fixed forward in an unrelenting gaze, and soon he was surrounded by a powerful comfort that touched him like a father's hand upon a young child's shoulder.

Before his journey north would be completed that morning, those words would be repeated several times.

A couple hours had passed, though the intensity of the drive continued.

"Please let me be there..." he spoke aloud, remembering all the times, words, and seasons of life in which Earl stood steadfast with him and his family. Pain shot through him when thinking of why he waited so long to visit him, and he feared the prospect of not having the chance to say goodbye.

Passing by open fields illuminated by the distant moon that emerged and hung on the horizon, Beau thought back to the passing of sweet Grandma Winnie—how he had not visited her in her final years that she spent in the nursing home before her soul departed from earth. Each time his mother returned from a visit, she told Beau how Grandma had asked how he was doing and how a big smile would come over her face when told that he was doing well and growing fast. Janet purposely withheld certain details of some of his less than straight and narrow ways, though it probably would not have mattered anyway. Grandma Winnie saw the good even in the worst of people.

Beau knew full well that if she was watching down on him from heaven, if it worked that way, she would hold no bitterness toward him for his distance in her final years. However, it still made him wince that he had to be so young and unaware of how much she meant to him until it was too late.

For whatever reasons, those memories of his grandma came to him in his first couple years of college, as if his heart was all of a sudden opened to it. For many nights he prayed earnestly while lying on his back before falling asleep, hoping that his grandma could hear him. He believed that, if it were at all possible, his request for forgiveness would get to her one way or another.

In time, of course, the pain would pass and be replaced by a sweet memory of her as the jubilant, healthy little grandma who was so full of love and who unselfishly filled their plates full of food and affection.

With that memory, Beau pushed down harder on the gas pedal, traveling fast enough to make a difference while not exceeding reasonableness, determined in his mind to beat death.

He knew inside, however, that death had already lost the race with Earl, even if it took his life this very moment.

> *Friday morn, nearing 4 a.m. Earl is in the hospital.*
> On I drive, night giving way to morn, glistening stars above, some dying, others being born.
> Desolate road, warm wind rushing in through the windows, gently crashing into my soul like mighty sea billows.
> Not yet, God, not yet, not yet this hour, though all things yours, all under your hand of love and power.

As the clock on Beau's dashboard revealed the time of 5:00 a.m., he pulled up to the brightly lit hospital that was surrounded by a dark, serene forest. He exited the car and ran through the dimly lit pathway into the building. Upon entering, he stopped at the information desk to find out Earl's room number. The nurse politely pointed him in the right direction, and he walked several minutes to the room—several minutes that felt like hours. Hope that his old friend might still be alive fueled him and kept his eyes fixed forward with each forceful step.

He approached the entrance to the room, slowing his pace and lowering his head for a moment to prepare his heart for whatever lay beyond. After a moment, he lifted his head again and stepped into the room, where he was met by both great joy and sorrow.

Earl was lying on his bed, still alive, though ailing. It appeared as if the breath of life was preparing to leave him. Seth, his two brothers and sister, Beau's father and mother, and his sister Anwen, whose tear-streaked cheeks were plain to see, were all gathered around the dimly lit room. The light morning breeze blew gently into the room through the cracked window, and a soft, quiet darkness remained as the first gleam of dawn had not yet become visible in the sky. A surreal, invisible fog hovered in the room, along with an unmistakable peace that was reminiscent of the times at Earl's cabin.

Beau sensed it immediately, and though it was not spoken of, everyone else felt it too.

He was warmly greeted by all upon entering, with quiet hellos and hugs from each that calmed his nerves after the long, intense drive. Beau's attention moved quickly to Earl. His eyes were closed and his chest moved slowly up and down, giving evidence of breath. Seth sat beside him with steady yet watery eyes that bore loyalty and a heavy heart.

They all sat around for a few moments, quietly reminiscing with one another. A few stories about Earl's life and his adventures brought soft laughter and joy to the room, though few words needed to be said as the familiarity between them provided so much comfort. Any walls or family strife, which might otherwise have interfered with transparency, were nonexistent, and no effort was made to hide tears or sniffles that needed to come out.

After several minutes Beau sat next to Seth at Earl's side. The old man's eyes eventually opened as his body, which had IVs running up and down his arms and chest and into his nose, remained still. It was a picture of a weak, helpless Earl that was most foreign to Beau. Despite his weakened state, however, an inner strength remained in him that went beyond the skin to overcome pity and ease the grief of everyone in the room.

Even in what appeared to be his final moments, he was able to comfort.

Seemingly unable to speak, a gentle smile came over his face as he turned his head just slightly and set his gaze upon Beau.

His fingers moved some as if trying to reach out to him. Beau noticed this and reached out to take his hand, feeling strength remaining in Earl's grip. At this, Seth motioned gently for all to leave the room to give Beau some time alone with him.

For just over ten minutes, they sat alone together. Time, as it often does, stood still. The whole time Beau just held his old friend's hand that continued to steadily grip his. Earl's old eyes opened and closed slowly, as if drifting in and out of sleep and time. Beau once heard that people sometimes say the most inadequate things in the deepest of moments, and this now proved true, for he had no words to convey a most visceral moment.

Yet the silence would be broken. Earl, mustering up strength, began to make noises, as if trying to speak. Beau leaned over, putting his ear close to him in order to understand what he was trying to say.

"I hear your life took a new direction, young warrior," he said with a frill whisper. Beau stood hunched over him, a smile crossing his face as he soaked in the words, not yet fully recognizing their significance. One day, not far away, he would.

"I did," replied Beau. "I meant to tell you sooner; just had so much to say and was waiting for the right time..."

Earl lifted his hand slightly to relieve Beau of explanation, motioning that he was going to speak. Beau leaned back, giving Earl room to release a cough. He then leaned over again to listen.

"It's okay, Beau. I knew you'd be coming up to share before too long." He stopped speaking, as if to prepare for what he was about to say next. "We all have our seasons...sometimes we just have to run, other times we have to stop and listen." He began to cough again. Beau feared for a moment that he may have just heard his final words.

Earl fought back and spoke again, however. "Chase life, Beau, and when you find her, chase her."

"I will," replied Beau after a few moments of silence. He was not expecting such content to come from Earl under the circumstances, and the words pierced him. Again, he was not fully aware of some of the deeper meanings and truths behind those words, though they would be revealed in time.

"Beau..."

"Yes, Earl?"

The old man began to speak again, now turning his head back on his pillow, looking toward the ceiling before closing his eyes.

"I can hear them…"

Beau sat silent for a moment, not sure how to interpret the words. "What?"

"I can here them singing,"

"You…you can hear *who* singing?

"The angels, Beau," he said, his eyes opening again. "I can hear the angels singing, loudly. Sounds almost like the cheering fans when I was standing just down the road from Lambeau Field last fall, right after Favre threw that touchdown pass, but…" his frail voice began to crack, eyes moistened, "but with so much more power and energy than anything I have ever heard. And I can feel the cool water of the river flowing over my ankles, coming up to my knees…"

Beau's own eyes began to moisten again. He squinted earnestly, desiring to understand what Earl was saying. A single tear emerged from his eye due to the simple, almost childlike passion and longing behind Earl's words. Beau didn't know what to make of it all.

"Ruth…" he whispered, his eyes closing. He then fell into a deep sleep after the last sound came from his mouth.

Beau leaned back, feeling as if he was briefly included in a great mystery of life, awestruck and silenced by the moment. He recalled the feeling he had years ago when that flower wilted before his eyes during breakfast at the cabin, only this time it was even greater.

He was unable to utter a sound and sensed that though Earl's life had not yet passed, his cognizance of Beau being in the room had vanquished despite their locked hands. A fear came over Beau simultaneously. A soft and inviting, ominous fear.

Just then, two nurses walked in and politely requested that Beau join the others outside the room while they attended to Earl. He slowly stood and placed Earl's hand, which continued to lightly grip his, on his thigh and pulled his own hand away. Tears began to break from his eyes as he walked away, though he wiped them away and breathed heavily as he rejoined the others in the waiting area.

The same quiet whispers and tear-streaked smiles previously seen in Earl's room existed in the waiting area. When Beau saw his other siblings, his heart was lifted, for he hadn't seen them in some time. His spirit was lifted even further by the sight of all the little ones—the extended family of his siblings and Earl's, his grandchildren and close friends, all who were one in accord that early morning.

Many greetings, many hugs.

After an hour of arduous waiting, those closest to Earl were called back into the room to be informed of his deteriorating condition. They entered the room, hoping for life to continue yet knowing a different truth was at hand. Sniffles resounded, tears fell, though a quiet, joyful sorrow overpowered death and its henchman, grief.

Seth and his two brothers and sister gathered closest to their father, taking his hands on both sides. The grandchildren stood on the perimeter with the Jamisons and a few others. For a brief moment, Earl's eyes opened slightly and looked about the room at all who were there. Another smile came over his face that captured everyone's attention. He then moved his head ever so slightly and gave in to the strong desire to surrender. As he did, the softest, most gentle and reassuring look came over his face.

As the first gleam of sun broke over the horizon and crept through the trees into the room, Earl Timmings, man of family, strength, compassion, and character, let out a long, deep breath that would be his last.

Many scenes under these circumstances are bitterly sorrowful, with spiraling emotions and cries of fear and despair.

This one was different.

Mourning and tears did take place. No one wanted to see him go. Yet an understanding of where he had passed to and a celebration and appreciation of his life reigned. Warmth, which went beyond human capacity and understanding, was now tucked away deep in the hearts of all who had the privilege of being a part of his life.

To the children, this was all new. It was their first taste of death, and they were uncertain as to what was happening to their beloved Grandpa. *"Was he really gone?"* they wondered. *"Will he be coming back?"* To all the others, who looked upon Earl and then the little ones, it was a vivid reminder of all that was important—a reminder of the value of life and that for everything there is a season. A time to live and a time to die.

Two days later, on a beautiful morning, the gun salute given at

Earl's funeral could be heard for miles throughout Cringle. All who stood there in the quietness surrounding the casket had tears left over to water the ground where Earl would soon be placed. There were others who were not present but could hear the distinct sounds of the gunfire, who knew what they represented and the man for whom they sounded. Honor and integrity travels far, touching many. They stopped whatever they were doing for a moment, looking deeply into the sky through kitchen and office windows to pay respect over the passing of one who stood for so much.

After the ceremony, they all went to the church that Earl so faithfully served, despite his many involvements, to sit and share one final meal together. Before the forks touched the food, Seth asked Beau to pray for the meal. Despite the large number present and various beliefs represented, all went silent as Beau gave thanks for the life of Earl and all who were a part of it, for the gift of life and hope, and for the food.

Later in the day, Beau and a few of the others went to the old cabin, where each of his children and grandchildren, as well as Beau and his siblings, were given the right to select an item of Earl's to take as a keepsake.

After confirming that neither Seth nor his siblings had their sights set on it, Beau took the Bible. For the sake of history, however, it should be noted that the Bible eventually found its way back to the cabin, where it was set beside the window to fill the cabin with light.

A few items remained restricted from that day on, like the faithful maul that was wielded so many times to keep visitors warm. And it would continue to do so, albeit with a few repairs to keep it going. Earl had willed the cabin and the land to his four children and a few close comrades at his church to use and maintain over the years to come. The Jamisons were included in this as well.

They each walked about the cabin, few words spoken. Soon they pulled themselves away to go their respective ways, each taking a longing look through weary eyes back at the cabin before entering the wooded trail that led to the cars. Beau remained for a time, walking about the woods before departing to rejoin his family, where a long, deep, and un- daunted nap was waiting for him.

The next morning, Beau and Dean went with their mother to the dump to get rid of some old items lying around her yard. In some strange way, this was always a thrilling occasion for their mother, for she so loved spending time with her two sons, especially when it involved outside work. Under the circumstances, it also acted as therapy to all their souls.

Afterward they stopped at the cemetery where old Grandma Winnie was buried at the request of her daughter. It had been a long time coming, and Earl's passing had rekindled the desire to visit. Though Grandma Winnie was still missed after all these years, no mourning was had there. Just some tears of joy and gratitude were had, along with a few laughs due to old, timeless memories.

Afterward they arrived back to the house, where the others had been waiting to see Beau off. More hugs, more partings. This was always the most difficult part for Beau. He was no good at goodbyes.

Just before he was to get in the car after walking out the front door, his mother came out to where he stood.

"Beau," she said in a lifted voice, walking quickly toward him with bare feet, "I have something for you." With that, she pulled an envelope from the pocket of her sweatshirt and handed it to him.

"Seth found it on Earl's table the morning he had the heart attack. He asked me to hold it and give it to you, in case he lost track of things with all the planning and coordinating. Now seems to be the best time..." Unable to say much more due to rising emotions, she simply gave him another hug and kiss on the cheek and returned to the house.

Beau held the letter in his hand and took a long look at it before slipping into the car and driving away. It would remain unopened until that evening.

Heaven Sent

Tuesday, August 8, 2001. A night beside the white lake.

The presence of nature is all around, captivating and inspiring my imagination, as it always does, as I sit under the tree branches before these tranquil waters. I believe it will continue to do so long after I close this journal tonight and throughout the rest of this week.

The sounds of bullfrogs and loons are ringing throughout the expanse, and the flicker of those mysterious fireflies are lighting up the shoreline. They are so close I can reach out and grab them, hold them in the palm of my hand, and peer inside to see the show of effervescent green. 'Tis something how these little creatures dazzle me now as much as ever.

Until recently, it seems that it has been so long that I have enjoyed them.

A glistening trail of bright white travels the distance of the water, leading from the sky where the moon rests and cast its glow upon all that lives and breathes, right up to the shoreline where I sit on this beached log. On either side of the trail I can see the reflection of stars in the water, though they are weakened by the powerful moonlight. I prefer the real thing, however, and simply look to the heavens in awe to watch them dance.

The island moon at Lake Wagatogabee years ago comes to mind, though this time an unmistakable peace rests within my heart and will not leave as I make my way to sleep.

Amidst all this, the memory of a country angel bombards me, as if carried to me by the soft breeze. Though she took me higher than any other before her, she is not the first to have flown into and out of my life with such force through the years. Not sure what to make of it as I sit here alone tonight. I hope she and the others have found their way to safe, fulfilling havens and that someday I will be able to share this beauty that surrounds me with another.

Someday, I pray.

I remember something Earl once told me 'bout how certain species of female fireflies send out signals with the frequency of their flickers that lure in hapless male fireflies. Mesmerized, perhaps seduced, the males come to the female, where they are devoured by them, literally. I never wanted to think of fireflies that way.

I don't believe that Amber was one of those types of fireflies but perhaps one whom lured me in innocently, unknowingly, to show me something without knowing it. Amidst all the sounds of the night, I can hear the soft sounds of piano taking my daydreams back to that weekend long ago at her house where that foggy field under the moon touched us. She still comes to mind, especially out here in the quiet open.

In times of strength I am so grateful—grateful for the experience and the growth it has brought me. Though in times of weakness I catch myself asking why things happened the way they did and if another could possibly come my way and move me the way she did. In the end, I have to concede that there is much I don't know and understand and hold fast to my faith that a greater plan exists, whatever it may be. I must persevere with the company of hope and patience that another may enter my life with a mightier gust of wind than she who causes my pen to move tonight. Either way, I have a race to run.

Right now I'm not sure if I am in a state of weakness or strength, though I know I am not completely alone.

Beau slowly closed his journal and returned his attention to the frigid Saturday morning in November, where he sat high above the forest floor in Cringle in one of his father's deer stands built years ago.

It was the annual hunting season, which carried him far from his residence in the big city. It was also far from the warmth of that night by the lake several months earlier while on vacation, when he penned those words with the aid of the moonlight.

He now sat quietly atop a small seat warmer on a five-gallon bucket, his body covered in blaze-orange gear from head to boot, crouched over slightly to keep the heat in. He sat still, listening closely for approaching white-tail deer that might fall into the sights of his high-powered rifle, which rested on his lap, ready for action.

Though he was to be attentive to the sounds of deer, he was much more interested in the awakening horizon. There was much to observe and admire; the exhilaration of witnessing the forest come alive on those mornings far exceeded even that of the hunt.

The forest, much like the lakes and rivers of summer, had a special way of providing relief from the city and the fast pace of life. He was able to gain clarity there, to sift through all the files that accumulate in the mind and make sense of some while throwing others away.

"The mind has a funny way of collecting dust when one is on the go…" he once heard.

Turning his attention from the forest, he looked over to his pocket-sized Bible that sat open next to him and read a few Proverbs, as he did each morning. Some mornings he would read other passages, if life called for it, though this morning was definitely fitting for words of the wise. In doing so, thoughts of Earl came to him. He remembered clearly the October dawn not all too many years ago when they were sitting out on the cabin porch, watching the sun rise into and above the trees, rays of gold breaking through the forest.

"I miss you, old friend," he said quietly to himself. A tender smile came over his face as he read over a few more sentences before looking up into the wood, the smile on his face remaining as he closed his eyes. "Much has changed," he whispered into the chilling wind.

Amidst the peace, however, there existed a stirring within him. For some reason, thoughts of Amber had entered into his mind in an unusually strong way that morning, even before reading through his journal just moments ago. The thoughts caught him off guard, and he couldn't make sense of them. After all this time, after all the growth and changes that took place in his life, she still came to mind, even when in the woods, far removed from everything.

Was he not letting go? Was he being a hopeless romantic stuck in a daydream? Perhaps he was living so fast that he couldn't see inside his own heart to know she was still there. Perhaps that was one of the reasons he was moving so fast.

"Release to increase," Earl once told him while fishing. Beau had caught a small trout that he wanted to keep, though the little slimy fellow would fill his limit and the fishing would have to end. Either he kept the trout and stopped fishing or let it go to make room for a better one. He begrudgingly let it go and a while later caught a bigger, fatter fish that did a fine job filling his stomach that night.

Recalling Earl's voice, he wondered of his motivations when saying that, how much more lay behind those words he spoke to the lad many years ago. It made Beau wonder about every single thing that ever came out of that old man's mouth.

Despite all this, the same thoughts of Amber always seemed to surface, causing a stir, even though the sting behind them had subsided. The same thoughts that he thought were successfully eradicated. Why she left behind the acquaintance after moving. Why she avoided his attempts to see her. Why this, why that. There was also a talk they had in one of their last phone conversations, which took place just months following the weekend at her place, one that he couldn't seem to let go of.

> "Do you think you could wait until marriage to have sex?" she asked hesitantly.
>
> "Are you kidding me?" he hastily replied without thinking twice. "I'm a twenty-three year old male..." Beau's voice trailed off, something not sitting right in him the moment after the words came out. Yet they came out, and there was nothing he could do to pull them back, the conversation fading thin until goodbye was said. A heavy, helpless burden pervaded him after hanging up the phone.
>
> "No sex until marriage?" The thought of it, he admitted to himself in the moments following that conversation, sounded right and good, even desirable. He wasn't very promiscuous, and saving that special physical act for one person would, without a doubt, be a gift. But it just seemed out of reach, unheard of, as close to impossible as anything could be. He knew of some "church people" who waited, though how he didn't know.

As Beau sat there in the deer stand, recounting that conversation, he thought about how his reply to her question would live to haunt him, regardless of her motives for asking. Had she been testing him for potential relationship, he would have crippled the opportunity to gain her hand. If she was just seeking direction in life, he may have slipped her poor, foolish advice that could influence her to travel down the wrong path with men in the future. He knew she was strong and likely would not, though even the possibility of his words altering her course in that direction made him shiver.

He also thought about comments that were made earlier in that same conversation.

"I wish you were here to help me unpack," she said to him shortly after settling into her new place in Ohio, the words completely catching him off guard. She also mentioned the idea of trying to get him a job at her company following his graduation. Beau, again feeling a lack of words and unknowingly silenced by a lack of inner confidence, said little in response. He was oblivious to the fact that she might have been serious and hoping for him to take action, again opening a door to him, though at the time he hadn't yet come to understand that it was primarily the man's responsibility to initiate and pursue.

This knowledge would come to him years later.

One comment she made grabbed him the hardest. Frustrated with the monotony of her new job and all the life changes, she spoke, "I'd like a life where I could just brush my teeth in the bathroom with the man I love, spitting on each other's hands..."

Those words would rivet him and cling to his soul in days, and years, to come.

Beau grimaced at the memory and shook his head as he sat up in the tree, mildly, if not exceedingly, frustrated when he recounted his lack of action and words in those conversations. Too long had these memories resurfaced, and as he sat there watching his breath dissipate in the cold air, he wondered if these and other thoughts of her would linger in eternity—the unspoken words and actions, the words spoken that he'd like to take back. The thought of all this forced him to believe he had to act now, regardless of all the time that had transpired.

He was not sure what or how, but something had to be done. Perhaps it was time for some simple, gentle, straight-up questions from the heart, aimed directly at the source.

And so it was. He left the woods that day with a clear purpose, aware of what had to be done.

On his way back south to Chicago the following evening, he decided to make a stop along the way into the small town where Amber and her family took him on his visit. There was this warm, rustic little bookstore beside a creek that he had discovered on a previous visit, near the old theatre and small waterfall. He returned to it, sat down, and began to write in his journal, collecting thoughts and preparing for what he was going to communicate to her, the questions that needed to be asked. Excitement and nervousness lingered, and the feeling in the air was anything but stagnant.

After an hour or so, he packed up and returned to the dark and desolate country highway to resume his journey south.

The next morning, Beau left his apartment and made his way to work with a heightened sense of purpose and determination. His electrified demeanor was much out of place on the crowded El train, where scores of young and middle-aged professionals sat and stood, many relatively unenthusiastic, with long, drawn faces that silently spoke of the dread in tackling the first morning of the week. After getting off at his stop and walking quickly down the bustling streets to his high-rise office building, he settled into his cubicle and released his courage onto the keyboard.

He typed Amber an e-mail, letting her know that there was something he hoped to talk with her about and that he'd be calling her that week. He wished her well and left it at that—short, simple, and sweet, not including more words than necessary or skirting the direct invitation for communication. He then clicked "send" without hesitation and leaned back with a sigh.

Beau intended on waiting a couple days to call her, mainly to allow time to clarify his thoughts. Wednesday morning, just two days after, arriving to work and sitting down with a cup of coffee, he opened his e-mail to discover the unforgettable reply from her that would eliminate the need to call.

"I got engaged on Saturday! We were at his parent's house, and he asked me to marry him." All Beau could do was stare at the words. The same Saturday that he encountered unusually poignant thoughts of

her and made the decision to go after her, she had gotten engaged to the man she met at work over a year ago.

The relationship between his thoughts in the deer stand, the subsequent mission to seek closure or a new beginning, and the news of her engagement seemed to go way beyond any measure of irony and left him with little to say.

Shock, sorrow, angst, joy, confusion, loss, and release...it was all there and running through his mind like wild horses on the range. After he could analyze the e-mail no longer, he got up to go for a walk. He went down along the Chicago River that ran through the crowded streets and a sea of faces, where a few tears crept up from within and found their way to the surface.

Saturday eve, mid-June, 2002. A long summer day.

The day of Amber's wedding has passed into evening, soon to be gone. I awoke today with emotions I cannot fully describe or understand. Emotions I wasn't expecting. Peace amidst uncertainty, the pangs of hopeless romanticism knocking on my door—a few times I thought of storming the castle, though thankfully the thought fled as quickly as it came. Seems my heart is now guarded by an adequate dose of hopeful reality that understands there is nothing more I can do. Since her engagement, I hadn't thought of her as often, though she and some of the questions that lingered have surfaced in my mind from time to time.

Today has been a long day, though with its end a strange and welcome feeling is upon me—like the breaking of ropes that were tied around my heart, ropes I didn't know still existed until I awoke this morning. Any trace of hope for something more with her, seen or unseen, was surrendered and replaced by a new hope for whatever lay ahead.

Beau closed his journal and walked outside onto his third-story porch that overlooked roofs and trees and provided a good view of the sky. He was met by a warm breeze and the usual sounds of the city that did not sound so bad at that moment. He stood out on the porch for a short time, allowing the wind to carry his burdens away. Sullenness was replaced by a quiet excitement for the future and thankfulness for the day, and days, to come.

Feeling expended, physically and mentally, he took one last look to the skies before returning inside. He prepared for bed and knelt down to pray before laying his weary head to rest. A prayer of blessing for Amber and her new husband could be heard in heaven.

Like the soft summer breeze, she flew into the young
man's life, drifting right into the center of his
thoughts and dreams.
She opened doors deep within him,
easily breaking through walls that stopped others.
She painted a vibrant portrait of life for him,
full of wildness, creativity, faith, and morals,
one that reminded him of how he wanted things
to be and felt they should be, hoped they could be.
She slowed him down while speeding him up,
adding tranquility and vitality to his soul.
Dreams and desires became clear,
while fog from his past began to disappear.
For a brief moment in time, he flew so high,
tasting the air above the clouds and near the
heavens,
though with the cool autumn wind, she was swept away,
only to return to him through his daydreams.
He continued to soar, though in times of quiet reflection,
he often wondered why she had flown away,
and why after all the passing time and changes in his life,
she still stepped into his thoughts.
In a search for answers he discovered,
that through her a better man he became,
and that while some things are not meant to be understood,
they do not happen without purpose, often revealed
through time.
She may have been guided onto his path, sent from Above,
to awaken his senses and open his eyes,

plant seeds within him that will help him grow,
and prepare him for the crown that is to come.

Sailing Home

June 2000

Dear Beau,

Well, my young fishing companion, the time has come for me to sit on one of these old rockers out on the porch and write you a letter. I have some thoughts that have been knocking at my heart's door to be shared, and not knowing when your next visit will come, I figured now is as good a time as any.

The sun has begun its descent in the west; we've spent enough times sitting out here that I know you can envision it in your mind as you read this. Our times out here will one day end, as I am fully aware you know, and it seems as if God has been giving me hints that the time could be near. My body has grown old. My soul has grown richer over the years, but my body has gone in a different direction—a fate we all must face at some point if not taken from this earth in another manner.

I write this not to alarm you, for I believe I have some valuable time left, and I hope and look forward to another cup of strong coffee with you out here. You will receive this letter after my passing, however, regardless of when that may be. After all, I hear that the writings of dead people are much more valuable...

On a more serious note, I know there is sorrow in death, and I hope that as you read this, you are celebrating my passing amidst any mourning that may result from it. The Lord has been good to me, Beau. I didn't deserve all He did for me. The journey through life I was sent on and the people brought into my life along the way...it is all worthy of spending eternity writing about, together with some new experiences, I suspect.

So rather than bring you sorrow, I write to refresh you and pass along a few things I have learned over the years. I also hope these words may in some way spur you on to live your life to the fullest for something bigger than yourself in the time you have each day, for you never know when your last may be.

Speaking of something bigger, I have recently learned of a choice you have made to walk a different path. As I sit here now, heaven drawing closer than ever before, I can think of nothing that brings to me greater joy. I remember wishing Ruth was here to share the news with me, though I know that she was dancing up above with me as I jumped around on the porch, hollering into the sky and woods. I do hope to see that little lady again soon, if that is the way God works things. I do wonder and hope, though either way I trust I'll be plenty satisfied up there.

I watched you search after life for many years, longing after that one true love that would satisfy you. I have also been a witness to you falling off course in the process as well. Seems someone had a mind to not let you fall too far, though, and now you have found the one true love that will allow you to experience it fully with another.

She will be special, Beau. Never let her out of your heart's sight, even before you meet her. And, Beau, when she does come your way, which I believe deep in my heart will happen at just the right time, pursue her with the same vigor that you are to pursue your faith. Use all your heart, mind, soul, and every ounce of strength you have, and don't stop doing so after she lets you put the ring on her finger and brings forth children to make you lose sleep at night and occasionally question your sanity.

Always pursue, being the gentleman you are in doing so, while taking her on the adventure of life with you. Love her, even when you feel you have no love to give. Remember, young traveler, love entails action and is much more than just feelings. Though do enjoy those too.

In the meantime, chase after true life, for it is then when you will find her, running alongside you.

By the way, old Ethel from the country store asked how you were doing. Told her you were a holy roller now and hanging out with those church folk. Thought she was going to jump out of her apron. "That boy is gonna sail a good ship!" she exclaimed with tears of joy in her eyes. She told me to tell you to stop in next time you're around. I told her I would, so do not let me down.

On faith. You must have some inkling by now that the road you have chosen will not be an easy one. There is an adversary; you've encountered him at various times and in various ways thus far in your journey, this I know to be true. And know that he will continue seeking to destroy, especially now that you are going against the tide and disrupting his agenda. He will never relent for too long. Trials, temptations that at times will seem unbearable, and moments of doubt will inevitably purpose to waylay your course. Times will fall upon you when it would seem much easier to quit and go the easier route, to do that which seems pleasurable and pleasing to others versus standing firm in the hard places where peace, purity, and perspective dwell.

But you know, through the empty life you lived in the past, that hope, happiness, and the zest of life fades away quickly on that path of compromise. God has given you a destiny, Beau, and the power to obtain it, and only in that will you find the life that is truly life, a joy that surpasses understanding. Hold fast to your convictions, fight for those you love, and remember to laugh, often. Don't take life too seriously, though do take seriously those things found in the pages of that book that you always peered into when coming to the cabin. Yes, I knew you were looking.

Like the river and lake near the cabin that get deeper the further out you go, so does life the further you step into it.

Beau put the letter down on his lap for a moment, remembering a time long ago of walking out into the river at Earl's when he was younger. The water kept coming farther and farther up his chest, nearing the opening of his waders. He kept following Earl, though, who knew how deep it was and kept encouraging him to continue following, stopping him before it became too deep. Over the years, Beau kept following him farther and always caught good fish when he did.

"Hmmm," he sounded, "so there was a lesson in that."

Take chances, lad, risk uncertainty, and venture into the deep waters and dark places where trial and joy exist together in ways you cannot comprehend without going there. In those places you will find your courage. Though do not go there alone, if at all possible. Know who your real friends are, those who stick by your side in hard times and you for them.

On wisdom. The more you grow, the less you ought to know. For many years I have both given and received counsel, and with each passing year, I realized I knew a touch (some years a lot) less than I knew the one before. Black and white areas often succumb, as they should, to gray areas in life. Within that paradox, wisdom does increase, and with it sorrow, for you will see that much is bent in this life that cannot be straightened, as well as old wounds that never completely heal.

Yet trees continue to grow, and hope is always the greater, and much peace exists for those who look up amidst wind and gloom. So again, don't take life too seriously, and live each day fully while preparing for the next, always willing and ready for a sudden change of course.

> *Get up, get out of bed,*
> *let your eyes look straight ahead.*
> *Sing, dance, fight, go, and do,*
> *fix your gaze directly before you.*

King Solomon penned some of those words, so I dare not claim them all as my own. But do understand you are in a fight. Be assured that storms will find you. Hard times come upon us all in our life, days full of evil and strife that fall upon us unexpectedly. You've been through some challenges, though greater ones lie ahead in ways neither you nor I can envision. I have lived through a war, one which made the world take more seriously the question of good and evil. I saw the best and worst of that which dwells in the hearts and minds of men, and it often gave me shaky knees when desiring a better world. It sometimes seemed so hopeless. So I say to you to walk steady through the times that come your way.

It is no surprise that the world, though still full of such life and beauty and opportunity, is not becoming a better place. There is always hope, though, and so much to live for when not living for yourself.

I need not inform you of the wars and famine, the decay of society and morals, all pointing to an eventual end that all will have to face. Though neither you nor I nor anyone else knows the time of this, and it is possible that your children's grandchildren and beyond will be preparing and waiting for that day. So continue in the fight to make it a better place while keeping your perspective. You are only a stranger passing through—a stranger with a mission, carrying a command given directly from a King. A wonderful King.

Persevere, young warrior, and follow the light that has burned in your heart ever since a child, a light I had seen in you very early in your life. A light that cannot be overcome, even in the greatest of darkness. You will stumble, though if you reach for strength and forgiveness, you will be lifted onto bright highways and fly high on wings like eagles. What you've been given cannot be taken away.

Do not forget those who brought you up and nurtured you or those whom you once played with in your early years, regardless of how far your roads may take you from one another. I can say from my own life, and my family that has long since passed, that roads often converge in later years in remarkable ways.

Above all, do not stray from those lakes and rivers that paint your heart, from fireflies and sunsets and the sound of wind. Fear that which created you, for in that fear, life will yield more than you could possibly ask for or imagine. Use and nurture your imagination, along with some daydreaming, for it is good for the soul.

I must leave you now, and I trust your voyage through life will be deep, long, and wide. You've been like a grandson to me, Beau, and I cherish the years I have known you and your family. The love I have for all of you brings tears to my eyes even now as I write.

Bless you, Beau, and may true love guide you forevermore,

Earl

P.S. If my sons or daughter are unable to take Jesse, please take her as your own. She always took a special liking to you and would make a fine companion in her golden years. And please split more logs for the fire, in case there are visitors.

Beau lifted his gaze up from the crinkled, time-worn letter in his lap. He sat motionless in the canoe, staring into the tranquil waters. The lake before him had grown calm again with the departing of the afternoon winds, and the skies now displayed a deeper shade of blue as early evening arrived. A few stars began to emerge. As he refolded the letter, using the same creases that were first used long ago, the memory came to him of when he held the hand of his old friend for the last time and the slice of eternity he was allowed to taste.

The letter also rekindled the memory of meeting a girl several years after Earl's passing. She smote his senses in such a way as never before, just as was predicted. Though Beau's eyes were open and ready at the time, the encounter still managed to sneak up on him. Through a series of unforgettable encounters and chivalrously reckless pursuit of her that came with its fair share of ups and downs, their relationship grew, spanning years and heartache and thrills, until finally they said a permanent hello.

This hello led them to Earl's cabin five years ago for a portion of their honeymoon, which has not ended but is rather going through various stages as they both travel down the same path through life.

However, those details are many and there is not the time to share them now.

It is known, however, that one early spring evening, as the sun was departing into the west, just days after young Beau sailed the perilous seas in order to reach her, a teardrop fell from her fair skin as she sat across from him in an old canoe. It was at that moment, on this very same lake in early springtime, that he opened a tiny box that guarded a very shiny stone that glittered in the waning sun and gently asked her the question that she had been longing to hear since she was a young girl.

Several months later, in the latter half of August, they wed.

He placed the letter back in his journal and returned it to the backpack.

As Beau, now a husband and father of two, approached the shore this evening, he could see this same young lady, now very much a woman, walking slowly down the path toward the dock. Little Alyssa walked next to her, taking many smaller steps while watching the ground before her. She looked up to see her dad as often as she could without stumbling. Those steps grew bigger each day, almost too fast for her parents to keep up with.

A smile grew on his wife's face when she saw him drawing

closer. She could tell by the soft expression on his face and the narrowness of his eyes that he had successfully endured some intense reflection and solitude. Others, perhaps, might not see this as readily, but she knew him far too well, and he no longer possessed any mechanisms to hide from her the things of the heart. He was an open book for her to read.

Beau was unexpectedly stirred within, in a most visceral way, as he watched the two walk down the trail. He looked down and away for a moment, his eyes becoming moist.

"Thank you," he whispered aloud.

He lifted his head again. His mind, which had grown weary from all the deep introspection, all of a sudden quickened, and an appetite formed for her companionship.

She read this on his face too, and her smile grew even more radiant.

"Daddy! You're back! Can we go fishing after supper?" yelled Alyssa from the dock as he paddled closer. Highway's tail began to wag excitedly at the sound of her voice, so much so that it rocked the canoe, and he now stood with his front paws on the bow of the craft. He missed the family.

"I'll take you out later, honey, I promise. First I am going to spend some time with your mother."

"Okay, but you promise?"

"I promise."

"Oh, okay...Highway!" He chuckled due to how the interest in Daddy was so quickly replaced by that of a canine.

They pulled up to the dock, where Highway jumped out of the canoe and greeted Alyssa over and over with a bunch of big wet kisses. While she squirmed in enjoyment, Mom cringed. Beau laughed aloud at the sight of it.

"You just can't stop love, darlin'."

"Nor do I intend to try," she said with a suggestive wink. "I was looking out the window and saw you coming. I missed you."

She went on to share of a few major events of the week from camp, like Wade getting rubbed up against a tree on a pony ride, and after crying a good cry, he grabbed the big animal by the mane and was about to let him have it. Thankfully, he was removed by the wrangler before doing so. They had to put him on a different horse after that. And

Alyssa, brave little Alyssa, cornered a snake in the cabin and picked it right up by the tail and carried it outside.

"She let it live?"

"She did. Apparently she doesn't share your distaste for them."

Beau mused, imagining the scene, as well as his wife screaming during the whole thing.

"Wade is alone in the cabin; we should get back up there. He was napping so soundly that I just didn't have the heart to wake him."

Beau stepped out of the canoe and wrapped his arms around her, holding her close and tight for a few long seconds. He then took her hand, along with Alyssa's, and began the short hike back to the cabin, where dinner and warm times awaited.

Over the years, Beau had learned that marriage and fathering came with more challenge than one could expect, no matter how much one prepares for that day. Hard times exist that test the relationship and every fiber of one's being.

Tonight was not one of them, though. As Beau walked on with his family toward the cabin, he looked back at the setting sun, whispering another "thank you" into the air.

Many other stories of people, places, and times exist to be shared that led Beau down the path to destiny and true love—more than could possibly be shared in one account. There also exist stories that have not yet come to pass, more than he could imagine. Many miles remain on his journey home.

However, these stories shall have to wait until another morning and cup of hot, strong coffee before calm waters.

"…whoever loses his life for my sake will find it."

Jesus Christ